I0600120

Valor Flakes:
Part of a Complete Breakdown

by Derek R. Bridges

Salt Circle Press

Valor Flakes: Part of a Complete Breakdown
www.eatvalorflakes.com

Copyright © 2025 by Derek R. Bridges
www.thebridgesarchive.com

ISBN: 979-8-9991674-2-2

Library of Congress Control Number: 2025911946

Disclaimer *This is a work of fiction. Names, characters, organizations, events, and belief systems are either products of the author's imagination or are used fictitiously. Any resemblance to actual persons, institutions, or ideologies—living, dead, or deified—is purely coincidental, symbolic, or redacted.*

Valor Flakes: Part of a Complete Breakdown *is a literary satire. It is not intended to promote or disparage any real-world faith, nation, or governing body. It explores how narratives of heroism, memory, and sacrifice can be manufactured, monetized, and sanctified. No drones were harmed in the making of this narrative. Any surveillance footage has been redacted for your safety. Proceed with caution—and a fortified breakfast.*

Printed Beyond Regime Jurisdiction
Salt Circle Press
Portland, Oregon

a Viaduct Publishing imprint
www.viaductpublishing.com

For Auggie & CeCe
(and all those working to create a better future for us all)

"Silence is the ultimate weapon of power."

-Charles de Gaulle

PROLOGUE

The apartment was too quiet for a holiday. Outside, distant hymns played from mounted street speakers, their volume regulated by algorithm: loud enough to reach the windows, soft enough to feel reverent. Inside, Sarah muted the Valor Network broadcast and sat cross-legged on the floor, surrounded by fragments of a life that no longer existed.

The screen in front of her glowed dimly. Her mother's face flickered into view, smiling, mid-sentence, interrupted by laughter from someone offscreen. Her father's voice followed, low and warm, asking someone to hold still for just one photo. The camera tilted. A hand reached out. Then static.

Sarah tapped the console again. Another clip loaded. A birthday. A school recital. A shaky ride through a garden Sarah hadn't seen since before the strike. Her mother's voice again, this time whispering a lullaby.

She closed her eyes.

The apartment had one window. Through it, the lightshow on the government tower played in subdued celebration. In the plaza below, families barbecued beside plastic flags. Children played with drone-shaped balloons. It was a day off work. A day of gratitude. Today marked another year since the attack on the Sacrificial Zone. The Valor Network called it a day of reverence. Of triumph over evil. They'd been honoring the dead all morning.

They'd never said her parents' names. Not directly. There were too many to name. A crawl of numbers scrolled along the bottom of the screen, clean, clinical, unspoken.

They could name the war, but not the dead.

Sarah leaned back against the couch. On the muted broadcast, a man in formal whites bowed his head while children in red uniforms sang before a monument that no one visited except on camera.

She turned back to the final video. Her parents stood in a kitchen. It was evening. The lights above them buzzed faintly, and a copper ibrik sat on the counter between them.

Her mother held up two fingers behind her father's head. He didn't notice. They both laughed.

She had left for college just weeks before the attack. Her mother had cried at the station, blubbering about how proud she was. Sarah used to laugh at her for being so sentimental. Her father told her to be brave. And to be still—just for once. He hugged her like he knew something she didn't.

In the background of the video—a missed call that Sarah hadn't answered—a sound. Like a freighttrain. Then: a flash. A window shattering inward. The video corrupted, then cut to black.

Sarah sat perfectly still.

The enemy's abrupt attack had launched the Republic into a war that defined the last decade. Over 19 million murdered in an instant. The largest single loss of life the world had ever seen, more than all known previous wars combined. Before there could be time for questions, there was a rush for retribution. It had reshaped the very fabric of life, everyone flocked to the flag. And under Hightower's guidance, the cross. Operators became folk heroes overnight, and real heroes in the months and years to come. They called the war sacred. Strategic. A necessary sacrifice. But that wasn't the footage they played on Martyrs' Day.

She reached forward and gently closed the file.

In the silence that followed, the hymns outside changed. A new voice filled the air, deep and clean, speaking of service, of sacrifice, of sanctity.

Her hand rested on the console. Still warm from the screen. Sarah didn't move.

She already knew the words.

She stood slowly. Moved toward the kitchen. Pulled the ibrik from its place beside the sink.

She needed a cup of coffee.

THE CEILING WAS ALREADY cracked before the first impact. The second one shook it loose. Dust drifted down in lazy spirals as a woman reached out to hush the child clinging to her side.

Outside, the sound was faint: a mechanical hum, steady and circular. The kind that arrived before you knew to run.

They didn't run. There was nowhere to go.

The walls trembled. The tin cup on the stove tipped, sending a thin line of coffee across the floor. The child flinched at the sound.

The walls were rough concrete. The floor had once been tiled. The furniture was salvaged, nothing matched. A decade of strikes would do that. The stove in the corner, hissed steam- burner still warm when the coffee hit it.

4

In the background, a radio crackled, half-buried in static. A flickering screen mounted above it displayed a regime broadcast she hadn't asked for. The language was familiar. The accent, familiar. The name, unmistakable.

A tribute. A voice spoke of sacrifice. Of cleansing. Of peace.

The woman turned her head. A familiar face, solemn, stared back from the screen.

The roof creaked again. She pulled the child closer. Held them steady.

She didn't speak. There was nothing to say.

The drone passed for the moment.

"...in honor of Daniel Eustasius Clymer..."

The child looked up. "Is that Dan from—"

"Shh," she said. "Be still. You are so brave."

She moved to the stove, reaching for a towel. The coffee had already begun to cool.

HE WAS UNDERGROUND again.

The dirt was still under his nails. His arms streaked with blood and dust, ash and grease.

Dan sat on the ground against the wall, knees bent, hands loose in his lap. His shoulders ached. His jaw. He hadn't spoken since—

No.

He kept wiping his hands. Jeans, sleeve, the floor.

Still there.

He wouldn't look.

Dirt. Blood. His. Someone else's.

He ground his palms against the rough concrete.

The blood on his hands wouldn't come clean.

And he knew it never would.

He screamed. He thought. Or maybe he hadn't.

The sound of it was still in his throat.

He hadn't moved in a long time.

After this, he didn't know how he ever could again.

"When fascism comes to America, it will be wrapped in the flag and carrying a cross."

-attributed to Sinclair Lewis

(ORIGIN UNCONFIRMED)

PART 1

1

Dan Clymer woke at precisely 0600, the soft chime of his alarm syncing perfectly with the morning bulletin flashing across the wall screen. The national flag—crimson, silver, and deep navy—rippled in slow motion, overlaid with the motto:

Strength. Honor. Victory.

A second later, Reverend Eli Hightower's face appeared. Smooth. Composed. Framed by flawless studio lighting.

"Righteous Patriots, welcome this new day." His voice was calm, unwavering. "With every sunrise, we reaffirm our commitment to faith and country, standing united against those who would seek to dismantle our way of life."

There was a pause, just enough to feel rehearsed.

"And remember," Hightower continued, "true strength starts with a strong body. Our friends at Valor Flakes are offering twenty percent off their protein-packed morning cereal. Fuel your mission. Fuel your faith."

Dan exhaled through his nose and sat up. The room was cold, the floor colder. He reached for his watch, a tactical black model, engraved with his service number, the same one he'd worn since his first commendation.

His apartment was orderly, impersonal, exactly as it should be. Framed certificates and medals lined the walls—a curated display of dedication. His nightstand held only the essentials: a well-worn challenge coin, a digital clock, and a single framed photograph of him with fellow operatives in fatigues, arms slung over each other's shoulders, grinning after what must have during training—the only time he had worn a field uniform.

Routine. Efficiency. Discipline. The makings of strength.

As the bulletin continued: mission updates, economic reports, a segment on patriotic investment portfolios. Dan moved to the kitchen.

He scooped the coffee without thinking, leveling the grounds with a soft tap against the Liberty Grounds™ tin's edge. The familiar weight of the moka pot felt good in his hands, solid and real. The smell of fresh grounds hit before the flame even lit.

The first drops spat into the chamber, rich and dark. The moment before the coffee finished was always the best part, a pause, a breath, the one thing in his day that didn't move too fast.

Then the pledge began.

Dan turned toward the hybrid flag hanging beside his certificates. Right hand over his heart, he recited in unison with the voice from the screen:

"I pledge my strength to the Righteous State, my faith to its leaders, and my devotion to the cause of our victory. We are one people, united, indivisible, and eternal."

The words came automatically. He had been saying them for a decade.

Dan poured his coffee into his In Service to Valor mug, lifting it to his lips as the morning feed scrolled through updates:

— Successful airstrikes neutralized key targets.

—Consumer confidence rose for the third quarter in a row.

— Vanguard Tactical™ was running a giveaway for five lucky winners to receive a limited-edition *Patriot Elite Combat Pack*.

A headline flickered past: "The Foreign Threat: How Righteous Patriots Must Remain Vigilant." Beneath it, a call to action: "Stock up on Fortitude

Flavors™ Frozen Meals. Dinner for a Stronger Nation."

Dan scrolled past another titled: "The Moral Duty of Conflict: Why Righteous Wars Strengthen the Soul."

He didn't click it. He already knew the message.

Strength came from service. Service meant trust. There was no room for hesitation in war.

His phone vibrated: MISSION PENDING.

Dan blinked at the screen.

The targeting interface was already live, pulsing faint blue. Four flagged heat signatures scrolled along the left, each tagged with a numeric ID, grid coordinates, and a flickering "Threat Assessment" score. Beside them, grayscale thumbnail portraits flashed, flat and low-res, barely more than silhouettes.

Dan didn't look at them.

He tapped the first.

"TARGET: ID #427-9B. AFFILIATION: SUBVERSIVE. THREAT LEVEL: MODERATE."

"ENGAGE PRECISION? [Y/N]"

He hit "Y."

A quick time-event circle bloomed in the center of the screen—ALIGN SCOPE TO HEARTBEAT.

He adjusted his fingertip on the sensor pad. The calibration blinked green.

"CONFIRMED: VITAL LOCK."

"STRIKE AUTHORIZED. +250 POINTS. +1 TACTICAL CHAIN BONUS."

Target two auto-queued.

"SPLASH RADIUS BONUS AVAILABLE. ENGAGE?"

"YES" and "ABSOLUTELY" were the only options.

He clicked "YES."

The kill zone map expanded.

A soft chime played, like leveling up in the *Patriot's Duty* video game.

"3X COLLATERAL CONFIRMED. CIVILIAN THRESHOLD: ACCEPTABLE."

"FAITH EFFICIENCY MULTIPLIER: +1.3X. PROCORE SPONSORED BONUS ACTIVATED."

Greg would've celebrated that one.

Dan just cleared the next target.

"FINAL SEQUENCE: SYNCHRONIZED STRIKE PROTOCOL UNLOCKED."

He hovered, then hit "EXECUTE ALL."

Three seconds. Orange countdown. Haptic pulse in his fingers.

"BLESSED ARE THE HANDS THAT KEEP ORDER," the system chimed.

"MISSION COMPLETE. FOUR ELIMINATIONS. CHAIN BONUS MAINTAINED."

And then—

digital confetti drifted across the top of the screen.

A tiny banner popped up:

"ELITE TIER: VALOR TACTICIAN. FAITH FIRST. GLORY ALWAYS."

Dan closed the window.

He reached for his coffee, took a slow sip, and didn't look at the screen again.

At the bottom of the interface, a soft corporate jingle played, followed by a final message:

"BROUGHT TO YOU BY PROCORE SOLUTIONS™—*your trusted partner in AI-integrated peacekeeping. Ensuring tomorrow, one precision strike at a time.*"

Dan dismissed it.

He drained the last of his coffee.

His phone buzzed.

—Reminder: Buy Fortitude Body Wash™.

He reached for the empty bottle on the sink. He had finished it in last night's shower, shaking out the last drops before tossing it aside.

Now he turned it over in his hands one more time before tossing it toward the trash.

It landed with a soft thunk against the other discarded containers: Liberty Grounds tins, PowerUp Patriot cans, the remnants of a good citizen.

Dan grabbed his wallet.

DAN'S BREATH CAME STEADY as his shoes struck pavement, his morning run tracing its usual path, past the towering Monument to the Fallen, down Victory Boulevard, where the morning pledge echoed over public speakers:

"In faith and in duty, we are united, one nation, one spirit."

The words blended into the hum of the city, a background noise as natural as the wind.

He veered toward the corner convenience store, its fluorescent glow spilling onto the sidewalk. Inside, the hum of refrigeration units mixed with the measured cadence of Reverend Hightower's voice over the speakers.

"A strong body builds a strong nation, Patriots. Never forget that your strength is a service to us all."

Dan walked the aisles with automatic precision. Milk, bread, Fortitude Body Wash. Same brand, same scent. No deviations.

Near the checkout, a PowerUp Patriot™ energy drink display caught his eye.

"Strength for Those Who Keep Us Safe."

The can's sleek design gleamed under the store's bright lights, its red, white, and blue logo bold against the metallic surface.

17

Dan grabbed one, placing it next to his other items. It felt like the right choice.

At the register, the clerk, a young woman with a bright but rehearsed smile, scanned his items. She hesitated for a split second when she noticed the operator insignia on his shirt.

Her expression brightened further.

"Thank you for your service."

Dan nodded. "Of course."

Routine. Expected. Like everything else.

The register pinged softly, and a small notification flashed across the payment screen:

— "Righteous Patriot Discount Applied—10% Off."

As DAN TURNED ONTO Independence Square, a small crowd had gathered around a digital broadcast display. President Knox's campaign slogan flashed in bold letters:

"Strength in Action. Faith in Leadership."

The ProCore Solutions™ logo appeared beneath it.

Hightower's voice played on a loop.

"Righteous Patriots, we must remain vigilant, at home and abroad."

Dan barely noticed. Knox's reelection was inevitable.

A murmur ran through the crowd.

Dan's gaze snapped toward a man standing on a bench, holding a battered sign. In the corner was a symbol. A red circle with two slashes beneath. His clothes were worn, his face unshaven, but his voice cut through the morning calm.

"How long will we pretend? How long before we admit what this war really is?"

Some people ignored him. Others muttered in disapproval.

Dan was about to walk past. Until the man's eyes landed on him.

"You." His voice sharpened. "You're one of them, aren't you?"

Dan stopped. Felt the weight of the attention shifting toward him.

The protester's gaze flicked to Dan's insignia, and his mouth curled into something between a sneer and pity.

"You tell yourself you're keeping us safe." His voice was calm. Too calm.

"But do you even know who you're killing?"

Dan's jaw tightened. His pulse remained steady.

"You follow orders," the man pressed, stepping down from the bench. "You press a button. People die. And you think it's war."

Dan held his ground. "It *is* war."

The protester's head tilted. "Is it?"

Something about the way he said it, like a challenge, like he knew something Dan didn't, made Dan's blood run hot.

"I protect this country," Dan said evenly. "I protect *you.*"

The man's expression twisted, like he was seeing something pathetic. "From what?"

Dan felt something coil tight in his chest. "The enemy."

The man laughed. Actually laughed.

"The enemy? You mean the one they tell you about?"

Dan took a step forward before he even realized it. He had lost friends- family- in the attack. Everyone had.

"I fight so people like you can stand here and say this bullshit." His voice was sharp now, no longer steady. "You don't have to like it. You don't have to understand it. But you damn sure benefit from it."

The protester held his gaze, unfazed.

Then, a sharp movement at the edge of Dan's vision.

Security.

Two men, plainclothes but unmistakable in their rigid posture, their clean efficiency.

Dan barely had time to register the protester's expression shifting, from defiance to something knowing.

The security agents were on him in seconds.

No weapons. Not here. Not in daylight.

Just a grip on the arm. A step to the side. A quiet removal.

The protester didn't fight.

Didn't shout.

Didn't make a scene.

Dan didn't know why that made it worse.

At the edge of the plaza, a group of schoolchildren stood in perfect rows, hands over their hearts.

"In faith and in duty, we are united. One nation, one spirit."

DAN SLID INTO THE SEAT across from Greg, still cooling down from his morning run. His hair was damp, the faint scent of Fortitude Body Wash™ clinging to him. The café was already busy, the hum of conversation mixing with the distant chords of a patriotic hymn playing over the speakers. The walls were lined with slogans of unity and faith, blending state loyalty with divine purpose.

Greg, halfway through his Liberty Grounds™ coffee, glanced up and smirked. "You're getting close to breaking 100K." He nodded toward Dan's tablet. "One more solid run, and they'll probably induct you into the Hall of Valor."

Dan smirked back, stretching his legs beneath the table. The thought wasn't unappealing.

Their breakfast arrived—high-protein platters, "Patriot Approved" stamped on the side of the plate. Dan picked up his fork, barely noticing the ProCore Solutions™ logo burned into the toast.

He sipped his Liberty Grounds™ and said, "They grabbed someone in the square this morning."

Greg flicked a sugar packet between his fingers, barely looking up. "Funny thing about the ones who ask questions, they always seem to disappear."

His tone was casual, but something sharp flickered in his eyes.

Dan chuckled lightly, shaking his head.

It was a joke. Just a joke.

He picked up his fork again.

Why had the guy laughed?

Greg was already moving on, tapping his tablet as a mission notification buzzed.

"Early deployment today. Let's see what we've got."

Dan followed suit.

The interface bloomed to life, clean lines, soft hum, three flagged targets flashing under a gold-bordered header:

—ProCore Solutions: Strike Authorization – Live Session

—Class II Offensive Deployment – Urban Grid C7

—Dissident Activity Detected – Threat Rating: Moderate

No names. Just grid points and indistinct pixelated photos.

No context. Just score potential.

Greg confirmed first. He flicked through the targeting prompts with practiced speed, finger taps, scope alignment, auto-queue. A chime rang out. His screen burst into a celebratory overlay of soft gold.

—Mission Complete: 3 Eliminations, 1 Injury, 0 Escapes

—Perfect Score Bonus Applied. Chain Multiplier Maintained.

—Elite Metrics: Valor Efficiency 98% – Confetti Unlocked.

Dan's session lagged half a second behind.

—Mission Complete: 2 Eliminations, 2 Injuries

—COLLATERAL WITHIN THRESHOLD. EFFICIENCY RATING: 82%

—CHAIN BROKEN. BONUS WITHHELD.

Greg grinned, already locking his screen. "Gonna have to do better than that if you want your name in the Hall."

Dan shrugged, feigning indifference, but the possibility lingered.

The Hall of Valor was no joke. There was no bigger recognition. A real mark on history.

Greg saw the pause and smirked. "What, not enough blood in your coffee yet?"

Dan snorted. "Just another day." He took another sip of his coffee, but the thought remained.

Greg nudged his plate aside, lowering his voice. "You know," he said, tapping the table with one finger, "word is, they're lining up a big event for high performers. Not just the Hall of Valor. Something bigger."

Dan glanced at him. "Like what?"

Greg smirked. "Not sure. But my guess? A Presidential Recognition. You make your mark on the leaderboards, you get a personal nod from Knox. Maybe even a handshake."

Dan set his mug down. "You think that matters?"

Greg shrugged, but his eyes gleamed. "Recognition always matters. Especially when things get unstable."

Dan didn't answer.

He reached into his jacket and pulled out a folded scrap of paper. A photocopy from an old military history text. Faint lines, half a paragraph: *To stand in the shield wall is not to seek victory, but to hold. That is honor.*

There was something about it. The simplicity. A time when soldiers faced the ones they killed. When they bled in the same dirt. When it cost something.

He remembered the first time he read it, back during training, in the off-hours when everyone else was passed out or watching feeds. He'd copied the quote from an old doctrine compendium, not because it was assigned, but because it stuck. He'd never shown it to anyone.

Now it was algorithms. Range. Collateral. And four new names blinking on a screen.

He stared at the paper a little longer, then slid it back into his pocket. It had been folded and unfolded so many times the edge had started to wear thin, a tear creeping down the crease like a split in armor.

His tablet chimed.

—*Briefing in one hour.*

25

He didn't know why, but it felt different this time.

2

The command floor hummed with quiet precision. Screens flickered, satellite feeds shifting, targeting grids adjusting in real time. Operators sat in rigid silence, their fingers tapping out the rhythm of war. No wasted movement. No hesitation.

At the far end of the room, the national map glowed red, its borders etched in sharp lines. Several vast blacked-out regions split the interior—voids where cities had once stood: New York. Los Angeles. San Francisco. Chicago.

Beneath the map, the words caught the light in gold:

THE ENEMY STRUCK FIRST. WE ENDURE.

To the right, a screen looped a familiar image, a skyline frozen in the instant of annihilation. The caption read:

NEVER AGAIN. NEVER FORGOTTEN.

Dan's jaw tightened. No matter how many times he saw them, the images never lost their weight. The searing flash. The rising ash. The bones of once-living cities.

A passing analyst nodded. "They've put the best on this one."

Dan nodded back.

Nearby, a younger operator, Marcus, fresh-faced and eager, muttered to a colleague, "I'd kill for a mission like this."

His partner chuckled. "You will. Keep stacking your numbers."

Dan glanced at them from the corner of his eye. He recognized the kid Marcus as one of the up-and-comers Greg had been training. He'd been out for drinks with them a couple of times.

A corporate screen above the break station flashed a rotating ad:

—*Fuel Your Mission with Dominion Provisions™ Dark Roast– The Strength and Energy to Prevail.*

—*Top Operators This Week Receive an Exclusive Sanctified Arms™ Elite Kit*

Dan barely glanced at it. He still drank Liberty Grounds Coffee™ for the loyalty points, but the perks weren't worth writing home about.

A technician tossed him a headset. "Locked in?"

Dan fit the piece over his ear.

"Always."

The tech smirked. "Then let's make today count."

He stepped into the mission station. The room dimmed, the screens aligning in a perfect arc before him, targeting overlays, live drone telemetry, data feeds folding into formation.

Across the screen, the compound emerged, dull and grainy, just shapes in ruin. The camera swept over broken rooftops, shadows clinging to fractured walls.

Greg's voice crackled through comms. "You'd think with all the funding, we'd get better cameras."

Dan replied without emotion. "The system doesn't need clarity. Just results."

"Still," Greg said, "a few pixels wouldn't kill them. Us, maybe."

Dan let the silence hold.

His fingers hovered over the targeting interface. The compound's main structure stood out, arched windows, a collapsed upper level. Something about it made his breath catch. A flash of something unplaceable.

A shadow moved. Small. Quick.

Civilian? Animal? Artifact?

He blinked it away.

"You good?" Greg's voice again.

"Yeah," Dan said. "Visual noise."

He centered the crosshairs.

One breath. One press.

The screen flashed.

Fire erupted across the compound. Stone, metal, and human silhouettes crumbling in unison. The console chimed:

—MISSION COMPLETE.

—EXCELLENT STRIKE.

— +97.5 Patriot Points.

Confetti animation danced across the interface. A digital trophy blinked:

"ProCore Salutes Your Service!"

Greg whistled through the headset. "Nice. Efficient. I told you that you'd hit 100K by week's end!"

Dan didn't answer.

The smoke still curled on-screen. Where the arched windows had been, now a void.

He stared at the empty space longer than he meant to.

"Just another mission," he murmured.

DAN WALKED HOME in uniform.

Not marching, just walking. The grid had quieted after curfew, and the glow from the mounted screens bathed everything in a wash of pale red and gold. Every few paces, a flag rippled under motion sensors, playing a soft chime of the pledge's opening notes. Dan didn't react.

He passed under the archway near Columbus Square, boots echoing faintly on the metal sidewalk. There were voices ahead. Low. Repetitive. Familiar.

A woman stood near the entrance to a midrise tower, kneeling in front of her daughter. The girl's hand was flat over her chest. Her small fingers trembled.

"Say it again," the mother said gently.

The girl's voice was high and unsteady. "I pledge my strength to the Righteous State... my faith to its eternal guardians... my vigilance to..."

She faltered.

"To the cause of sacred victory," the mother supplied, sharper this time.

Dan stopped a few steps away. Not intruding, just still.

The girl looked up. Her eyes were wide. Not with fear, exactly. But with effort. The kind it took to remember the right thing at the right time.

The mother noticed him and straightened. Her voice shifted to public tone. "Officer. She's just learning. We practice every night."

Dan nodded, not smiling. "She's doing fine."

The girl pressed her hand tighter to her chest. Her voice came quicker now: "To the cause of sacred victory. I am loyal. I am ready."

"Good," the mother whispered. She gave Dan a small, forced smile. "Thank you, sir."

He nodded again, then kept walking. The wind carried a few stray words after him.

"I'm sorry, Mama."

"You mustn't forget. Not ever."

The sidewalk quieted behind him. He didn't look back.

The mural waited at the corner, as it always did. Soldier and child, cast in golden light. This time, he noticed the child's expression. Blank, eyes fixed forward, mouth slightly parted. Just...waiting.

Dan adjusted the strap across his chest. He moved through the gate toward his building.

The final screen of the block looped the day's closing benediction: "Let our deeds speak for our beliefs. Let the strong protect the faithful."

Dan didn't say it aloud.

But he mouthed the words anyway.

3

Sarah Bishop woke to the muted hum of city life filtering through the cracked window of her apartment. The space around her was a study in contrasts: bohemian and vibrant, with mismatched furniture and handwoven textiles that clashed with the sterile conformity of the modern world beyond her walls. The sun cast long rays across shelves crowded with worn books and small clay figurines, each with its own story. A framed charcoal sketch of an unidentifiable landscape hung above her bed, its smudged edges a testament to its handmade origin.

She stretched, her fingers brushing the patterned quilt stitched by her grandmother, a rare relic of the past. In moments like these, wrapped in layers of comfort and memory, she felt a sense of grounded defiance. But beneath that warmth, something colder lingered. There were mornings when she could still feel the absence of her parents as if it had only just happened. They had died in the strike, *the* event that changed everything. She had been seventeen.

The broadcast of Reverend Eli Hightower's morning blessing droned on from the apartment next door, muffled but unmistakable.

"Grant us the courage to uphold the path of righteousness, to safeguard our nation, and to question only when the answers have already been given," his voice proclaimed, deep and commanding.

Sarah's eyes flicked toward the wall as though she could see through it, a habitual eye roll accompanied by the smallest, wry smile. She had heard those words, or variations of them, for years, but their meaning was no less hollow to her now. The familiar cadence, meant to inspire obedience, instead settled in her chest like a stone.

She should have believed them. After all, hadn't the enemy taken everything from her?

But there was something off. Always had been. Too many sealed records. Too many blank spaces in the official story. Too much theater in the way grief was packaged, commodified, weaponized.

Her mornings began without the rigid patriotism that marked most of her neighbors' routines. Here, in the quiet cocoon of her apartment, she allowed herself to be simply Sarah. She took her time preparing her coffee with an ibrik, an act of ritual and care that connected her to memories of shared moments with her grandmother. Sarah hand-ground her coffee beans to an ultrafine size, beans she had obtained through a discreet black market contact, a quiet rebellion against the corporate, patriotically branded coffee that dominated store shelves. She crushed a single dried cardamom pod between her fingers, its papery husk giving way with a gentle snap, and added the aromatic seeds to the grind, an old habit she'd picked up from her grandmother. The scent bloomed as she mixed in two spoons of sugar, then filled the ibrik halfway with water.

Placing the long-handled pot on the stove, she watched intently, listening for the subtle stirrings as the liquid began to foam. The rich, heady scent of coffee filled the kitchen, mingling with the earthy aroma of sandalwood from a candle sputtering on the windowsill. As she waited, Cleo, her sleek, gray cat, padded into the kitchen and wound herself around Sarah's legs, purring softly. Sarah smiled and nudged Cleo with her foot, the warmth of the cat's presence adding comfort to her morning ritual.

"Morning, Cleo," she whispered, the cat's soft fur brushing against her ankle like a familiar reassurance.

At the precise moment before the coffee boiled, Sarah pulled the ibrik from the heat to preserve the crema. She dumped hot water from the prepared cup, returning the ibrik to the flame. The liquid foamed up quickly, and she removed it with practiced precision, pouring the gritty, aromatic brew into her pre-warmed cup. Cleo leapt gracefully into Sarah's lap as she sat by the window, and Sarah rubbed behind the cat's ears while taking a sip. The bitter-sweet flavor grounded her, a private act of defiance and joy that pushed back, if only slightly, against the world outside her door.

After a moment of quiet indulgence, Sarah briskly turned the cup onto its saucer, studying the remaining grounds that clung to the sides. She tilted it, watching how the dark patterns settled. Though she wasn't a true believer in divination, reading the telva, the shapes left behind, was a lighthearted ritual that gave her mornings an added layer of meaning and a subtle rebellion against the state-imposed faith that dictated unquestioning loyalty. Today, the grounds formed...well...she couldn't exactly say, but something in the blurred shapes gave her stomach a slight twist. She smiled faintly, but the smile didn't quite reach her eyes.

"Looks like it's another day to tread carefully," she muttered to Cleo, though her voice carried less certainty than usual.

Cleo, now content after her lap time, leapt gracefully from Sarah's lap as she stood. Sarah reached down to scratch behind the cat's ears once more before filling Cleo's dish with food. The cat purred in appreciation and began to eat, brushing against Sarah's leg in a familiar gesture of affection.

Her morning ritual complete, Sarah stretched, glancing once more at the framed sketch above her bed. The unmarked landscape, with its blurred and undefined horizons, spoke to her in a way the regimented city outside never could. It seemed to whisper of freedom. Not the polished, state-approved freedom touted in public broadcasts, but a raw, uncharted kind that defied control.

After rinsing the ibrik, she opened the small drawer beneath the bookshelf and reached behind the stack of state-approved devotionals. The book was there—thin, sun-faded, its corners softened by years of rereading. Her father had given it to her on her first birthday, the year the rivers flooded and the power went out. Inside the front cover, in his tidy, slanted script, he'd written: *For Sarah, may you always*

walk the harder path, even when it disappears beneath your feet.
It wasn't a political book. Just a quiet story about a
girl who leaves a green valley to follow a river out
beyond the known borders, losing, changing,
remembering. He used to read it aloud every night
until she memorized the ending. When the regime
rewrote the curriculum and banned anything that
didn't end in salvation, this one disappeared without
a trace. She'd already taken it to college by then,
tucked in her backpack. Concealed and safe, but
accessible, and always with her.

Normally, she just kept it hidden these days—
because it remembered who she was, and who they
had been, and because she had never found another
ending that felt more honest. But this morning,
something about the telva had unsettled her. A
restlessness she couldn't name. She slipped the book
gently into the lining of her satchel, censorship laws
be damned, before turning to the small wardrobe
that held her collection of clothes, a mix of practical,
subtly eclectic garments that mirrored her
personality.

She lightly brushed a patterned shawl before
choosing a loose, earth-toned blouse and a pair of
worn jeans. She changed out of the oversized
sweatshirt and cotton shorts she slept in, the familiar
fabric pooling at her feet before she kicked it aside.

Cleo watched from her spot, tail swishing contentedly as Sarah dressed.

With a quick pat on the cat's head, Sarah stepped back to the mirror, adjusted her blouse, and tied her hair back into a low ponytail. The reflection that stared back at her was both familiar and foreign, a woman who had learned to navigate a world of silent resistance, where small acts held as much weight as bold proclamations. She took a steadying breath, bracing herself as the contentment of her private sanctuary faded, replaced by the stoic readiness needed to face the regimented day.

Outside, the city pulsed with structured energy, the rhythmic march of a society bound by its rules and rituals.

The unmarked landscape above her bed, a relic of a freer time, lingered in her thoughts as Sarah exhaled slowly and stepped into the machinery of the world beyond her door.

THE COMMUNITY AID CENTER buzzed with quiet efficiency. Sarah's boots clicked lightly across the polished floors as she stepped inside. The building was spotless by design, gleaming tiles, crystal clear windows, and the ever-present scent of government-issued disinfectant. Large digital displays rotated between curated success stories and looped speeches from President Knox and Reverend Hightower.

Posters lined the walls:

"Unity Through Service."

"Dissent Is Disobedience."

"Faith Makes Us Strong; Order Keeps Us Safe."

Behind the slogans, security cameras blinked red in steady rhythm.

"Morning, Sarah!"

Marla's voice rang out with a warmth that felt out of place in such a sterilized space.

"Morning," Sarah answered with a faint but genuine smile.

She moved to her desk, placing her bag gently down. As she settled in, she glanced once at the nearest camera, not from paranoia, but habit. Resistance had trained her in the art of awareness.

The day unfolded in a familiar monotony: processing paperwork, sorting requests, and navigating a steady stream of quiet, weary citizens. Each person was a case number before they were a face. But Sarah refused to let them blur.

She leaned forward when an older woman, trembling slightly, stepped up with her forms. Her cardigan hung loose over bony shoulders. Her fingers shook as she held out the documents.

Sarah met her eyes, softened her voice.

"This first page is where you list dependents. They want it in this exact order: eldest to youngest, with middle names. Don't know why. Just how it flags less often."

The woman blinked, confused, but nodded.

Sarah kept her voice low, pretending to scan the rest. "Skip section three. It's a trap question. If you mark 'unsure,' it flags you. Leave it blank."

The woman's eyes widened. "But..."

"Trust me," Sarah interrupted gently, sliding the forms back. "Now take this to the clerk at station four. Don't ask for clarification. Just tell them you were pre-processed."

A flicker of understanding passed between them. Gratitude. Fear. Trust.

The woman nodded once, tightly, and moved on.

Sarah exhaled and returned to her terminal. It could cost her everything. But withholding help felt worse.

A lull followed. Marla disappeared into the back for inventory checks. The room hushed.

Sarah reached into her bag, fingertips brushing the folded slip she'd hidden under her notes. She hesitated. Then slid it out and read it again.

Black text on white paper. No logo. No name.

Just a single line:

"Deliverance will come not by way of the faithful, but by those who seek truth in all things. The road shall open before them." —Isaiah 67:19

Beneath it, small and faint, was the mark: a circle with two diagonal slashes beneath.

The original had been slipped inside a bag of her coffee beans by the vendor, a woman in the market called Nama. No explanation. Just a glance— sharp, deliberate—and a nod.

Sarah had printed twenty-five copies. It had taken hours to find a terminal not logged in the central registry. She had passed 2 to a friend to post.

Each flyer felt like a match.

An act of war.

She rose slowly, pacing to the exit under the pretense of a break. Her heart thudded as she passed the front camera, keeping her face composed. Outside, the bulletin board fluttered with government ads: calls to service, reminders to "report all suspicious activity," and announcements for Martyrs Day events.

She lifted the edge of a crowded flyer, slipped her own beneath it. Not hidden, just slightly veiled. Waiting to be seen by someone who needed to see it.

The door creaked open behind her.

"Sarah?" Marla's voice called.

She turned, voice steady. "Just getting some air. Be right in."

A BOY APPROACHED the desk near the end of Sarah's shift, lanky and jittery, no older than sixteen. He wore the standard-issue uniform of a citizen aide, but it hung loose on his frame like it belonged to someone else. He clutched a sheaf of forms tightly, edges bent and sweaty.

Sarah offered him a calm, practiced smile. "Step forward. Let me take a look."

He didn't speak as he handed them over. His hands were trembling.

She flipped through the pages, scanning quickly. Her eyes paused at Section Six.

"Relatives not currently registered," she murmured under her breath.

The line was filled in. One name: an uncle, noted as last seen during a supply run.

She lowered the form and looked up at the boy. His mouth twitched, eyes darting once to the red blinking light of the security camera.

"They said to be honest," he whispered.

Sarah kept her voice even. "Honesty is... complicated."

She slid the form back across the desk. Her pen moved quickly as she circled the offending section.

"This will flag you. It's automatic. Secondary review, and they'll open a profile on your whole family."

He blinked, lips parting. "But I didn't do anything. He just... disappeared."

Sarah nodded. "I know. Doesn't matter. Here's what you do. Leave that part blank. If they ask later, say you weren't sure what they meant. Keep it vague. But confident."

The boy hesitated, then scratched out the line in a shaky hand.

She took the form back and stamped it with a code reserved for rush processing. Then she leaned in slightly, lowering her voice further.

"Take it to Station Four. Don't speak unless asked. Say you were pre-screened."

He nodded. Not quite understanding, but trusting. He started to turn, then paused. "Thank you."

Sarah gave a small nod. "Good luck."

He walked off quickly, shoulders still tight with fear.

Her screen pinged.

FLAGGED CONTENT: Form 117D – Previously Modified

She dismissed it with one tap, her expression unreadable.

And moved on to the next name in the queue.

4

Dan stood alone in the control room, the glow of the mission console dimming as the system powered down. The final strike data lingered in the air like smoke, each line fading one by one:

—*Confirmed Targets Neutralized.*
—*Structure Integrity: 0%.*
—*Collateral Impact: Minimal.*

Minimal.

He stared at the word, watching it blink once before vanishing. Clean. Sanitized. Final.

The support team had already dispersed, their polite nods and murmured congratulations swallowed by the sterile quiet. He was left with the ambient hum of dormant machines and the subtle thrum still echoing in his chest. Not adrenaline. Not exactly. Something quieter. Slower. Something that felt like it didn't belong.

He peeled the headset off and placed it gently on the console, the movement careful, almost reverent. For a long moment, he didn't move. He just stood there, watching the screen's faint afterglow. A ghost image. Like the compound. Like the heat signature tucked into that low-priority quadrant. The one that hadn't moved. Not until the last second.

It had flickered—barely. Small. Irregular. The system flagged it as non-combatant—possibly an animal, a glitch, or residual thermal noise. Nothing actionable.

Still.

He shook his head.

He had done everything right. Every parameter checked. Every protocol followed. Every target cleared. Every risk assessed. There was no room for improvisation, no incentive for second-guessing. Doubt wasn't just inefficient, it was dangerous.

He told himself that as he walked the corridor, boots striking against the polished floors in mechanical rhythm. The hallway was empty, save for the posters that lined the walls in perfect intervals, their slogans glowing softly beneath motion-triggered backlights:

"Precision Protects."
"Faith Makes Us Strong."
"Your Eyes, Our Shield."

Dan stopped at the end of the hall, facing a large mirrored window overlooking the city. Towers stretched skyward, wrapped in corporate emblems and glowing banners already preparing for Martyrs Day. Stylized missiles launched in digital unison on repeat, their smoke trails blending into holographic doves.

He took out his phone.

A message blinked on screen.

Greg: *Drinks tonight? You earned it, Top Defender. Marcus is already buzzing.*

The title lingered, Top Defender, framed in digital laurels on his Patriot Points app. He should've felt proud. He did. Sort of. But something about it felt off now. Like he was being applauded by people who hadn't seen the screen flicker. Who hadn't felt that flicker in their chest.

Another buzz.

Marcus: *BIG night. Greg says drinks are on the house now. You in??*

Dan smiled faintly. Marcus never did anything halfway. He tapped out a reply.

Dan: *On my way.*

He slid the phone into his pocket and glanced once more at the city. Martyrs Day displays shimmered across the skyline—red, white, and deep navy. Fireworks, families, freedom. Unity through sacrifice.

He thought again of the heat signature. Of the way it had hesitated. Of the way he hadn't.

Just a flicker.

He pushed it down.

Tonight was for celebration. He was a hero. He had done everything right.

He turned from the glass, let the door hiss shut behind him, and stepped into the synthetic night, where neon prayers lit the streets and sirens sang beneath the static drone of broadcast blessings.

5

The office itself was immaculate: polished marble floors, a massive mahogany desk, and walls lined with artifacts that blurred the line between altar and armory. A gilded eagle clutched a silver cross above the mantle. In the far corner, a locked cabinet held priceless chalices, each one engraved with both scripture and the seal of the Office of Faith & Patriotism. Every inch of the room was designed to communicate dominion. Not just spiritual, but cultural, political, economic.

Reverend Eli Hightower's reflection shimmered faintly in the glass as he stared out. He no longer flinched at the memory of his father's voice, but it lingered anyway, a rasp etched into his mind: "Spare the rod and spoil the child." That voice had shaped him. Through beatings and forced confessions, fire-and-brimstone sermons that stretched for hours, and leather straps inscribed with scripture.

He had been forged in that furnace. But now, he was the fire.

A soft chime broke the silence.

His senior advisors filed in, dressed in tailored clerical jackets: black with crimson piping, each adorned with a patch that combined the nation's seal with a crossed sword and cross. They settled wordlessly at the long oak table, their expressions a blend of reverence and calculation.

Hightower moved to the head of the table, each step deliberate. "Brothers," he said smoothly. "We have much to finalize before today's broadcast."

A nod from Brother Simon cued the projection on the wall: slides of Hightower's upcoming Daily Blessing, interspersed with targeted sponsor placements. Valor Flakes, Sanctified Arms, Dominion Provisions. Each had purchased a line of scripture. The slogans were already drafted, fused into psalm-like rhythms."

"We're leading with divine vigilance today," Simon said. "Framing the strike as preemptive sanctification."

Hightower clasped his hands behind his back as he paced. "We tie the enemy's aggression to moral decay. We pair sacrifice with salvation. And above all, we elevate the mission.

And what about Dan Clymer?"

"Top of the hour," said Brother Marcus. "He's polling at 97% recognition among patriot-confirmed families. The mission footage will run mid-sermon. Framed as ordained action."

Brother Jacobson shifted in his seat. "Reverend, the footage includes... a civilian heat signature. Children, possibly."

The room stilled.

Hightower's gaze sharpened, unblinking. "Then it is fortunate we do not broadcast thermal."

Jacobson paled. "Yes, of course, Reverend."

Hightower said nothing further. He turned slightly, gaze fixed on the stained-glass cruciform embedded in the far window, its reds and golds casting the light in sanctioned fire. A pulse tapped low in his throat, but he did not allow himself to note it. Children. Possibly. He let the words hang just long enough for everyone to feel their weight, then dismissed them with a blink. The mission sanctifies itself, he thought. If the optics held, the rest would burn away. He closed his fist behind his back until the flutter stopped.

"Besides," Hightower added coolly, "our President will be joining the ceremony. The theatrics demand a spotless script."

As if summoned by cue, the double doors swung open and President Alexander Knox strode in, flanked by two aides. He grinned, the practiced smirk of a man who believed his presence elevated the room.

"Morning, gentlemen," Knox boomed. "Hope I'm not late to church."

"President Knox," Hightower said with a nod of polite welcome, masking the clench in his jaw.

Knox moved to the display and pointed to the operation schematic still glowing on-screen. "Is this the Clymer compound?"

"It is," Hightower said. "The footage will run beneath the blessing. Paired with footage of his commendation and family archive. A full profile piece."

Knox nodded. "Good. It'll make a strong lead-in to the Hall of Valor induction. We want people crying in their kitchens, Eli. Kids reciting his name like he's Moses with a missile launcher."

A ripple of forced laughter spread through the room.

Knox turned to one of his aides. "Remind me—we're set to unveil the new drone at the ceremony, yes?"

"Yes, sir," the aide replied. "Design is finalized. It'll be featured alongside the tribute video."

Knox looked back at Hightower, smirking. "We're naming it after Clymer. The DAN- Defensive Action Neutralizer. Sleek, sharp, easy to remember."

Hightower raised a brow. "And you're sure he's the right face for a line of unmanned death machines?"

"Absolutely," Knox said. "He's clean. Marketable. Obedient. Best part? He actually believes the shit we're selling. Doesn't get more patriotic than that."

A few chuckled. Hightower didn't.

"And he looks good on a box of cereal," Knox continued. "Miniatures, patches, commemorative pins are already in the works. Maybe a limited-edition action figure for Martyrs Day. Make the kids beg their parents to support the war effort." He winked. "Sanctified Arms is ready to sponsor the rollout...just need your people to bless the branding."

Hightower gave a practiced smile. "Naturally. We'll wrap it in providence."

Knox clapped him on the back. "Knew I could count on you. Always good to let the spirit guide the spending."

Hightower said nothing. The room returned to quiet hum as aides took notes and synchronized schedules. Knox basked in the attention, unaware, or perhaps uncaring, that Hightower had already brokered half the sponsorship deals behind his back. To Knox, this entire machine ran because he allowed it. To Hightower, Knox was a mouthpiece. Loud, crude, effective.

Knox approached the projection, advancing to the next slide and jabbing a finger at the drone. "This thing'll make Clymer a legend. Can't wait to slap a medal on him."

"A medal," Hightower said, voice light. "And a market."

Knox didn't hear the edge in his tone. "Exactly. Wrap the ceremony in patriotism and God-talk. Schools, churches, parades. We'll have kids pledging to drones by the end of the month."

Hightower smiled tightly. "What a blessing."

The President turned toward the exit. "Keep it clean, Reverend. Nothing too heavy in the blessing. I want fire, not fallout."

"Of course," Hightower said again, and watched the door close behind him.

The room exhaled.

Hightower returned to his desk as the room emptied and unlocked the bottom drawer. Inside, ledgers bound in fine leather detailed his financial entanglements: investments in supply chain firms, defense tech companies, and media outlets tied to the Valor Network. Everything was cross-stitched: scripture and subsidy, benediction and branding.

He flipped to a fresh balance sheet. Revenue from Dominion Provisions™ was up twenty percent after the last strike blessing. Valor Flakes™ had already purchased ad time during the drone unveiling. Each sermon reinforced the sale. Each blessing drove stock.

He ran a finger along the drone schematic left by Knox, sketched beside a speech draft. "The DAN," he muttered. "May it strike true, in the name of profit and providence."

The ceremony details lay nearby. Timed applause, product reveals, military hymns adapted into praise songs. Knox would bluster. Dan would blush. And Hightower would consecrate the entire performance as divine truth.

A knock broke the silence.

A young aide stepped inside, head bowed. "Reverend, the broadcasting chamber is ready for final checks."

Hightower nodded. "On my way."

He took one last look around the office, smoothing the collar of his robe. His reflection stared back at him in the glass—stern, immaculate, godlike.

He walked down the corridor flanked by portraits of past religious leaders—Constantine, Calvin, Luther...hell, even St. Peter himself—none of whom had ever wielded this level of control. None of whom had turned faith into a fully monetized weapon of state.

Inside the broadcasting chamber, technicians scrambled to their marks. The altar was lit, banners unfurled, the camera angles pre-set.

Hightower stepped into the pulpit, clipped the microphone to his robe, and cleared his throat.

The red light blinked to life.

He smiled into the camera, his voice smooth as velvet.

"Good morning, faithful citizens. Today, we walk together in the shadow of sacrifice and the light of victory. Let our faith be unmoved, our resolve unshaken, and our unity eternal..."

6

By the time she left work, the afternoon sun slanted across the city's clean, ordered streets. Sarah made her way to the small café tucked between two towering buildings emblazoned with military advertisements. The storefront was a familiar spot, its sign worn but welcoming, promising a reprieve from the rigid structure that framed their days. Inside, the air was warm, tinged with the scent of cinnamon and roasted coffee beans, a comforting aroma that masked the subtle tension ever present in the world outside.

"Sarah!" Marcus waved from a corner table, a grin lighting up his face. He was already nursing a cup of dark coffee, the steam curling up as he adjusted his glasses. Marcus was always early, his enthusiasm both endearing and a reminder of how deeply he believed in the system Sarah quietly questioned.

"Hey," she greeted him, sliding into the chair opposite. The café hummed with quiet conversations, the clinking of cups, and the soft, controlled laughter of patrons. Patriotic branding was everywhere, from the disposable cups emblazoned with "Victory Brew" to the framed poster announcing, *"Powered by Precision: Your Trusted Patriot Beverage Partner,"* proudly noting its sponsorship of missile strikes. Sarah reluctantly ordered a cup, grimacing as she read the label and the overzealous slogans. It was sub-par, a bitter echo of the real coffee she cherished at home, but it was part of the routine, a small act that made her blend in.

"You look tired," Marcus said, his eyes narrowing with concern.

Sarah shrugged, managing a small smile. "Long day at the Center. You know how it is."

Marcus nodded, his expression softening. He leaned forward, the earnestness in his eyes unmistakable.

"I heard they're planning to expand the Sacrificial Zones. The broadcasts said it's to secure new boundaries, a necessary step to keep us safe." His voice held the quiet awe of someone who accepted the narrative without question.

Sarah's fingers tightened around her cup, the warmth seeping into her skin, grounding her. "Yeah, I heard," she replied, careful to keep her tone neutral. The words barely made it out. Her throat felt tight, like the words had to squeeze past something lodged deeper down. She thought of the footage from that day. Grainy, sanctioned, too clean. Her dorm had smelled like floor polish and burned popcorn while she watched the flames erase her street. The regime's logo sat in the corner of the screen, quietly insisting: Remember who did this. But even then, she'd known something was missing. No screams. No chaos. Just a drone's eye blinking from the sky. She pressed the cup tighter between her palms and smiled so Marcus wouldn't see the heat behind her eyes.

Marcus was more than a friend; he was a true believer, an unwavering supporter of President Knox's regime. Their friendship was a delicate balance of shared moments and unspoken divides.

"It's incredible, isn't it?" Marcus continued, oblivious to the flicker of discomfort in her eyes. "We're so fortunate to have leaders who protect us."

Sarah's gaze drifted to the street outside, where uniformed guards patrolled with the casual authority of those who mistake compliance for belief. Their uniforms were absurdly macho, blending deep crimson and navy blue with emblazoned gold eagles clutching both olive branches and arrows, a visual testament to power. Religious symbols interwoven into the fabric, crosses that merged with the sharp lines of military insignias, reminded passersby that patriotism and piety were one and the same. Each guard wore a stern expression, eyes scanning for any hint of dissent, as if they embodied the righteous fury of the state itself. She looked back at Marcus, his boyish enthusiasm both a comfort and a burden.

"Fortunate," she echoed, forcing the word past the knot in her throat. A ValorNet ad looped above the drink station—drones distributing relief packs in slow motion, set to a hymn arranged with synthetic strings. The tagline read: Mercy, Delivered. Sarah looked away, not fast enough. That was the thing now. Relief and destruction blurred on the same screens, in the same fonts, delivered by the same hands. A woman behind her blessed her cup before sipping. Sarah pressed her lips together and let the heat of the coffee remind her she was still here. Still pretending. Still watching.

There was a silence that last a half-second too long, filled only by the ambient noise of the café. Marcus's smile faltered as he noticed her hesitation.

"Sometimes I wonder," he said, lowering his voice, "if you worry about things more than you should. It's not safe to question too much, you know."

Sarah's heart thudded, the warning wrapped in care. She met his eyes, searching for any hint of suspicion, but found only concern.

"You're probably right," she said, lifting her cup to mask the tension in her expression. She took a sip, the strong brew biting at her senses, giving her a moment to collect herself.

Marcus reached across the table, his fingers brushing hers for just a second—an innocent gesture that lingered between them. His gaze softened, and the unspoken affection in his eyes was almost palpable. Sarah pulled her hand back, not unkindly, but with the quiet certainty that they both recognized. He cared for her deeply, but she couldn't let him know how far her doubts truly ran.

"You're a good friend, Marcus," she said, the words carrying a kind of finality he didn't hear.

His smile returned, a touch of color rising in his cheeks. "Anything for you," he replied, the sincerity so clear it made Sarah's chest ache.

As the conversation shifted to safer topics, shared memories, small frustrations at work, Sarah noticed a shift in his posture. His hand, resting below the table, began to fidget. Not with his cup, not with a spoon, but something more deliberate.

She glanced down and caught a flicker of movement—his fingers rolling over a worn leather bracelet with small, faded beads.

She didn't say anything. Just took note. A nervous habit, maybe. Something old and meaningful. Something that grounded him.

Marcus cleared his throat. "Hey, by the way, some of us are going out for drinks tonight. Greg got a table. It's kind of a thing for this guy Dan, he hit some milestone or whatever. You should swing by. If you want."

Sarah blinked, the shift catching her slightly off guard. "Oh?"

"Yeah. No pressure. Just thought you might want to come. It'll be fun."

She offered a small, noncommittal smile. "I'm supposed to meet up with some of my girlfriends later, but we'll see."

Outside, the city buzzed with its usual orchestrated calm. Digital banners scrolled updates on Martyrs Day preparation, ads for government-approved holiday gear, and a looped message from Hightower: "To question is to betray."

Marcus held the door open for her as they stepped outside.

"You coming to the vigil?" he asked, more as an afterthought.

Sarah hesitated. "I'll think about it," she said, knowing full well she didn't intend to. Not in the way he hoped.

They parted ways, Marcus walking with the upright posture of someone who believed deeply in what he was told, and Sarah with the burden of knowing that belief was a luxury she couldn't afford. She slipped her hands into her pockets, a small shield against the onslaught of religious militarism beaming from each sign.

Behind her, she heard the subtle chime of a public broadcast switching over. Hightower's voice filled the air once again.

And somewhere beneath it, she imagined the soft sound of beads clicking together in a nervous rhythm.

7

The chapel was always empty this time of night. Dim orange light bathed the altar's marble lip, casting long shadows across the inlaid scripture etched beneath it. The walls glowed faintly with backlit engravings, tactical maps reframed as holy relics. Missile trajectories rendered in gold. Blessings overlaid on battle diagrams. A stylized portrait of Saint Benedict the Defender loomed overhead, haloed in flame and fiber optics.

Hightower moved slowly, deliberately. He wore his signature uniform of robe and collar even here, pressed and perfect. The room recognized him by retina scan, unlocking the inner drawer below the altar with a soft mechanical click.

His father had once called televangelists false prophets. Said if the Church ever sold war, it'd damn itself by breakfast.

And now Hightower's blessings aired in 4K across every screen, synchronized with the launch of branded drones.

He reached inside and removed a black leather folio, unfastening the magnetic clasp. Inside were the most sacred texts he owned—not scripture, but spreadsheets. Profits from the drone initiative. Projected revenue from the upcoming DAN line. Defense contractor tithe breakdowns. Margins from state-aligned coffee growers.

He flipped through page after page, pausing only when the speakers embedded in the altar crackled to life.

"Only through fire do we find purification."

The voice was his own, recorded during last year's Martyr's Day celebration.

Hightower allowed himself a brief smile.

Beneath the ledger, tucked behind a stack of donor projections, was a faded photograph.

Three people, frozen in sun-bleached grain. A boy, maybe ten, stood stiffly between a tall, unsmiling man and a woman whose face was turned just enough to blur.

He hadn't looked at it in years.

His fingers hovered.

Then he reached for the match.

The flame caught quickly, curling the edges, distorting the faces. The man disappeared first. The boy took longer.

He dropped the ash into the bronze basin.

The speakers looped again. "Only through fire do we find purification."

Hightower snuffed out the match and closed the drawer with quiet precision.

He did not pray. He had numbers to review.

8

Dan Clymer exited the command center alone, the sterile blue overheads reflecting off polished floors that gleamed like mirrors. His pulse still hummed from the strike—a faint, controlled throb behind his sternum. The glow of the "MISSION COMPLETE" screen lingered in his vision, a phantom blinking in sync with his blinks.

He rubbed his temples as he walked. The gesture was automatic. The unease wasn't. It pooled low and slow in his chest.

The corridor walls were lined with murals. Drone operators rendered as titans, posed beneath stylized eagles and flaming crosses. Each tableau etched with slogans:

"Guardians of Freedom."

"Faithful and Unyielding."

"Strike First, Stand Eternal."

Most days, they filled him with pride. Today, they buzzed like static.

"Dan!"

Greg jogged up, his grin easy, familiar. "*Everyone's* already heard about your op. Elite-level, man. Crisp execution."

He clapped Dan on the shoulder. Solid, reassuring. Dan allowed a faint smile.

"Thanks. Just followed the brief."

Greg gave a half-laugh. "Yeah, well, Command's already whispering about your numbers. Word is you'll be front and center for the Hall of Valor ceremony. Knox wants another poster boy."

Dan's smile didn't grow. "It's just a rumor."

"Sure," Greg said. "And drones fly themselves."

Dan didn't answer. The praise didn't quite settle. It hovered instead, uncomfortable, like a detail he couldn't shake. The small movement in the footage that he'd only noted at the time, but lingered now, vague and persistent.

Greg seemed to catch the pause. "Hey, don't spiral. You did your job. That's what matters. The rest —that's above our pay grade. And remember- they struck first. It's divine retribution."

Dan nodded faintly. "Right."

Greg started to turn, then paused. "Oh. Marcus texted. Said we're meeting at Valkyrie's tonight. Reserved a table. Drinks are on me."

Dan raised a brow.

Greg smirked. "He's bringing someone. Says it's 'someone special.' You've been warned."

Dan exhaled through his nose. "I'll be there."

THE DRIVE HOME WAS SMOOTH, quiet, except for the sermon loop rolling through the dash speakers.

"And remember," Reverend Hightower intoned, rich and certain, "Operators are the righteous flame, burning away doubt, sin, and the foreign hand that dares reach across our sacred soil. Support our brave warriors today with your purchase of Fortitude Body Wash™, part of the ProCore™ family of brands

Billboards loomed along the highway:

A drone mid-strike: "Justice Flies on Sacred Wings."

A missile morphing into a dove: "Your Security, Our Priority – Sponsored by Liberty Motors."

Dan's gaze snagged on the second. The missile-to-dove transition felt jarring, like a hymn written by committee.

He turned the volume up, letting Hightower's cadence fill the silence.

The apartment was spotless, as always. Keys on the counter. Boots off. Jacket hung. The rituals of control.

Digital frames cycled through national slogans. Above the kitchen counter, his Patriot Points tally glowed:

107,432 – ELITE RANK ACHIEVED

He tapped the screen. A short fanfare played.

"TOP DEFENDER: CONGRATULATIONS, DAN CLYMER."

Golden laurels spun slowly. A new pop-up: *"You are eligible for induction into the Hall of Valor. Details forthcoming."*

He stared as highlight reels played. No sound, just target confirmations and blast radii. Crosshairs. Detonations. Motion blur of bodies.

The image stuck: the structure collapsing in the moment of detonation—just before the blast, the flicker of motion barely registered. Small. Quick. The system hadn't flagged it. Just noise, the analysts said. Nothing worth reviewing.

He closed his eyes. Then opened them.

The newsfeed scrolled across the kitchen wall:

"Martyrs Day Vigil Schedule Finalized."

"Sacrificial Zone Expansion Ratified."

Hall of Valor Ceremony to Feature Live Address by President Knox."

His tablet buzzed.

Supervisor: *"Clymer. Congratulations. You've been selected for Hall of Valor induction. Ceremony details incoming. Expect direct contact from the President's team."*

Dan stared at the message. No ceremony details. No congratulations. Just confirmation.

He paused, then typed:

Dan: *"Honored. Awaiting instructions."*

He stood in silence, the words echoing faintly in his head. Not pride. Not quite doubt either. Just... weight.

The strike was over. The reward was coming. The path was clear.

So why did it feel like something had shifted?

Dan splashed water on his face and stared into the mirror. The man looking back seemed unbothered—calm, clinical. Steady. Composed. Loyal. But his jaw was just a little too tight. His breath just a little too shallow.

The room was clean. The banners were bright. The message was clear.

But the flicker...

He still saw it.

Above the door, the alert screen lit up:

"Honors Pending. Induction Confirmed. Celebrate Accordingly."

Dan stared for a moment.

Then grabbed his jacket.

Time to celebrate.

9

Sarah closed the door to her apartment with a soft click, letting the lock settle into place before leaning against it for a moment. Cleo meowed from the armchair, barely lifting her head.

"Hey, girl," Sarah murmured, nudging her boots off. She crossed the room, giving the cat a gentle scratch behind the ears. "Just grabbing a few things. Hold down the fort."

Outside, the light had dimmed to amber. The sky was streaked with navy clouds, the first signs of evening settling over the city. Sarah tugged on her coat, grabbed a reusable bag, and slipped into the crowd.

THE NEIGHBORHOOD MARKET buzzed with early evening activity. Patriotic slogans scrolled across LED screens mounted above vendor stalls:

—"Faith Feeds the Nation."

—"Buy Righteous. Buy Local."

State surveillance drones floated overhead, scanning with idle indifference. Music played softly, an instrumental remix of the national anthem, but it couldn't quite mask the murmur of quiet deals and whispered warnings.

Sarah kept her expression neutral. Nama's stall was tucked near the back, away from the main path. The herbs were fresh. The coffee was real.

"Evening," Sarah said.

Nama looked up, her sharp eyes narrowing slightly before softening. "New shipment. Didn't touch the register."

Sarah gave a small nod, brushing her fingers across a burlap sack of beans. "You hear anything?"

Nama's voice dropped. "Same rumors. More movement near the outer zones. Some say they're preparing to expand."

Sarah kept her expression blank. "They always say that."

"Yeah," Nama said. "But this time... I don't know. Something feels off."

Sarah handed over credits and tucked the beans into her bag. "Be careful."

"You too," Nama replied. "Tell your friends to lay low."

BACK HOME, SARAH set a pot of lentils to boil and poured the coffee beans into her grinder. The rhythm steadied her. The scent grounded her. Cleo stretched on the windowsill, eyes half-closed as if bored by the world's chaos.

Sarah made her brew slowly, deliberately, spooning in sugar and cracking the cardamom, watching the crema rise. Her thoughts flicked back to Nama's words. To the whisper about the Sacrificial Zone. To the flyers still hidden in her dresser.

When the coffee was done, she settled into her kitchen chair and pulled a light shawl over her shoulders. Her dinner sat cooling in front of her. The crema rose slowly, curling at the rim like it was reluctant to settle. She cupped the mug and brought it close, inhaling until the heat prickled her eyes. For a second, she wasn't in the apartment. She was in her father's kitchen, younger, watching him scrape the sugar flat with the edge of a butter knife, like it was a science he didn't want to get wrong. But the memory didn't hold. Not really. It came with too many overlays now—footage, slogans, that tight metallic whine the drones made when they passed too low. She stared at the wall while the newsfeed began to scroll, letting the bitter steam anchor her before the words could take over. The newsfeed flickered across the wall:

—"Martyrs Day Vigil Schedule Finalized."

—"Sacrificial Zone Expansion Ratified."

—"President Knox to Honor Top Operator Dan Clymer in Upcoming Hall of Valor Ceremony."

Sarah stared at that last line. Then laughed, quiet and bitter.

A hero behind a screen. Another name fed to the machine.

10

Dan stood in front of his mirror, the muted glow of the bedside lamp casting half his face in shadow. He fastened the last button of his jacket, the subtle patriotic symbols embroidered along the lapel catching the light, a small eagle, wings outstretched, a quiet nod to his service.

The room was still, save for the muffled symphony of the city humming through the closed window. In the distance, sirens and the low rumble of traffic blended into an urban lullaby.

His phone buzzed.

Greg: *See you there, brother. Ready to toast to you!*

Marcus: *Big night, Dan! Hope you're pumped. I'm bringing a special guest. You'll love her.*

Dan smirked. Of course Marcus was bringing someone. The kid never missed a chance to turn an ordinary event into a minor spectacle.

He picked up the small medal that hung from the edge of his mirror, his first commendation. Worn, a little tarnished, but steady in the hand. He slipped it into his pocket, its weight familiar.

A final breath. He turned out the light.

THE STREETS WERE ALIVE with artificial color. Neon reflected in rain-slicked pavement, stretching patriotic hues into every puddle. Digital billboards played highlight reels of drone strikes over corporate logos. The ad for Liberty Motors featuring a missile turning into a dove.

Dan walked past it all. Some people recognized him. A few nodded. One man gave him a thumbs-up without breaking stride.

A newsfeed scrolled across a shopfront: *President Knox's approval surges ahead of operator recognition ceremony.*

Another: *Faith & Patriotism's Martyrs Day Event to Feature Live Induction.*

Dan's chest lifted slightly.

VALKYRIE'S WAS ALREADY humming by the time he arrived. Flags, streamers, and branded banners turned the bar into a low-lit shrine to national valor.

Screens above the bar cycled through footage of drone strikes with a heavy metal soundtrack. The voiceover was smooth and reverent.

"ProCore Solutions™: Defending Freedom, One Strike at a Time."

"Top Defender Dan Clymer: A Hero for Our Times."

Greg stood near the corner booth, pint in hand, waving him over. "There he is!"

Dan returned the grin. "Mr. Glory himself," Greg added, holding up his glass.

Dan joined them, offering a modest smile. He shrugged off the attention, settling into his seat without fanfare.

Marcus appeared with a tray of drinks, his energy unmistakable. "Drinks are on Greg tonight. And me. And Hightower, technically."

"Nothing says holy endorsement like discount bourbon," Dan said, twisting the glass slowly in his hand. He didn't drink right away.

They toasted.

"Big things coming," Greg added, lowering his voice. "They're planning a rollout. Ceremony, sponsorships, the works."

Dan took another sip.

Marcus, meanwhile, couldn't sit still. He kept glancing at the door, his knee bouncing, fingers drumming the side of his glass, voice always a half-step too loud. He talked over Greg to tell a story about Dan's last mission, how Command had cleared the room when they found out Dan was coming in. How the briefing officer actually used his name as a verb: 'He Clymered the whole sector.' Greg snorted into his drink. Marcus didn't stop.

Dan shifted in his seat. The laughter and lights felt like overexposed footage—too bright, skipping frames. It reminded him of the command floor, just after a strike, when the room went quiet except for the soft whine of the cooling fans. This place had that same static edge to it. Except here, they filled the silence with noise. With Greg. With Marcus. With all of it.

"I'm serious! They're already using his footage in the next training sim. I saw a test run—had the tagline and everything. Like, 'Precision is Dan-defined.' I'm telling you, it's nuts. He's going to be more famous than Knox."

Marcus finally slowed, just long enough to glance at his messages. A flicker of uncertainty passed over his face.

Dan raised an eyebrow. "Special guest?"

Marcus nodded, then winced. "I mean—not like that. Just... someone I admire. She's sharp."

Dan chuckled. "You nervous?"

Marcus rolled his eyes. "You'd be too if you saw the way she cuts through people's nonsense. She's... different."

At the bar, someone let out a cheer. A moment later, a nearby table erupted in applause. Dan glanced over just as a woman in a red ProCore jacket tapped her wristpad and muttered a confirmation code into her glass.

A chime sounded overhead.

"MISSION CONFIRMED."

The nearest screen updated. A drone was already inbound.

Nobody stopped drinking.

The screens looped again: another compound leveled, the footage sanitized and glorified. A voiceover praised precision. A logo flashed: Sanctified Arms™: *Faith, Firepower, Future.*

Greg gestured with his glass. "You realize this is the peak, right? Hall of Valor, trending status, ad slots lined up. Next step: sainthood."

Dan didn't respond right away.

And somehow, that made the whole room feel a little louder.

THE NEXT ROUND ARRIVED, and with it, a louder toast from a nearby table. Dan raised his glass reflexively, but his eyes weren't on the drink.

Marcus was still checking the door every few seconds. His fingers brushed something at his wrist, a habit, maybe, or a tic Dan couldn't quite place, but he never looked down.

Dan leaned back slightly, gaze tracing the edges of the room. Coasters etched with "In Strength We Stand." Screens blinking out strike highlights and patriotic ads in seamless loops. A silent promotion for a new line of deodorant: Victory Vibe – Sentinel Sandalwood. The tagline beneath it read: "Stay fresh. Stay faithful."

He took a slow sip. The celebration hadn't ended, but it had taken on a rhythm that felt less like joy and more like obligation.

"She's different," Marcus had said.

Dan found himself watching the door.

He didn't know who she was.

But he was starting to wonder.

He turned back to the screen as a familiar blast rippled across the display. A drone. A detonation. A logo.

He raised his glass to no one and drained it.

Tomorrow, the ceremony.

Tonight, noise.

He could already feel the medal around his neck, tightening like a noose.

11

Sarah glanced at the oversized clock on the wall of the bar, its neon glow casting a subtle pulse over the room. The hum of conversation mixed with clinking glasses and the bass of distant music, creating a comforting buffer between her and the world outside. She wrapped her fingers around her cup, willing her muscles to untense. Tonight, she had promised herself, would be a reprieve. A night out with her friends, a momentary escape from the weight that came with living in the shadow of patriotic fervor.

"Another round?" Amelia leaned over the table with a mischievous grin. They had known each other since childhood, before the relocations, before everything changed. In a world where permanence was a myth, Amelia was one of the few constants

Sarah had left. The neon lights reflected in her eyes, making them sparkle as she spoke.

Sarah smiled, even if only fleetingly. "Why not?"

As the evening deepened, the bar filled with patrons seeking relief from the ever-tightening rhythms of duty and loyalty. Sarah noted the subtle signs of regime influence creeping even here: drinks named Valor Vodka™ and Liberty Lager™, coasters etched with slogans like *"Raise a Glass for Righteousness."* Everything wrapped in a veneer of service.

From the next table, a voice carried: "They're saying Dan Clymer's getting inducted into the Hall of Valor."

Sarah's chest tightened. The name had drifted in and out of her orbit since Marcus first mentioned him, a face plastered across recruitment ads and televised sermons, always framed in firelight or beneath fluttering flags.

"I heard they're hosting it at the same event Knox is using to formally kick off the re-election," another voice added.

Amelia caught Sarah's eye, smirking. "It's all so performative."

Sarah managed a small nod. "Exhausting. Like there's always a spotlight waiting for a slip."

Amelia reached across the table, resting a hand on Sarah's. "That's why tonight's about us. No politics. No slogans. Just a night to be human."

Sarah smiled again, this time more genuinely. But the feeling faltered as her phone buzzed. A message from Marcus:

Out with Dan and some of the guys. You should come by. It's going to be a night to remember.

Her pulse quickened.

"It's Marcus," she said. "He's out with coworkers. Dan Clymer's there."

Amelia's eyebrows rose. "*The* Dan Clymer?"

Sarah nodded. "Probably just a lot of talk about missions and medals." She tried to sound dismissive, but the hook had already set.

"You should go," Amelia said. "See what they're like when the cameras are off."

THE AIR OUTSIDE was cool, thick with the scent of wet pavement and overcooked street food. Sarah hugged her coat closer, weaving through the crowd. Neon light spilled from every doorway. Flags hung like garlands, casting faint shadows over window displays stacked with Martyrs Day specials.

Ahead, Valkyrie's glowed. Laughter spilled from the open door. Screens flashed with looping footage of drone strikes and glowing mission stats. Sarah paused at the curb, watching the revelers inside. She slowed just short of the threshold. From this distance, the celebration felt less like a party and more like a ritual, each laugh and burst of applause part of a choreography she had never learned. The footage flickered across the windows, casting explosions across her coat sleeve. For a second, she felt like a shadow in someone else's story.

She could still turn around.

She didn't.

As SARAH WALKED toward the entrance, the familiar buzz of surveillance drones hummed overhead. The door was guarded by a pair of officers in crisp uniforms, scanning patrons as they passed through. As she approached, the tall officer held up a hand.

"Bag check," he said, his voice mechanical. Sarah's heart skipped.

"Shit."

She paused, trying to keep her expression neutral, her fingers brushing the edge of the book hidden in the lining of her satchel. For a split second, her breath caught. How could she have been stupid enough to bring her father's book *here* of all places.

The officer's eyes moved over her, as he peered into the bag. The small metallic chime of the scanner confirmed there were no obvious threats. She quickly slipped her hand over the edges of the book, hiding it under a bundle of pamphlets—only her small, brief movement caught in the officer's peripheral vision.

"Everything alright?" he asked, slightly too focused on her bag.

Sarah nodded, the words suddenly heavy in her throat. "Yeah, just…nothing to see."

He nodded and gestured for her to move on, the scanner beeping again as she passed. Her body stiffened as she stepped through the doorway, feeling the weight of the book like an anchor. She hadn't even realized she was holding her breath until it came rushing out, the crowd's noise enveloping her.

Close. Too close. She swore under her breath.

INSIDE, THE HEAT HIT FIRST. Then the sound. Then the eyes.

Not everyone turned, but it felt like they did.

Marcus saw her first. Relief broke across his face. He elbowed Greg, who gave her a brief nod before returning to his drink.

"Sarah!" Marcus called. He stood and waved her over.

She moved carefully through the crowd, avoiding the glances, the slogans, the spotlight.

"You made it," Marcus said.

"I did."

Dan looked up.

Their eyes met.

For a moment, the bar faded.

"Welcome to the party," he said, raising his glass in a half-toast.

Sarah nodded. "Looks lively."

The corner of his mouth twitched. Not quite a smile. Not quite not.

12

Greg grinned.

"Looks like this night just got interesting."

Marcus gave him a nervous smile.

Sarah slid into the booth beside Marcus, who beamed like he'd just won the lottery. He immediately launched into introductions, his words spilling over themselves.

"This is Sarah," Marcus said, practically glowing. "She's been running circles around the aid center since college. I mean, she knows the city better than half the regulators...and she's got a way of talking people down without ever raising her voice. Saved my ass more than once."

Sarah gave him a side glance. "That's... a stretch."

Dan offered a nod. "Nice to meet you."

"Welcome to the inner circle," Greg said, flashing a grin. "Don't worry, we don't bite."

"Some of us don't," Marcus added, laughing a little too loud.

Sarah adjusted in the booth. Dan watched her carefully. There was something in the way she carried herself. Not guarded, exactly, but distant. Like she was trying to learn something without letting anyone know she was studying.

Marcus launched into a mission story before anyone could stop him. He gestured with wide arms and shifted the tone halfway through to include a funny mishap with a glitchy comms unit that somehow became a triumphant win. Dan had heard it before, twice this week, but let him go on. Marcus needed the airtime. Sarah listened, her expression unreadable. When the retelling got to Dan's role, Marcus leaned forward.

"You should've seen it. Textbook. Minimal collateral. Straight from the manual."

That word again. Minimal. It crashed into Dan like a garbage truck.

Sarah looked at Dan. For a second, she thought she saw doubt. Or was it empathy? It vanished quickly.

Greg pivoted, giving her a nudge with his elbow. "What about you, Sarah? What's your day job when you're not gracing us with your presence?"

"I work with people who need help," she said simply, avoiding the specifics.

Marcus leaned in again, that same flicker of admiration in his eyes. "She's one of the good ones."

The group murmured approvingly, but Dan sensed something more complicated beneath it, something Sarah wasn't saying.

The attention, all directed her way now, felt a little too warm, a little too close.

She started to rise, brushing a loose strand of hair behind her ear. "I'm going to grab a drink."

Before she could step away, Marcus blurted, "I'll get it," already halfway up. Too eager, like he'd been rehearsing the offer in his head for the past ten minutes.

She hesitated, halfway between standing and retreating, then sank reluctantly back into her seat. Marcus scurried off.

"I'll leave you two to it," Greg muttered, slipping toward the restroom, leaving her alone with Dan. *The* Dan.

When the others were gone, the air between them changed. Dan felt it immediately. Quieter... heavier.

"So," he said. "What did Marcus promise to get you here tonight?"

Sarah smiled faintly. "Nothing. I was out with friends. He just said it might be worth a detour."

Dan nodded. "Glad you made the turn."

A pause. Then—

"Must feel good," Sarah said, gesturing subtly at the room. "Being the center of all this."

Dan exhaled slowly. "It's part of the job."

She tilted her head. "But don't you ever think about it? What it means to be a hero and never be in danger?"

Dan stiffened. Not angry. Just exposed.

"You think I don't ask myself that?"

"I think you're good at what you do," Sarah said. "But it's a different kind of heroism. Clean. Distant."

Dan looked down at his glass. "It's still real," he said, though the certainty in his voice wavered. "The consequences, the responsibility, they're as real as they've ever been."

Sarah's eyes softened, just a fraction. "I don't doubt that. But real for whom, Dan? For you?"

For the first time in what felt like ages, Dan found himself without a ready answer.

Marcus returned with her drink. "You two look intense," he said, handing it over.

"Just getting to know the legend," Sarah said lightly.

Marcus laughed and slid back into the booth. But something in his glance lingered. Measured. Uncertain.

Dan raised his glass again.

The drink tasted colder now.

13

As the bar crowd began to thin and the night wound down Marcus lingered near the door, his voice a little too casual: 'You heading out?

Sarah nodded. "Yeah, I should."

"Mind if I walk you?" he added quickly. "Just to make sure you get back okay."

"I'll be fine," she said.

"Right. No, yeah. Of course. Just figured..."

But she didn't stop him from following.

THE STREETS WERE QUIETER now, the city humming in its after-hours rhythm. Streetlights pooled golden on the wet pavement. They walked side by side without speaking.

Marcus kept fiddling with something on his wrist.

Sarah glanced over. "What is that? You keep touching it. You were touching it the other day, too."

He looked down like he'd forgotten it was there. "Oh. Just something my abuela gave me. From when I was a kid."

"She gave you a bracelet?"

"Yeah," Marcus said, his voice softening. "She was everything when I was a kid. My mom was gone most of the time, and my dad... wasn't around much either. But my abuela, she always made space for me. She used to say the world would try to make me forget who I was."

He held up his wrist. "So she gave me this. Said if I ever felt lost, I should hold onto it. That it would remind me."

"She sounds lovely."

Yeah, she was great. He touched each of the three worn beads, slower now. "Uno por coraje. One for courage. Dos por esperanza. Two for hope."

His voice dropped, more fragile than before. "Y tres... por no perderte. Three so I don't lose you."

"You said she *was* great...I take it she's gone now?"

"Yeah," Marcus said quietly. "She didn't make it through the attack." He stared at the ground, fingers moving across the beads.

Sarah didn't speak for a long moment. Her voice was quieter when she finally responded. "I lost my parents in the Zone attack."

Marcus looked over, surprised, but didn't say anything.

"I don't usually talk about it," she added. "But I have a friend. Amelia. We grew up in the city together. She's stayed with me ever since. Makes sure I don't drift too far."

She gave him a half-smile. "Courage...hope...I guess she's my version of the bracelet."

Marcus smiled, warmer this time. "She sounds like someone worth holding on to."

They stopped at her corner.

"Thanks for walking me," she said.

"Anytime."

She paused at the door, hand on the handle. "Goodnight, Marcus."

He looked up. "Goodnight."

She offered him a soft smile, something real, if not quite a promise, then slipped inside.

Marcus lingered at the bottom of the steps, staring up at the door long after it had closed. He shifted his weight, glanced down at the bracelet on his wrist. He traced the third bead, but didn't say the words this time.

Then, with a quiet sigh, he turned and walked into the night. When he got home, he locked the door behind him, the bolt sliding into place with a muted click.

14

His apartment was too quiet. Not peaceful. Sterile. It smelled faintly of lemon solvent and recycled air, like a room that had been scrubbed too many times without ever being lived in.

He set his bag on the bench near the entryway and unzipped it slowly, removing a sealed meal pouch, a worn prayer card, and a regulation booklet titled Strength Through Obedience. He placed each item on the shelf by the door in perfect alignment. It was muscle memory. Habit. Survival.

The wall screen flickered to life. The closing blessing had already begun.

"May your loyalty be your shield, your faith a guiding flame..."

Marcus stepped out of his boots. The sound of Velcro echoed too loudly. He crossed to the far shelf, where rows of devotional books stood in pristine formation. He adjusted one slightly to restore its symmetry.

Then, he hesitated.

He reached behind the row and pulled out a small, tattered book. The cover had once been deep blue. Now it was nearly gray from wear. Inside, the pages were scribbled with notes in two hands: his, and his mother's.

Underneath it lay a photo, creased and fading. A boy with wide eyes, standing beside a woman in a field. No flags. No salutes. Just sun and wind and a kite held between them.

The broadcast intoned: "All glory to the Founders, all peace to the faithful."

Marcus replaced the photo. Closed the book. Slid both back into hiding.

He turned toward the screen and stood still.

The final pledge scrolled across the bottom in crisp white letters. He placed his hand over his chest and began to mouth the words. No sound, no conviction, just motion.

"I pledge my strength to the Righteous State, my faith to its eternal guardians, my vigilance to the cause of sacred victory."

The camera light blinked red in the corner.

He finished the line, eyes blank.

"Amen," he said softly.

15

The room was dark, bathed in the soft glow of a few strategically placed lamps. Heavy drapes blocked out the late afternoon sun, casting long shadows that danced over the rich mahogany of Reverend Eli Hightower's desk. The scent of polished wood and old books mingled with the faint aroma of incense lingering from the morning's private prayer. The only sound was the gentle ticking of the antique clock on the wall. A reminder that time, like power, must always be managed.

President Knox sat across from him, legs sprawled like he owned the place. His tailored suit was impeccable, but it couldn't hide the smugness that radiated from beneath every cuff and collar.

"Dan Clymer," Knox declared, fingers drumming a lazy rhythm. "He's exactly what we need for the next phase. The public loves him. His Hall of

Valor induction couldn't be timed better. We get him on stage with you and me during Martyrs Day—boom, new cabinet appointment. The face of the next era."

Hightower steepled his fingers. His expression was calm, but there was ice behind the stillness.

"The idea has potential," he said after a deliberate pause. "But potential doesn't equal readiness. Has he been tested?"

Knox scoffed. "Tested? He's killed more people than half the command floor combined."

"Yes. But that's not the test I'm referring to."

Knox shifted slightly. "He's obedient. Loyal. Exactly the brand we need."

"Loyalty," Hightower murmured, "is most guaranteed when it's unexamined."

The room fell quiet again, the clock ticking like a metronome between their silences. Knox's aides didn't speak. Hightower's never even looked up.

"Symbols rise fast," Hightower said, almost to himself. "But it's the unseen hand that teaches them where to point."

WHEN THE MEETING ENDED, Knox left in a wave of tailored fabric and overconfident swagger.

Hightower stayed seated, hands still folded.

He waited until the footsteps were gone, then stood, moving to the window.

Below him, the city churned in regulated motion: drones in formation, crowds funneling through civic checkpoints, billboards rotating between scripture and state-sanctioned slogans.

Hightower closed his eyes. Somewhere beneath the city's rhythm was a boy in a hot room, kneeling on a wood floor while his father read scripture with a belt in his lap. Obedience was not natural. It was beaten into men. Forged like iron. He could still hear the snap of the belt before the scripture finished—obedience was measured in bruises, not blessings.

"Let's see what you're made of, Mr. Clymer," he murmured.

He returned to the desk and picked up the phone, its polished receiver cool against his palm. A few quick taps, and the direct line to Dan's personal number was dialed.

The call was unexpected. And that was exactly the point.

The first time...no answer. On the second call it rang twice before Dan answered, his voice steady, professional.

"Reverend Hightower," he said, the faintest hint of surprise threading through the formality.

"Dan," Hightower began, infusing his tone with the warmth that had captivated millions. "I wanted to personally congratulate you on your induction into the Hall of Valor. A rare honor. Earned."

There was a pause.

"Thank you, Reverend. It's... appreciated."

"You've served with discipline. Integrity. Faith." Hightower's voice took on a steely edge. "We are entering a time that will test those virtues. I trust you'll rise to the occasion."

"I'll do my part," Dan said. His tone was careful.

Hightower narrowed his eyes slightly. "Good. Because a true defender knows what's at stake. And knows the faithful are always watching."

"I understand, Reverend. I won't disappoint."

"I know you won't," Hightower said. Then he hung up.

THE ROOM WAS QUIET again.

He pressed a button on his desk.

"Prepare the media release," he said. "Frame the Hall of Valor induction as divine recognition. Emphasize that loyalty is sanctified by service."

"Yes, Reverend," came the reply.

He turned toward the framed verse on the wall: The righteous path is narrow, and only the steadfast may walk it.

He spoke the next line softly, more to himself than anyone else: "May our hands be guided by the divine, our actions blessed with purpose, and our hearts unwavering in faith."

16

Dan stirred awake to the thrum behind his eyes, the kind of headache that didn't wait for permission. Light leaked through the half-open blinds, slicing across his apartment in harsh geometric lines. Empty bottles cluttered the table. The air smelled faintly of warm liquor and stale beer.

He sat up slowly, fragments of the night trickling back: Marcus, loud and hopeful; Greg, laughing at his own jokes; Sarah, sharp as flint. Her words had stuck like burrs in the dark, quiet, reasonable challenges that refused to leave him alone.

He shuffled into the kitchen, fingers moving on instinct. Water. Coffee. The moka pot clicked into place. He opened the tin of state-branded coffee, Liberty Grounds: Strong Flavor, Stronger Faith, already preground, vacuum-sealed for freshness and conformity. The smell hit first: bold, burnt, familiar. It filled the silence like a hymn.

He reached for his phone while the coffee gurgled. Notifications blinked across the screen: congratulations, endorsements, algorithm-curated praise. A headline scrolled past: "Valor Is a Choice—Clymer's Heroism Sets New Standard."

Then he saw it.

Missed call: Reverend Eli Hightower.

His pulse ticked faster.

The phone buzzed again.

Incoming call.

He answered. "Reverend Hightower."

"Dan," came the voice. Smooth, composed, unmistakable. "I wanted to personally congratulate you on your induction. The Hall of Valor...you've earned it."

Dan swallowed. "Thank you, Reverend. I'm grateful."

"This isn't just a commendation," Hightower said. "It's a symbol. You embody the faith that keeps our people secure."

Dan stared at the counter. "I understand."

"Good." The word hung like a blade. "The world watches. And it's men like you who must stand resolute. Your induction is more than honor, it's a message. To the faithful. And the wavering."

Dan said nothing. The silence pressed in.

"I won't disappoint," he said.

"I'm certain of it." The line cut.

Dan stared at the screen. He hadn't realized he was holding his breath. It wasn't the praise that unsettled him, it was how much it sounded like a warning.

The coffee was done. He poured a cup and stood at the window. The city outside was already in motion. Orderly and watchful. Loud in all the wrong ways. Sarah's voice rose in the back of his mind: "Do you ever think about what it means to never face the people you fight?"

He took a sip. It tasted hollow.

HE CHANGED INTO SWEATPANTS and an academy sweatshirt. The emblem across his chest—swords crossed beneath a rising sun, framed by laurel and scripture—used to make him feel proud. Now it felt exposed...naked. On display for everyone to see.

The morning was sharp and bright. The city thrummed with orchestrated patriotism. Billboards pulsed with slogans: "Ever Faithful." "Stand With Strength." "Believe and Prevail."

Dan ran. Feet against pavement. Heart pounding harder than the propaganda speakers overhead. His breath synced with the rhythm, but his thoughts wandered.

Marcus had texted him, he'd seen the missed call. Dan hadn't answered. He couldn't. Not yet.

A schoolyard passed to his left. Children stood in rows, reciting the Daily Blessing. Their hands were folded. Their eyes forward.

"Loyalty is strength," they said in unison.

The city shouted, but inside him, something had gone quiet.

Dan ran faster.

He passed a vendor selling red-white-and-gold pastries beneath a banner that read "Feed the Faithful." Across the square, a holoscreen replayed part of Hightower's latest sermon: "Our soldiers, seen and unseen, carry the weight of salvation."

His chest tightened.

He pushed harder.

Was this salvation? Sarah would've called it theater. Marcus would've believed it without question.

He thought of those old texts he'd studied. Spartans. Huns. Persian generals. Men who had to stand eye to eye with death and still move forward. Blood, dust, steel. None of it sanitized.

He had a touchscreen phone and a medal.

Was that valor?

Was it even war?

A statue loomed ahead. President Knox, ten meters high, hand raised in solemn command. Dan slowed. The shadow stretched long across the street. Cold and clean.

He stopped beneath it. Chest heaving. Hands on his knees.

No doubts, he thought.

His phone buzzed again. Marcus. Dan didn't answer. Not yet.

He looked up at the stone face.

But comfort didn't come.

Only silence.

17

The early light traced familiar lines across Sarah's room, touching the cascading plants in terracotta pots and the stacked books on crowded shelves. Cleo stretched lazily by the window, catching the morning sun in her fur. The room was still and calm, a sharp contrast to the world outside. Sarah rolled over and sat up slowly, a slight throb in her forehead reminding her of the night before.

Rising with a sigh, she wrapped herself in an oversized cardigan and padded into the kitchen. Her fingers moved automatically. She reached for her grinder, already knowing the steps by heart. In a world built on convenience and conformity, even the act of making her coffee from scratch felt like resistance. Quiet. Intentional. Hers.

The rhythmic grinding filled the silence, a meditation that slowed her thoughts. She added a pinch of cardamom and two spoons of sugar to the ibrik before filling it halfway with water. Placing it on the stove, her mind began to wander as she watched for the mixture to froth, pulling it off just before it could boil.

As the rich, spiced scent of the coffee curled around her, Sarah leaned on the counter and let the events of the previous night replay in her mind. She'd left the bar with a strange mix of emotions—confusion, curiosity, and something else she couldn't quite name. Dan's presence had been more captivating than she'd expected. Beneath his calm, confident exterior, there had been moments when his eyes clouded, as if warring thoughts stirred just beneath the surface. And then there was Marcus's unabashed admiration of him, so fervent it bordered on worship. She remembered the way he fidgeted with the bracelet on their walk home, and how gently he'd explained it when she asked. He could be sweet, but it was apparent he wanted something more from her. She felt bad for leading him on, but didn't know how to let him down without breaking something fragile between them.

A knock on the door pulled her back. She poured the thick coffee into a small, pre-warmed cup and opened the door to find Amelia standing there, smiling, with a loaf of bread tucked under one arm.

"Morning, sunshine," Amelia said, breezing in like she owned the place. "I brought this, figured you'd need carbs."

Sarah laughed and gestured to the kitchen. "You know me too well. Coffee's ready."

They settled in the living room, Cleo weaving between their legs. Amelia took a sip and raised an eyebrow. "You and your contraband coffee," she teased. "So? How was the big night?"

Sarah's eyes lingered on the steam rising from her cup. "Eventful," she said. "Marcus was there. And Dan."

Amelia arched a brow. "I believe you mean '*The Dan Clymer*.'"

Sarah tried not to smile. "He's... interesting. There's more to him than the uniform."

Amelia's playfulness dimmed slightly. "Be careful. The ones closest to the state rarely know how deep they're in it."

The air between them shifted. A quiet seriousness returned.

"I heard something," Amelia said, lowering her voice. "There are whispers. People might be alive in the Sacrificial Zone."

Sarah's hand paused mid-sip. "That's not possible."

She remembered the headlines from years ago: chemical strikes, total casualties, full evacuation. Her mother had still been chasing a story back then. Her father had refused to leave the city—said people always overreact. After the strike, neither had answered her calls. The government declared the area uninhabitable the next day. She never got answers. Only silence and a closed file.

"Is it?" Amelia asked. "You work with people. You see how easy it is to erase someone. You see the names fade from their files. You see the way they stop being seen—become unfindable."

Sarah stared into her cup, the sediment curling in slow spirals.

"If it's true..."

"It means the state is lying," she whispered. Saying it out loud felt like opening a door she couldn't close again.

Amelia nodded. "And if Dan's already questioning things?"

Sarah didn't respond immediately. But Dan's eyes flashed behind her own. Calm, uncertain... deeply human.

Reverend Hightower's voice sliced through the quiet, spilling into the room from the vents. His blessing echoed across the neighborhood: "May we walk in faith, uphold the truth of our nation, and stand ever vigilant against those who would seek to unravel our sacred unity."

The voice spilled from the walls like smoke; sweet, suffocating. Hightower's words used to wash past her. Now they stuck.

Sarah forced a smile. "It was one night. With the attention he's getting, I doubt I'll see him again."

She reached for Amelia's hand. "Same time after work?"

Amelia nodded. "Same place. Stay safe."

Sarah stood, still holding her cup. The dregs swirled. The light was brighter now, drawing sharp lines across the room. She stared into the dark sediment, as if somewhere in the swirl, the cracks were starting to show.

18

The heavy doors closed with a muffled finality. Reverend Eli Hightower stood at the window of his private study, watching the orderly morning procession of citizens funneling through the checkpoint gates. Their movements had the precision of a ritual.

President Knox crossed the room with less ceremony, scrolling through a secure tablet. His face was tight, unreadable.

"The foreign campaign footage is holding," Knox said flatly. "Patriot Points engagement is up seven percent. No leaks. No unauthorized images. Clymer's profile is clean."

"As it should be," Hightower murmured, hands clasped behind his back. "We give them only what they're meant to see."

Knox scowled. "There's chatter in the civilian channels. Not organized. Not yet. But we know how fast rumors grow."

Hightower turned slowly. "Then root them before they take seed."

Knox tilted the tablet toward him. "I've authorized increased ground sweeps in the outer sectors. More random loyalty checks. Additional grid scans near the market district."

Hightower gave a faint nod. "Good. Quietly. Subtle disruption maintains faith better than overt suppression."

Knox eyed him carefully. "You're sure about this timeline?"

Hightower stepped closer to the window. The giant screen across the square lit up with the Valor Network's morning programming: Dan's pristine image overlaid with soaring patriotic slogans.

"It must appear organic," Hightower said softly. "Spontaneous adoration. They must believe they discovered him. Not that we placed him there."

Knox sighed. "You're betting a lot on faith."

"Faith is nothing but controlled narrative," Hightower replied. "And we still hold the pen."

There was silence between them as the anthem rose faintly from the city speakers. Then Hightower smiled thinly.

"Let them sing. The curtain is almost ready to rise."

A KNOCK STARTLED HER. Cleo barely blinked. Sarah rose carefully.

When she opened the door, Marcus stood there, holding a paper bag. "Thought you could use dessert. Pre-vigil indulgence."

Sarah stepped aside. "You didn't have to."

He grinned, stepping into the familiar space. "They're from the new kiosk near the square. You should've seen the line. Everyone's feeling festive."

She opened the bag. Two pastries, each sealed with a government-issued sticker: a stylized dove and a blade entwined beneath the words Sweets of Sacrifice.

Of course.

Marcus wandered the room like always, eyes briefly scanning the decor. No flags. No posters. No slogans.

"Still cozy in here," he said, sitting lightly on the edge of her couch. Cleo jumped into his lap, surprisingly tolerant. Marcus smiled.

"So... what did you think of Dan?" he asked.

Sarah kept her expression flat. "Quiet. Polite. He listens well enough."

"He's a legend," Marcus said. "Every cadet runs his missions in the sim. I was there when he conducted the last one. It was—flawless. Dude's unreal."

She sipped her coffee. "He seemed... practiced."

Marcus didn't catch the edge in her voice. "Yeah. He's clean. Like... above the rest of us. You know?"

She gave a small nod but didn't reply.

Marcus glanced at the time and stood. "We're heading to Valkyrie's again after the ceremony. Greg reserved a booth. Dan doesn't know—it's kind of a surprise. You should swing by. Bring your friends if you want."

She hesitated.

"No pressure," he added quickly. "But... I'd like it."

Sarah nodded. "Maybe. Depends how things shake out."

Marcus paused at the door. "He meant what he said, you know. About the war. About the loss."

She didn't answer, and he didn't push it.

"See you at the induction ceremony??"

"Maybe."

She closed the door and locked it behind him. Then leaned her forehead against the frame.

Cleo rubbed against her shin.

Sarah turned back toward the kitchen. The headlines still glowed.

She picked up her shawl, pulled the flyers from her drawer, and stared at the one on top.

Maybe tonight, she'd leave a few more behind.

19

Reverend Hightower paced the grand hall of his private chambers, the polished marble floor reflecting light from towering stained-glass windows. Each pane depicted triumphal saints with armored wings, standing over faceless enemies cloaked in shadow. The air vibrated with reverence as chants from the daily service below rose and fell like tides.

President Knox sat at the long mahogany table, fingers tapping the carved wood. His suit was immaculate, his expression anything but. "How long will this take, Eli?" he snapped. "The campaign event's at prime time. No surprises. We can't afford an optics blunder."

"It won't be a surprise," Hightower replied, his tone velvet over steel. "It will be a revelation."

Two weeks had passed since Dan Clymer's surgical strike elevated him from faceless operator to folk hero. Tonight, his image, projected across rooftops, broadcasts, and pulpits, would crystallize into something larger than life. A monument. A myth. A legend.

Hightower stopped beside Knox, resting a hand on his shoulder. "Dan Clymer's induction into the Hall of Valor, alongside the unveiling of the DAN drone, will fuse faith and security into a single narrative. It's more than ceremony. It's doctrine."

Knox scoffed. "Let's hope he understands the weight of the stage. The people love him, but love's fickle. It needs guidance. And we're the ones holding the reins."

An aide entered and bowed. "The press is ready, sir. Media representatives are in place."

Hightower's robe shimmered as he turned, embroidered gold thread catching the light: In Unity, Faith. He cast Knox a beatific smile. "Before the spotlight finds us, you'll meet our hero in the flesh. He's waiting just beyond the doors."

As they moved down the corridor, the chants from below reached a crescendo. It wasn't music. It was control.

DAN ADJUSTED THE COLLAR of his ceremonial uniform. Gold epaulets caught the light. The air in the waiting room was dense with incense and something colder—polished brass, stone, expectation.

He stared at his reflection in a full-length mirror. Clean lines. Measured breath. A soldier, a symbol. He didn't recognize his own eyes.

A soft knock at the door jolted him back to reality. An aide's voice followed. "Mr. Clymer, Reverend Hightower and President Knox will be with you shortly."

Dan nodded. No one saw.

He stood beneath the flag and the cross, both hanging from the wall as guardians of the State. The door creaked. Footsteps echoed.

Hightower's voice led the way. "President Knox, allow me to introduce Mr. Daniel Eustatius Clymer, our honored defender and today's living testament."

Knox's gaze landed on Dan, calculating, indifferent. The appraisal of a pawn awaiting its role. He approached like a man rehearsing sincerity, his handshake firm, his smile functional.

"Operator Clymer," he said. "With men like you, I don't just see valor, I see potential. Influence. Maybe even something more permanent, politically speaking."

"It's an honor, sir," Dan replied, his voice smooth, if not entirely his own.

Hightower stepped forward. "Let's dispense with the pleasantries, gentlemen. There is more to today than ceremony. Dan, we invited you here not just to honor your achievements but to offer you a place in the president's cabinet as the next Minister of Peace and Security."

Knox's expression twitched. "Reverend, we should've discussed..."

Hightower's glance silenced him. It wasn't aggressive. It was absolute. The room tightened with an unspoken understanding of their hierarchy, Knox's objection dissolving in the weight of Hightower's presence.

Dan's thoughts scrambled for footing. He masked it well, but the word peace echoed strangely in his head. As did security. As did minister.

He paused. "Thank you, Reverend."

Hightower's laughter broke the tension, a low, confident rumble that seemed to fill the room like the deep toll of a bell. The corners of his mouth lifted, eyes glinting with the gleam of a man who wielded power effortlessly.

"No need for hesitation. We'll speak more in the days ahead."

Knox said nothing. Dan saw it then. Not just the politics, but the resentment. The shifting power. The leash tightening.

Hightower turned to both men. "The world is waiting."

Hightower swung his arm to urge Dan ahead, side-by-side with him as the two men made small talk down the corridor to the waiting reporters. President Knox followed a few steps behind, glaring at the back of Hightower's head, fuming.

20

The plaza was unrecognizable.

Where yesterday there had been concrete, today there were banners—red, navy, and blinding white. Screens blinked with slow-motion footage of drone launches and patriotic hymns. Giant posters bore Dan's face, rendered in high-contrast monochrome, with words like HONOR and SACRIFICE bleeding into the corners.

Children filed in by rank, dressed in miniature uniforms. Not for combat, for optics. They carried miniature flags and lyric sheets. A conductor in a government vest clapped his hands to bring them to attention.

Dan stood at the edge of the main stage, off-camera, a shadow in his own celebration.

From the far side of the plaza, a media director pointed toward the podium. "We want the medal moment tight. Zoom on the eyes. And don't cut to Knox until after the clasp. We're selling humility first, then strength."

Someone ran cables. Someone else readjusted a cross-shaped banner where it had started to lean. The air smelled like hot metal, electricity, and something too sweet. Victory Grounds, probably.

A group of children began to sing:

"In glory and in duty, Our heroes rise above, With hand to heart and eyes to flame, We follow those we love."

Their voices were pure. Perfect. Too perfect. Dan watched them without blinking.

One girl in the front row turned slightly, her eyes scanning the perimeter. They landed on him. Not recognition. Not reverence. Just observation. The kind of look you give a statue.

Dan shifted his weight. The medal pinned to his chest caught the light and flared.

He stepped back from the edge of the stage. Just enough to disappear from the sightlines.

Behind him, the children continued:

"O Patriot, O Lord above, Lead us ever true, We pledge ourselves in faith and strength, In service, blood, to you."

Dan didn't mouth the words. He didn't move at all.

SARAH ADJUSTED HER SCARF against the evening chill as she stood beside Marcus in the crowded square. She hadn't wanted to come. This kind of thing wasn't her scene, but Marcus had insisted. And she hadn't been able to say no. Amelia had flatly refused the invite, leaving Sarah without an ideological buffer. The square, normally a bustling commercial center, had been remade into a spectacle. Banners lined the buildings, spotlights swept the crowd, and enormous screens loomed over everything, casting a cold blue light.

Speakers blasted patriotic music, drowning out the low murmur of the assembled citizens. Marcus stood tall, wide-eyed, waving a miniature flag absently like a kid at a parade. Sarah scanned the crowd, families, vendors, schoolchildren in uniform, all gathered in reverent anticipation. The state emblem fluttered everywhere: the rising sun behind the cross and sword, etched in gold. Her fingers tightened around her scarf.

"This is it," Marcus said, nudging her. "They're about to start."

The screen crackled to life. President Knox appeared on a grand stage framed by martial banners and glowing scripture. Just below, a grinning animated soldier popped up with the caption: "Presented Live by Defender Dental—Defending Your Mouth Against Cavities!"

The crowd roared. Marcus whooped. "Dan's going to be inducted into the Hall of Valor! Can you believe it?"

Sarah forced a smile. "Yeah. It's something, all right."

Knox raised his hands for silence. The square quieted.

"We gather tonight," he began, "to celebrate the brave, the loyal, and the righteous. To honor those whose sacrifice builds the very foundation of our Republic."

Applause erupted. On-screen, Reverend Hightower took the stage, robes gleaming under spotlights.

"Our strength," Hightower intoned, "is in our unity. And tonight, we recognize not just a hero, but a symbol. A man whose faith and valor illuminate the path for all."

Sarah glanced at Marcus. His face was rapt, eyes shimmering in the glow of the screen.

"You don't look convinced," he said.

"It's a lot," she admitted. "All this spectacle." She hesitated. "Don't you ever wonder if there's more to the story they tell us?"

Marcus frowned. "What do you mean?"

She kept her voice low. "I've heard rumors... people surviving in the Sacrificial Zone."

He laughed lightly, shaking his head. "Come on, Sarah. You don't actually believe that stuff, do you? No one survived out there. You know that."

Sarah looked away.

The screen changed again. Dan stepped forward in full dress uniform, solemn beneath a cascade of white-gold lights. His image towered above the crowd.

"Ladies and gentlemen," the announcer boomed, "it is my honor to present Daniel Eustatius Clymer—our newest inductee into our esteemed and cherished Hall of Valor! Sponsored by Armory Assurance: When the Fight Comes Home, We've Got You Covered."

More cheers. Fireworks exploded overhead. Marcus cheered until his voice cracked. "There he is! Dan Eustatius Clymer. He deserves this."

Sarah kept her gaze on Dan's projected face. His posture was perfect. His expression was unreadable. He looked like a man trying not to flinch under the weight of his own legend.

Knox stepped forward to shake his hand. "Tonight, we honor true courage," he said. "True patriotism. True leadership. An honor rarely bestowed, and only on the absolute best our Republic has to offer"

Sarah's eyes narrowed. More logos scrolled across the screen: insurance, weapons contracts, patriotic fashion lines. Even bottled water. Everything branded.

Then Hightower reappeared.

"Let us give thanks," he said, his voice rising like a sermon, "for a moment unlike any in our nation's history. For the first time, we honor a soldier not only in spirit, but in steel. Tonight, we unveil the DAN drone, Defensive Action Neutralizer, named in honor of Operator Daniel Eustatius Clymer.

This is no ordinary advancement. This is the most sophisticated, precise, and powerful autonomous weapon ever conceived by man. Guided by our values, forged in our image. A sleek, righteous instrument of defense and deterrence, sanctified by purpose and perfected by design.

To name such a weapon for one man... that is not commendation. It is canonization. A mark of faith, bestowed only upon one whose courage and conviction eclipse all others. Let the world remember that name: Clymer. A guardian made immortal, a symbol of divine justice in a world too often ruled by chaos."

The screen lit up with the drone's reveal. Sleek. Sharp-edged. D-A-N stenciled across its metallic side in blood red.

The crowd roared. Marcus grinned wide. "See? He's a legend now! Immortal."

Sarah couldn't look away. "Perfect," she said quietly, a chill rolling down her spine.

The ceremony went on. More prayers, more pledges, more slogans. Knox spoke again, this time framed by cascading streamers and digital flames. Hightower offered a final blessing.

Marcus turned to her, full of conviction. "This is why we believe. Everything they do...it's for us."

She nodded, not trusting herself to speak.

"I still want to see the Zone someday," Marcus added, his voice quieter now. "Just to understand what it cost. I mean... my abuela was lost there. And your parents too." He looked down at his flag, twisting it once between his fingers. "It's sacred, isn't it? To see the sacrifice it took to make our world what it is."

Sarah smiled faintly. "Maybe. One day."

He beamed.

Dan stood frozen in salute, flanked by Knox and Hightower. The final image faded to the national seal, now pulsing with light, as fireworks ignited above the crowd.

Around her, people clapped and cried and cheered. But Sarah stood still, the sound crashing around her like waves. She kept her eyes on the screen, but her thoughts were miles away.

21

Dan stood alone in the small, dimly lit room behind the stage, the echo of the crowd still lingering in his ears. He let out a slow breath, staring at the polished medal draped across his chest. It was heavier than expected. More metal, more meaning. The Hall of Valor. He had been canonized. Immortalized. He was supposed to feel pride. But all he felt was hollow.

He caught his reflection in a mirror on the far wall. The uniform fit perfectly, every button aligned, every fold crisp. But it looked like a costume. The man inside it—tired, tight-jawed, hollow-eyed—didn't look like a hero. He looked like someone pretending.

A knock. He straightened instinctively.

A young aide entered, her smile precise and polished. "Mr. Clymer, congratulations again. The President would like a word."

Dan nodded. "Of course."

She led him down a fluorescent-lit corridor, heels clacking. The echoes faded into the hum of machinery and distant crowd noise. They arrived at a pair of grand double doors. The aide knocked once, then pushed them open.

Inside: gold trim, velvet drapes, dignitaries and donors sipping from branded glasses. The smell of cologne and ambition hung thick in the air.

President Knox greeted him first, flanked by military brass and Hightower, whose presence seemed to glow under the lights.

"Dan! Our man of the hour." Knox gripped his hand. "You were magnificent. Truly inspiring."

Dan offered a tight smile. "Thank you, sir. It's an honor."

Knox guided him forward. "Come, meet the real power behind the curtain."

He gestured toward a display of branded merchandise: Valor Flakes cereal, Sanctified Arms tactical home defense bundles, Defender Dental kits, and Armory Assurance brochures. A small mountain of patriotically packaged loyalty. A man in a navy suit stepped forward, beaming, holding a box of Valor Flakes with Dan's image on the front.

"Mr. Clymer," he said, "it's an honor. You're the embodiment of modern courage. With your face on our campaign, we're not just selling cereal, we're shaping patriots."

Dan took the box. His own face smiled back at him, overly lit, digitally smoothed.

"Thank you," he said, voice flat. "It's… humbling."

Hightower stepped in, hand on Dan's shoulder. "Let us not forget the spiritual side of this moment. The DAN drone will be our sword of justice, guided by righteous hands."

He turned, still smiling, working the small crowd. "Did Knox tell you? Operator Clymer will be taking the role of Minister of Peace and Defense."

The words hit like a blunt instrument. Around them, a few people clapped.

Dan's smile tightened. "It was… unexpected."

"A divine opportunity," Hightower said, eyes gleaming.

Dan's smile had never taken so much effort to maintain.

The rest blurred. Knox slapped his back. Donors shook his hand. A woman thanked him for keeping her children safe. Everyone smiled too wide.

Eventually, Dan drifted toward the back of the room. He stopped by a window that overlooked the square. The last of the ceremony crowd was dispersing. Streamers drifted through the street like shed skin.

His forehead touched the glass.

Sarah's face flickered in his mind, steady, questioning. She hadn't looked at him with awe. Just curiosity. That had stayed with him.

He looked down at the medal again, then out at the city. Somewhere out there, people believed in this. In him. In the drone.

He thought of ancient warriors. Generals who fought with blade and blood, who faced their enemies and knew the weight of each death. Their names echoed in marble and history books. And here he was: immortalized not by valor, but by marketing. Not a sword, but a drone.

Was this heroism? Sitting in a control room, watching lives end through a screen? There was no risk. No weight. Only distance.

A soft knock.

The aide again. "Mr. Clymer, your car is ready."

Dan nodded. "Thank you."

He followed her out. The air was cool now, the city humming. He looked up, the stars smothered by the glow of artificial light.

He climbed into the waiting car and let the door shut behind him. The drone that bore his name loomed in his thoughts, not as a triumph, but as a warning.

"The most effective way to destroy people
is to deny and obliterate their own
understanding of their history."

-George Orwell

PART 2

22

The crowd was thick, the cheers still echoing in the square as the ceremony wrapped up. Sarah and Marcus moved through it side by side, shoulder to shoulder, but worlds apart. Marcus's energy practically bounced off the pavement. He waved his little flag with uncontainable enthusiasm, flushed with excitement.

"Did you see that? The DAN drone! Named after Dan!" Marcus shouted over the noise. "It's perfect."

Sarah nodded, lips tight. "Yeah. I saw."

She kept her gaze on the crowd, how easily they moved from awe to amusement, how quickly reverence bled into laughter. She had expected a spectacle. But the corporate banners, the precision of the speeches, the product launches... it wasn't just reverence. It was choreography. Orchestration. Manipulation, even.

Marcus nudged her. "Don't be like that. Dan's a hero. He's going to keep us safe. That's what we operators do."

"I know," Sarah said softly. Her voice caught, barely audible. "I get it. It's just... when they started talking about the Zone again up there, it hit different."

"What?" he asked, his grin faltering just a little.

She hesitated. "Don't you ever wonder if it's all just... too polished? Too easy to swallow? The drone, the music, the slogans. And the Sacrificial Zone, like it's just a symbol now—not a place where people died?"

He laughed, but there was an edge to it. "Sarah, come on. That's conspiracy junk. The Zone is... it's ashes. You know that. We both lost people there."

But she was watching him closely. That flicker in his eyes wasn't disbelief. It was hesitation.

"What if it's not?" she said. "What if people are out there, trying to survive?"

Marcus slowed, weaving toward the edge of the crowd. "You really think that?"

"I don't know," Sarah admitted. "Amelia mentioned it. Quietly. She's not the type to chase stories. But it stuck with me. I'm not saying we should do anything stupid... just that it's hard not to wonder sometimes."

Marcus stared at her, his flag lowered now, twisting in his hands. He glanced back toward the square where people were still laughing, still shouting praise for Dan.

Then, as if the idea landed before he fully thought it through, he said, "Maybe we should go." He said it like a joke, but then stopped walking, blinking like he'd surprised himself. "No, really. Why not?"

Sarah blinked. "Go where?"

"To the Zone. Just to see." He gave a breathless laugh, trying to hide the edge in it. "I know how it sounds. But just once, don't you want to stand there? Just to feel it. To see what's real. To know something for sure."

She didn't answer. Her throat tightened. Her parents had vanished into that place. There was no grave. No recovery. Only a silent absence that lived in her very bones.

"You're serious?" she asked quietly.

Marcus nodded. "Look, I don't want to break rules just to stir the pot. But don't you want to know? If something's there. If the state lied."

Sarah looked away. Something clenched tight in her chest. The words Sacrificial Zone always stuck in her throat. Her parents had been there that day. That was the end of their story, and somehow, the beginning of everyone else's. Amelia had mentioned rumors. There were whispers in the market, too, but Nama was elusive and guarded. The silence was its own kind of scream.

"We should do it... make our mark. Don't worry, I'll make sure you... we're safe."

His phone buzzed. He checked it. "Greg's heading to the bar. Want to come?"

Sarah stared at him. He looked so certain. So lit up.

She didn't want to encourage him—not really. Especially with all of this talk about the Zone. But her thoughts were swirling too fast, her doubts too loud, and somewhere beneath it all was the quiet ache that had never gone away. Maybe going along was easier than explaining why she shouldn't. Maybe part of her wanted to see if the silence would crack.

"Sure," she said. "Why not. As long as you stop talking crazy about going into the Zone."

He grinned and slipped the phone away.

"I'm not making any promises," he said jokingly. But not.

He reached for her hand without thinking, but she was already walking, threading through the crowd. He caught up quickly.

They didn't speak much as they walked. But the silence buzzed with something unspoken. Something risky. Something real.

And though Marcus didn't say it aloud, a thought settled into him quietly: If he took her to the Zone—if he showed her something no one else dared to see—maybe she'd finally see him. Not just a loyal operator. But someone brave enough to chase the truth.

23

The apartment lights flickered on automatically as Dan entered, but the space felt dimmer than usual. The silence wasn't comforting. It pressed in around him.

He set the commemorative box on the counter with a soft thunk.

Inside:

- His Hall of Valor plaque, engraved with his name.
- A sealed Fortitude Blend mug with his image engraved in gold.
- A miniature drone replica, the DAN model, in chrome.
- A medal, heavy and cold.

He lifted the medal, turning it over in his palm. The front bore his name: Daniel E. Clymer – Valor Beyond Measure.

Beneath it, smaller lettering read: Presented in Recognition of Historic Patriot Point Accrual.

On the reverse, the logo of Dominion Provisions™ was etched in precise relief, flanked by a stylized QR code linking to his sponsored tribute broadcast.

Dan stared at it. Then set it down.

The wall screen blinked to life without prompting.

"Relive Today's Moment of Glory!" it proclaimed.

His own face appeared, smiling, frozen mid-handshake with Knox, applause roaring behind them. A pre-recorded narration played underneath: "One man. One mission. A legacy built on obedience and precision."

Dan watched it in silence.

He didn't remember smiling. Not like that.

He muted the feed, but the image lingered. He tapped the remote, and the screen turned black. The room filled with stillness. Finally.

He sat. Not at attention. Not upright. Just... down.

The glow of the Patriot Points tally pulsed faintly from his watch: 100,017. Elite status. Lifetime rank secured. No new missions assigned. For now.

His phone buzzed. Dozens of messages. Congratulatory texts. Media tags. At the top: Greg.

Come meet us at the bar. You earned a drink, man.

Dan stared at the message.

After everything... maybe distraction wasn't a betrayal. Maybe it was just survival.

The medal lay beside him, glinting under the overhead light. He reached for it. But didn't lift it.

The silence stretched.

Then Dan stood. Slowly. And turned the screen off at the source.

A quiet, final click.

He didn't need to see it again.

What he did need? A drink.

24

The bar was crowded, alive with noise and movement. Music pulsed through the floorboards, and voices rose in bursts of laughter and clinking glasses. Dan stepped through the door in jeans and a t-shirt, a sharp contrast to the dress uniform he'd shed an hour ago. The medal from the ceremony sat buried in a drawer at home, out of sight, right where he wanted it.

He didn't know what he was doing here. Greg had texted to celebrate, but Dan wasn't sure what there was to celebrate. Being turned into a symbol? Having his name etched onto a drone? He needed the noise. The distraction.

He spotted Greg near the back, surrounded by other operators.

"Dan! Over here!" Greg shouted, raising a drink.

Dan slid into an empty seat, nodding as Greg passed him a tallboy of Valor Lager Light: Fewer Calories, More Courage!

"To the man of the hour!" Greg bellowed. "Hall of Valor inductee. Drone namesake. The whole damn legend!"

Everyone cheered and clinked glasses. Dan raised his beer and offered a muted smile. "Thanks, guys."

Someone asked, "So how does it feel? Being the poster boy for the next generation of tactical destruction?"

Dan shrugged. "It's... a lot."

He didn't know how to say it felt like he was watching someone else live his life.

His eyes scanned the crowd. That's when he saw them.

Marcus. And Sarah.

They stood near the bar, Marcus talking with animated energy, hands moving fast, smile wide. Sarah listened, her expression soft but unreadable. Dan felt a flicker of something, maybe surprise, maybe guilt, maybe something deeper.

"Be right back," he said, setting down his drink.

He crossed the room, weaving through the crush of bodies, and called out, "Marcus! Sarah!"

Marcus turned, lighting up. "Dan! Man, you were incredible tonight." He clapped Dan on the shoulder. "The Hall of Valor! The drone! They're literally naming history after you."

Dan gave a faint smile. "Yeah. Something like that."

His eyes met Sarah's. "Didn't expect to see you here."

Sarah's smile was small, careful. "Marcus convinced me."

There was a pause, just long enough for Dan to notice Marcus's hand fidgeting with the bracelet on his wrist.

Dan turned to Marcus. "Celebrating?"

"Of course!" Marcus said, practically vibrating. "This is huge. We figured we'd come raise a glass or three."

Before Dan could answer, Greg appeared behind him. "Dan, come on, everyone wants to hear about the drone. You've got to tell us more... you've got details, right?"

Marcus perked up, chiming in with his own questions, his voice already shifting toward the larger group.

Sarah leaned toward Dan, voice low. "Can we talk outside?"

Dan nodded. "Sure."

165

He touched Marcus on the arm. "Back in a sec." Marcus waved him off, already caught up in Greg's storytelling.

Outside, the cold hit instantly. The city's neon glare bled into the fog hanging low over the street.

Sarah stopped just beyond the side exit and turned to him. "I need to talk to you. About Marcus."

Dan's chest tightened. "What about him?"

"He's been talking about going into the Sacrificial Zone. He hasn't committed to anything, but... I don't know, it's more than a joke to him it seems He first mentioned it after the ceremony, but he hasn't stopped bringing it up since we got here."

Dan blinked. "The Zone?"

Sarah nodded. "I tried to brush it off, but he kept circling back to it. He thinks it's not that dangerous, that if he can just get there, he'll prove something. Like it's a test of conviction."

Dan looked down the street, jaw tight. "He knows that's insane, right?"

"He trusts the state too much to believe survivors exist. But not enough to leave it alone. It's like... he needs to prove...something? That it's really empty, I guess."

Dan shook his head. "When?" He had more than a slight idea of what Marcus needed to prove.

"I don't know. Soon." Her voice dropped. "He wants me to go with him."

Dan turned toward her. "And?"

"I told him I'd think about it. I'm scared he'll go alone."

"You told him you'd consider it? Did you mean it?" Dan asked with more than a tinge of urgency.

"Of course not. It's just... I have a hard time telling that guy no."

Dan nodded slowly. "So I've noticed. Listen, let me talk to him. I'm sure it's all bravado. You know how Marcus can be. A bit... intense."

Sarah's eyes searched his face. " I don't know, this time he seemed different. More determined. Don't tell him we talked, okay? He'd feel betrayed."

"I won't."

Their eyes held for a moment longer than necessary.

"Come on," Dan said. "Let's get back before Marcus thinks we're plotting."

Sarah smiled, tension cracking. "Yeah. Wouldn't want that."

"Here's my number in case he tries anything crazy. Don't let him get into any trouble without calling me."

They reentered the bar, swallowed again by warmth and sound.

"Dan! Get over here, man!" Greg shouted. He and Marcus had their arms around each other, laughing, each holding a shot glass.

Sarah leaned in close to Dan, her voice low. "Thanks." Then she pulled back, gave a small wave to Marcus, and mouthed, "I've got to go."

Marcus didn't see it, too caught up in the moment.

Dan returned to the table. But he couldn't shake the weight in Sarah's voice.

THE STREET WAS MOSTLY empty by the time Sarah reached Amelia's building. She climbed the stairs, her hands deep in her coat pockets, her mind still buzzing.

She knocked a second time before the door opened. Amelia stood in pajama pants and a sweatshirt, blinking at the hallway light.

"Sarah?"

"Sorry. I just... I wasn't in the headspace to go home and didn't know where else to go."

Amelia waved her inside. "Of course. Come in."

The smell of clove tea and toast filled the air.

They sat at the kitchen table. Sarah rubbed her hands together, not from the cold but from nerves.

"It's Marcus," she said finally. "He wants to go into the Zone."

Amelia raised her eyebrows. "The Sacrificial Zone?"

Sarah nodded.

Amelia let out a low whistle. "That's insane."

"I tried to talk him down. He thinks it's not that dangerous. He wants me to go too. And I'm scared if I don't, he'll go alone."

Amelia reached for Sarah's hand. "You're not going with him."

Sarah swallowed. "I don't want to. But if he does decide to go, I can't let him go alone. He's my friend. And I just... I don't want to be the reason something happens to him."

Amelia sighed. "He doesn't know what he's asking of you."

"I don't think he really sees it. Not the way I do."

Amelia nodded slowly. "Sarah..." Amelia hesitated, her fingers tapping once on the table. "Are you absolutely sure he's serious? That this isn't just one of Marcus's dramatics?"

Sarah hesitated. "No. But I've seen that look in his eyes before. He's already halfway there."

Amelia exhaled through her nose, frustrated. "Then maybe you need to stop him, not follow him."

"I've tried."

Amelia studied her a long moment, jaw clenched. Then, reluctantly: "Alright. If you're going to do this, we're going to do it smart. You'll need supplies. A map. Some idea of where the blind spots are."

"You'll help me?"

"Of course I'll help you. But I don't have to like it." Amelia paused, then added, "I've heard more rumors. Not just static on the fringe...real stuff. Someone swore they saw old state ration crates being traded in the underground markets. Said the barcodes were recent dates. I didn't want to believe it... but lately, I'm not so sure anymore. What about your coffee lady? Where does she get her beans?"

Sarah gave a tired smile. "Nama? I've never asked. She's not the type to like questions.

Listen, you've always been the one who keeps me from losing my way. The one who reminds me what matters."

Amelia rolled her eyes, but her smile was warm. "Damn right I am."

Sarah's smile faded slightly. "Just... promise me you won't let me do anything stupid."

Amelia reached across the table and squeezed her hand. "Only if you promise to come back."

She held Sarah's gaze. "And promise me you'll try one more time to talk Marcus out of it. Before it goes any further."

They sat like that for a long moment, in the quiet, just two people trying to map out the impossible.

Just in case.

25

Reverend Hightower stood beneath the vaulted ceiling of the Hall of Valor's private chapel, his gaze fixed on a stained-glass panel depicting Saint Michael the archangel, sword in one hand and olive branch in the other. Candles flickered in golden sconces along the stone walls, their glow casting long shadows that danced across the mosaic floor. Incense still lingered in the air, a remnant from the blessing given just before the ceremony.

President Knox leaned against the communion rail, a folder of polling data in one hand and a half-finished drink in the other.

"Well, Eli," Knox said, voice full of satisfaction, "we pulled it off. The Hall of Valor, the DAN drone—Dan Clymer's face is everywhere. We've turned him into a national treasure."

"They see what we've taught them to see," Hightower replied. "A loyal operator made holy by the pageantry of sacrifice. A blade, polished and paraded, cloaked in reverence drawn from myth, not merit."

Knox smirked. "There's a cartoon now. The DAN drone teaches kids civic duty."

Hightower didn't flinch. "That needs to be shut down. We're not marketing cereal. We're codifying loyalty."

"There's a prayer going around too," Knox added. "The Voice, the Light, the Shield. You, me, and Dan. Our holy trinity. It's gone viral in the southern parishes."

Now Hightower turned. His smile was tight. "That's not a blessing. That's a warning."

"They're worshipping us," Knox said with a shrug.

"No," Hightower corrected. "They're worshipping him. The moment he believes it, we lose control."

He moved to the side of the altar and poured wine from the ceremonial decanter into a small crystal glass. "Reinforce the narrative. He is the product of our providence, not a prophet in his own right."

Knox leaned back against the rail. "So what's your read on him?"

Hightower paused. "He hesitated tonight. Just for a moment. Not enough to alarm anyone, but I saw it. A question formed behind the eyes. That's how it starts."

Knox chuckled, though not convincingly. "It's probably nothing. A little nerves. The DAN drone rollout's already overtaken every other campaign push we've launched. Kids have backpacks that light up red and say his name. He's not just a symbol, he's a sensation."

"A sensation is volatile," Hightower said. "And sensations don't take orders."

"The Minister position," Knox mused, glancing down at his tablet. "It's already politicized. We can't let it slip. Too much invested now. I wish you had told me you planned to..."

"Alex, it's fine. This was the moment. We had to present him as part of the State. As part of *us*. Before the public consecrated him *without* our blessing.

Knox tapped his tablet and turned it toward Hightower. "There's noise about the Sacrificial Zone again. A flagged image just crossed trending thresholds. Grainy footage. Might be real."

Hightower moved closer, studying a flickering heatmap of keywords and viral nodes. "It started in underground channels. Possibly smuggled. Possibly fake. Doesn't matter."

"Why not?"

"Because it gives shape to doubt," Hightower said. "And doubt is contagious."

Knox glanced toward the flickering candles. "So more patrols?"

"No. That shows fear. We make the Zone feel like ancient history. A sealed tomb. A failed memory."

He stepped back, wine in hand. "Frame it as mercy. Sanctified containment. We mourn the lost, we don't question the loss. We've already passed legislation to expand the Zone."

Knox frowned. "Still... maybe Dan could help contain the noise. A PSA, something scripted. Friendly. Harmless."

Hightower's smile didn't reach his eyes. "That would give him ideas, Alexander."

Silence.

Knox straightened. "I'm still President."

"Of course you are."

Hightower raised his glass toward the flickering altar.

"To strength and security. And to keeping our symbols silent."

Knox clinked his glass, lips tight.

"To staying in control."

The two men drank as incense curled in the candlelight. Outside, the square faded to shadow, but within the chapel walls, a new doctrine was already taking form.

26

Marcus hadn't planned on doing it that day. Not really. Not yet.

But sometime between midnight and dawn, the restless energy overtook him. He couldn't stop thinking about Sarah's voice in the bar, the quiet defiance in her questions, the way she didn't look at Dan like everyone else did. It burned in his chest—a need to do something bold, something unforgettable.

He lay awake in his apartment, staring at the ceiling, the dull glow of the streetlight catching the edge of his commendation badge on the nightstand. It looked hollow. All of it did. What good was glory if it didn't mean anything to the people who mattered?

Sarah had said it was a ridiculous idea. Spent the better part of the walk to the bar trying to talk him out of it. But if he were to pull it off...if he were to *know*, and to show *her* in the process...well, she'd have to see him in a different light. Right? And once she saw that Knox and Hightower were right, that the Zone really was empty, then she could move on from the conspiracy theories and finally be content. At peace. And he would be there for her. The one who gave her that gift.

So he got up. They wouldn't get any sort of wireless service there, so he printed a few files that he had clearance to access, satellite screenshots, archived access points, gaps in drone patrols. A map. Nothing solid, but enough. Enough to prove a point.

He packed quickly. Water. Food. A burner ID. A pair of basic air filters—more symbolic than necessary, but it made him feel prepared. They'd only be in for a few hours, take a few photos, prove a point, and get out before anyone even knew they were gone.

Before he could talk himself out of it, he messaged Sarah.

Marcus: "Change of plans. Picking you up in 30. Be ready."

No explanation. No apology. Just momentum.

SARAH HADN'T SLEPT WELL. After her conversation with Amelia, she still hoped Marcus was kidding, or might change his mind, or at least wait a few days. She tried to convince herself it had just been talk, the kind of late-night bravado that faded by morning. But deep down, she knew better. Marcus didn't let things go. Not when he thought it might impress someone.

The message came just after dawn.

Marcus: "Change of plans. Picking you up in 30. Be ready."

No explanation. No details. Just that signature confidence.

She stared at the screen, bile rising in her throat, the taste of acid burning the back of her tongue. She texted back once, then deleted the message. There wasn't time to reason with him now. She had to decide.

Her hands shook as she pulled on her boots and grabbed her pack. She'd prepared for this in theory, with Amelia's help, but that didn't mean she was ready.

Then she did what she'd promised herself she wouldn't: she called Dan.

It rang long enough that she thought he wouldn't pick up. Then, finally...

"Sarah?" His voice was groggy, confused.

"It's happening," she said. "Marcus is coming. Today."

There was a pause, then the rustle of sheets.

"He's really doing it?"

"He thinks it'll prove something. That we'll see it's safe. He won't wait. He won't listen."

Dan exhaled, slow and heavy. "Are you going with him?"

"I don't know what to do," she said, her voice cracking. "I'm not sure I have a choice. He's already on his way here. I thought we had more time. I thought maybe I could talk him down. But if anything were to happen to him, I don't think I could..." She trailed off.

Another pause. Then: "Where are you?"

I'll text you my address.

"I'm on my way."

Sarah closed her eyes. "Dan..."

"We'll figure it out," he said. "Don't let him leave without me."

She ended the call, sent the text, and moved to the window, heart thudding. The sky was gray and low, the city still groggy from the night before. She hoped, briefly, that Marcus would be late.

He wasn't.

The car pulled up fast, too fast, and he leaned across the passenger seat to wave her in. "Let's go!" he called, beaming. "Sun's up, boots on!"

He looked like he was headed to a music festival, not an illegal crossing into a condemned territory.

Sarah stepped outside slowly, shouldering her pack.

"You sure you've got everything?" she asked, trying to stall.

"Food, water, a couple of burner IDs, and some basic filters," Marcus said, his voice full of confidence. He grinned, tapping the dash. "GPS is scrubbed. We're ghosts. Invisible."

"Maybe we wait an hour," she tried. "Check the perimeter again."

Marcus laughed. "It's fine, Sarah. Trust me."

She hesitated, hovering beside the door. "Are you sure we can't wait just a little longer?" she asked, her voice tight.

Marcus gave her a look. "What for?"

"I don't know. Just... I don't feel good about this."

"You said you'd come."

"I didn't say when."

He reached over and popped the door open. "Come on, Sarah."

She lingered one more breath, then finally slid into the passenger seat. As he pulled away from the curb, she glanced once more down the street.

183

A dark sedan rounded the corner at speed, tires whispering against the curb. As he saw them pull away, Dan eased off the gas, keeping just enough distance to stay out of Marcus's sightline.

Sarah's breath hitched, but she said nothing. Marcus was so giddy about his adventure that he didn't notice.

Behind them, Dan switched lanes and followed, eyes locked on the car ahead. He didn't have a plan yet. Just a conviction: He couldn't let Marcus's recklessness put them in danger, especially not Sarah.

THEY DROVE IN SILENCE for most of the two hours. Marcus kept the music low, fiddling with the dial between stations, occasionally humming under his breath. Sarah stared out the window, watching as the buildings thinned into scrubland and signs of civilization gave way to silence. Dan held back, just keeping Marcus's car in sight.

They reached the outer perimeter around mid-morning.

The road dead-ended into a concrete barrier, scorched and overgrown. Beyond it, a fence wrapped in rusted razor wire and scorched state emblems stretched for miles. A faint tang of burnt wire and rusted iron clung to the breeze.

Marcus parked behind a half-collapsed billboard and killed the engine. "Okay. On foot from here."

Sarah got out slowly, stretching her legs. Her mind racing.

"There's a blind spot in the northeast section," Marcus said, slinging his bag over his shoulder. "I pulled some old satellite data and cross-referenced the drone flight paths. The security tower's been offline for years, cameras are out. Just motion sensors and warning signs. If we move slow and low, we'll be invisible."

"Warning signs," Sarah repeated.

"They always exaggerate. Radiation, collapse risk—it's just theater. We're in, we're out. Quick trip."

Sarah didn't answer. The silence was unnatural, no birds, no wind, just the brittle rustle of weeds against metal. A chill passed through her despite the warm air. She brushed her hair out of her face and followed.

Dan arrived a few minutes behind, parking just out of sight and moving fast. He saw their footprints in the dust. Saw the fence in the distance.

He didn't hesitate. Just pulled his collar high, secured his bag, and headed in.

Somewhere ahead, Sarah paused to touch the top of the fence.

She thought of Amelia, of their talk the night before, of how her world used to feel safe even when it wasn't honest. Then she murmured, "Last chance."

But Marcus was already ducking through the breach.

She followed. Dan wasn't far behind.

And behind them all, the wind carried the faint static hum of a forgotten security drone. Still watching. Still listening.

27

The air changed the moment they crossed.

It wasn't just the smell, though that was different too, drier, tinged with metal and ash, it was something in the silence. The world beyond the perimeter felt suspended, stripped of motion. No birds. No wind. No human sounds.

Dan's breath caught in his throat. The last time he'd seen a place this still, he was watching it burn through a grainy monitor.

Marcus stepped forward with purpose, already ten paces ahead. He walked like a man fulfilling a prophecy, not breaking a federal law. The cracked asphalt beneath his boots had once been a road. Now it was a fracture, part nature, part ruin, part memory.

Sarah trailed behind, every step heavier than the last. Her eyes scanned everything: rusted signage, a long-dormant checkpoint booth, the skeletal remains of a billboard still stood near the checkpoint. Most of the image had been weathered away, but the corner of a cartoon cereal bowl and the words THEY'RE GRRRRREAT! were still visible beneath the rust.

Dan caught up just beyond the breach. Marcus moved with momentum, already ahead when Dan's boots crunched the gravel behind them. Marcus froze.

"You followed us?" he asked without turning around.

Sarah glanced back, relief flickering across her face. Dan adjusted his pack and nodded once.

"Someone had to."

Marcus turned slowly, squinting. "We don't need a babysitter."

Sarah's voice was soft but firm. "I called him."

Dan let the silence stretch before speaking. "I'm not here to stop you. Just to make sure you come back. But you know this is a bad idea."

Marcus looked like he wanted to argue, but he didn't. He looked past Dan, toward the fence now behind them, then back at Sarah. The tightness in his jaw softened a hair, but not enough to hide the edge of resentment creeping into his voice.

"Right," Marcus muttered. "Wouldn't want Dan Clymer to miss a headline opportunity."

Dan didn't rise to it. He closed his eyes, trying to think. Pressed his lips together momentarily. Then, "Lead the way."

Marcus gave him a glare that was halfway between defiance and disappointment, then turned and pressed forward, faster now, like he could outrun the tension.

Dan brought up the rear, moving slowly, methodically. He paused near the sign, eyes lingering on it longer than the others noticed. He pulled his collar higher.

"Which way?" Sarah asked, her voice low.

Marcus pulled a folded page from his pocket, smoothing it against his thigh. A rough map printout. He glanced at Dan, just for a second, as if daring him to question it. "Northwest quadrant. Closest urban remnants. Used to be a school there, I think. Might still be something left."

Dan said nothing, but his eyes never left Marcus.

They moved forward in silence, weaving through overgrowth and collapsed infrastructure. Everything had a half-melted, half-forgotten look. Broken power lines snaked through the ground like skeletal veins. The ground was soft in places, still blackened with ash.

Marcus talked more than he should have, his fingers finding each wooden bead as he spoke.

"Can you believe how quiet it is?" he said, adjusting the strap on his pack. "Not even a drone overhead. It's kind of beautiful, honestly. Pure."

Sarah didn't respond.

"I used to think about this place all the time," he continued. "Not just the Zone. The idea of it. Something untouchable. Sacred in a way."

Sarah stopped. "Sacred?"

Marcus faltered, catching her tone. "I mean... sacred, yeah. But not in a religious way. Just... untouched. A place of remembrance. Of what we lost...outside the noise."

Dan finally spoke. "Outside the surveillance, you mean."

That landed heavier than it should have.

Marcus turned to him, defensive. "I'm not saying it's good. I just think we're seeing something most people never will. And that means something."

Sarah shook her head. "We shouldn't be looking for meaning in ruins and destruction."

A long silence.

They kept moving, but the terrain shifted quickly. What began as a narrow road dissolved into a maze of collapsed structures and overgrowth. Concrete gave way to broken stone and ash-covered soil. Landmarks disappeared behind them, blended into the sameness of ruin.

As they continued through the desolate landscape, Sarah's nerves began to fray. She had lived with the weight of the regime's surveillance for so long that she couldn't ignore the quiet whispers in her gut, the sensation that eyes were watching them from every cracked wall and ruined doorway. But she couldn't pinpoint why.

Her hand brushed against her satchel again, just to make sure the book was still tucked safely beneath the fabric. It was fine, she told herself. But the thought of the losing it here, where she had already lost so much, made her feel even more exposed.

"It's not safe," she murmured, trying to shake the feeling off. "We shouldn't be out here. We need to turn back."

Marcus shot her a quick glance, his enthusiasm for the Zone barely contained. "It's just ruins, Sarah. The worst is over. Relax."

She didn't respond, but the tightness in her chest only grew.

They made their way through the crumbling ruins, every step echoing off the broken concrete. The silence between them stretched long, but Sarah couldn't shake the sense that there was something beneath it all. Something unseen and unsaid.

A distant sound, a shift in the rubble perhaps, caught her attention. Her eyes darted toward the shadows, but nothing moved. Just the wind, rustling through the twisted remains of what had once been a settlement.

Still, the unease lingered. She could feel it pressing down on her, the faintest sense of something watching them from behind the shattered walls.

Marcus was talking again, his voice upbeat, but it sounded far too loud in this empty place.

"Hey, we should check over here. Maybe we can find some supplies..."

Sarah's voice cut through his chatter, sharper than she intended. "We need to keep moving."

A flash of movement in the corner of her eye made her heart skip. But when she turned, there was nothing. Just the wind tugging at the ragged remnants of a flagpole.

Nothing.

But the feeling gnawed at her, relentless.

Dan slowed, scanning the fading horizon. "We'll need a better way to mark our path," he murmured.

"We're not going that far," Marcus replied, brushing him off. "We'll be back before dark."

But even he glanced behind them, and for the first time, the way back didn't look familiar.

They paused beside a gutted vehicle, its frame twisted inward. Sarah reached in, brushing away shattered glass from what had once been a child's car seat. She didn't say a word.

Marcus stared at the mural on a crumbling wall: WE NEVER LEFT.

He let out a short, nervous breath that might have been a laugh. "Guess the cartoon cereal tiger didn't make it."

Nobody responded.

Sarah stepped closer to the mural, fingers brushing against the wall. The texture of the charcoal caught on her skin. She turned away quickly, blinking harder than she needed to.

"That's not state messaging," Dan said quietly. "And definitely post-strike."

Sarah looked at Marcus. "Still think no one's here?"

He opened his mouth, then closed it. The words didn't come. For the first time since crossing, Marcus didn't have an answer.

28

By late afternoon, the light had shifted. It wasn't fading so much as retreating. Drained of warmth, drawn into the haze that clung low over the Sacrificial Zone. Everything looked washed out, as if the world had lost some essential layer of contrast.

They hadn't spoken much since spotting the message on the wall. If Marcus had come to prove the Zone was empty, he had to admit doubt now. And if it wasn't empty then *who was here*? The question remained unspoken between them, but it propelled them forward.

Marcus still walked ahead, but slower now. Sarah stayed close to him, though her eyes kept drifting to Dan, as if silently checking he was still with them. He was.

The ground beneath them had turned soft and uneven, damp with ash and the slow decay of long-forgotten things.

They passed the remnants of a market—wooden stalls scorched and splintered, steel awnings crumpled like paper. Dan crouched near one, brushing aside dust to reveal a ceramic bowl still intact beneath a layer of ash. He turned it over once and set it back down without a word.

"Do you know where we are on the map?" Sarah asked, breaking the silence.

Marcus glanced at the paper again, brow creased. "I think so. These side roads just don't match the satellite view anymore. Must've collapsed, or the data's just old." He flipped the paper over, then back again, squinting. "Some of the reference points are missing. I swear there was a tower marker here."

Dan stepped closer. "That's the problem with ruins, they don't stay still."

The sun began to dip behind the haze, low enough to cast the city in long, angular shadows. Light fractured through suspended dust. They hadn't gone far, but it already felt like they'd crossed a psychological boundary, not just a physical one. Every structure leaned inward, as if the Zone itself were trying to fold in on them. Sarah kept glancing over her shoulder, tracing the path they'd come. It was already lost in the sameness.

"We should turn back," Dan said. "Before we're wandering in the dark."

Sarah scanned the crumbling skyline behind them. "I think it's already too late," she said, the edge in her voice sharper than she intended. Her patience, already stretched thin by Marcus's impulsiveness, was fraying. "We've been circling collapsed blocks and duplicate intersections for half an hour. Everything back there looks the same. And if we try to retrace our steps now, we'll just get more lost." She didn't say it aloud, but part of her feared they weren't alone. Not anymore. "We're better off waiting until morning."

Marcus hesitated, then pointed toward a shell of a building ahead, a two-story structure missing most of its upper floor.

"There," he said. "Good sightlines. Partial cover."

They stepped inside carefully. The roof had caved in over one corner, but the interior was dry, the air still. Dan checked the back wall and found an intact stairwell that led nowhere, but gave height. They chose a spot near the base of it, settling in behind chunks of collapsed drywall.

As twilight deepened, the wind picked up. A dry, listless sound that stirred old paper and dust into the corners of the room. Sarah sat with her back to a concrete pillar, arms folded tight. Dan leaned against a piece of broken shelving, eyes half-lidded but watchful.

Marcus was pacing.

He kept checking the sky as if it might give him directions, though the movement was more anxious than purposeful. His fingers fidgeted restlessly at his sides, then found his wrist. He began turning the bracelet again, bead by bead, not consciously. When he realized what he was doing, he stopped, then resumed more slowly.

Dan watched him for a moment, the frustration building. "This was your plan," he said finally. "You wanted to come here. You wanted to see it for yourself. Well, here we are."

Marcus didn't answer. He only paced a little longer, then stepped quietly to a darkened corner near a half-collapsed beam.

There, under his breath, he began to murmur the old lines.

"Uno por coraje. Dos por esperanza. Y tres..." His voice caught. "Por no perderte."

He wasn't sure if Sarah or Dan had heard. Maybe he didn't care.

"Marcus," Sarah said gently. "Sit down."

He didn't, not at first. But finally, after another long moment, he slid to the ground.

No one spoke.

Then, the stars appeared.

At first, just a few. Brighter than city stars. Colder too. But as the darkness deepened, the sky exploded into light. A brilliant, jagged smear of stars spilled across the heavens: the Milky Way, sharp and sprawling.

Sarah tilted her head back. She hadn't realized how small she'd felt until now. Under this sky, the state felt far away. Almost imaginary.

"It doesn't feel real."

Dan looked up too, something soft flickering in his expression. "You never see skies like this anymore."

Marcus stared upward, his voice quiet. "No one we know ever has."

The wind quieted. Time seemed to stretch. Tomorrow they would work their way home, but now, in this moment, there was no rush.

Dan let out a slow breath, his gaze tracing the familiar shape of Orion, the hunter. He remembered learning about the constellations as a child, but it had never felt real—not like this. Here, with the cold air biting at his skin and the weight of the night pressing down on them, it felt different. The stars weren't just distant points of light; they were part of something much greater, something timeless.

Despite his recent induction into the Hall of Valor, despite being hailed as a national celebrity and hero, Dan knew his story would never be written among the true heroes in the stars: Orion, yes. But also Perseus, Hercules...Jason's ship, the Argo. He had been celebrated for acts that, in the end, felt hollow. The heroes of old faced their enemies, fought against impossible odds, and had their deeds immortalized in the constellations above. Dan's so-called heroism came from pushing buttons, from a distance so vast that he couldn't even see the people his actions affected. There would be no legends told about him, no stories that inspired awe under a sky like this. That he was avenging the destruction that now surrounded him gave Dan a small amount of comfort.

"Heroes had their stories written in the stars," Dan said, almost to himself. "They faced trials, and their deeds were remembered forever. It's strange to think that they looked up at this same sky, that they found meaning in the same constellations we're seeing now."

He turned his head, meeting Sarah's gaze. For a brief moment, the fears and frustrations of their journey seemed to fade, replaced by a quiet connection, an understanding of how small they were in the grand scheme of things.

The three of them sat there, side by side, their eyes turned to the sky. The vastness above them was humbling, a reminder that despite everything—the fear, the uncertainty, the danger—they were still part of something much larger. And for that moment, it was enough to soften the edges of their frustrations, to bring a fragile sense of peace.

Then, in the far distance, a soft mechanical buzz.

Faint.

But unmistakable.

Not the hum of the wind. Not the creak of ruins. Something unnatural.

Dan sat up sharply.

"Do you hear that?"

29

Dan focused his attention beyond the ruins, towards the sky, towards something unseen.

The mechanical buzz came again. Low and rhythmic. Too regular to be anything natural. Marcus turned, wide-eyed. Sarah was already on her feet, her breath catching.

"That's not wind," Dan said.

The sound grew louder by the second. A rising whir that vibrated in the bones. Mechanical wings, sweeping in slow arcs.

"Drone," Marcus confirmed under his breath.

They moved on instinct. Bags slung over shoulders, knees bent low, feet soft against the debris-littered floor. Dan led them back through the hollowed entrance and into the open, hugging the shadows of broken walls and rusting steel.

The buzz shifted, now hovering. Searching.

"Stick to cover," Dan said. "No sound. No lights."

Sarah stayed close behind him. Marcus lingered at the rear, casting glances skyward as the sound circled overhead.

"Do you think it's armed?" Sarah whispered.

Dan didn't answer right away. He was scanning the skyline, looking for movement, reflections, the red blink of a signal light. "If it is, we're already exposed. Keep moving."

They crossed what used to be a narrow intersection, now choked with collapsed signage and the skeleton of an old checkpoint booth. Marcus ducked behind a rusted bollard, then froze.

"Ten o'clock," Dan said, crouching low. "Red indicator light. It's old...SST-2."

Marcus nodded quickly. "Exactly. Legacy surveillance model. Definitely unarmed. The red light gave it away. It was changed in later versions to reduce night signature."

Dan didn't respond. His jaw was tight.

Sarah glanced between them. "So it can't shoot at us?" The drone hovered just above the rooftops, its limbs angular and silent except for the hum. A soft beep emitted from its undercarriage.

"Reporting back," Dan said, voice tight.

"So what do we do?" Sarah asked.

"We wait," Dan said firmly. "If it's surveillance-only, we don't run unless we have to. Let it pass."

Marcus fidgeted. "They don't deploy armed drones for passive zones, right? It's just tagging. That's what SST-2s do—they catalog movement, log heat signatures, maybe trigger a remote alert."

He shifted again, this time too quickly, his foot scraping against a shard of tile, the sound sharp and unnatural in the silence. All three of them froze. Sarah's eyes darted to Dan, then back to Marcus. The heavy silence dragged on, stretching as if it could snap at any moment.

Dan's jaw tightened. The drone buzz changed pitch.

Marcus muttered, barely audible, "Too visible for frontline ops... definitely a surveillance model."

But his voice had lost all certainty.

Dan bristled. "And what if they've upgraded the chassis to carry payload? You think they're still using two-generations-old models to monitor the Zone?"

Marcus looked unsure now. "It could be for redundancy. Even old models report intel. We're not worth missiles, just tagging."

Dan clenched his jaw, weighing the risk. "We stay out of sight. If it tags us, we're burned."

They ducked beneath the arch of a collapsed wall, pressed tight to the earth. The buzz shifted again, closer this time. Sarah's breath was quick and shallow. Marcus's hand was on the bracelet again.

Dan looked to the sky. "You hear that tone modulation?"

Marcus nodded. "Adjusting scan parameters. It's looking harder now."

Then: a soft red blink, directly above them.

"Move," Dan snapped.

They broke into a run. Not toward safety. Just away. Away from the light, the sound, the certain eyes in the sky. Dust kicked up around them. The whir followed.

Behind them, the drone beeped again, longer this time.

Sarah stumbled, caught herself, kept going. Her lungs burned. The buildings blurred past, indistinct forms in the dark.

They darted into a shell of an apartment block, breathing hard, backs pressed against flaking tile.

"It knows," Dan said. "It marked us."

Marcus slumped against the wall, his breath ragged. "They'll know we're here now. Not just a blip —anomaly flagged. They'll follow up."

Sarah leaned forward, her hands braced on her knees. "I don't know what that means. What happens after a tag. Do they send in another drone? Something worse?"

Her voice wavered slightly. "You wanted this, Marcus. Thought it would mean something."

He didn't respond.

Dan didn't answer right away. He was staring at the spot where the drone had disappeared into the sky. "It means we're on the map now."

He exhaled, slow and deliberate. "They'll pull heat maps. Scan patterns. They'll see how we moved, that we moved together. We won't be just anomalies anymore. We'll be a narrative. Narratives can be foreshadowed...followed."

None of them moved. The silence pressed in again, only now it didn't feel sacred. It felt surveilled, parsed, like something unseen was cataloging their every breath.

30

They didn't speak for a long time.

The drone was gone, but the sky still felt full of it. Of its buzz, of its lens, of the unseen connection tracing their path back to whatever feed it was transmitting to. Sarah pressed her back to the wall, trying to steady her breath. Marcus stood a few paces away, rubbing his hands together, trying not to look shaken.

Dan was crouched near a broken window, eyes fixed on the skyline.

"It logged us," he said finally. "That model doesn't just tag movement, it triangulates ID signatures. If we were in the periphery of any cross-feed with facial recognition overlays, we're flagged."

Marcus's head jerked up. "Wait. You said those drones had garbage resolution. Low-tier optics, low-rank priority. Remember? When we were talking with Greg..."

Dan shook his head slowly. "That was about the strike drones. Different specs. Surveillance units are sharper. They're made for this. Quiet airspace, long dwell, high-fidelity scans. We were lit. Probably the best look they've gotten of anyone in the Zone for years."

He hesitated, then added, "It's not just that we were seen. It's that someone's watching that feed right now. Logging it. Making decisions with it. Turning us into something they can measure and track."

Sarah looked between them. "So... we go back? Now? Before they send anyone?"

Dan hesitated. "We try."

They set off quickly, retracing what they thought were their steps. The cityscape looked different now. Shadows had shifted, streets they thought they knew ended in deadfalls or impassable wreckage. Every corner looked like the last. Every alley led nowhere.

Marcus pulled out the folded printout of his map again, frowning. "I don't recognize this turn. Did we come through here?"

Dan scanned the broken signage on a streetlamp, its lettering half-eaten by rust. "No. This isn't right."

"We should've seen the building with the mural with the birds by now," Sarah added. "I remember it from earlier. It had that strange fire escape still standing."

They backtracked. Then turned again. Every block blurred into the next. At one point, Sarah paused, frowning. "Didn't we just pass that sign?"

Dan didn't answer. The rusted placard was identical to one two streets back. Or maybe it was the same one. The skyline had started to warp in his periphery, familiar outlines repeating where they shouldn't be.

Dan stopped suddenly, his jaw tight.

"We're not getting out tonight."

Sarah stared at him. "What are you saying?"

"We've been looped. This place... it disorients. What's left of these roads doesn't connect the way it should. Especially not in the dark."

Marcus looked down at the map again, his voice small. "I thought it'd be more linear. That we'd just... turn around."

He laughed once—short, brittle. "Maybe we're not worth their trouble...?."

"We can't stay here," Dan said. "If they tagged us, they'll come back. To confirm. Or worse."

Marcus looked up. "You think they'd send a strike drone?"

Dan didn't answer right away. "I think they've got our faces. And if Hightower's watching the feed, anything's on the table."

Sarah's voice was hoarse. "So what do we do?"

Dan scanned the skyline again, then nodded east. "We move. Now. Get as far from here as we can before they send anything with teeth. Movement sensors will trigger if we stay exposed."

They didn't speak as they started walking. The silence between them wasn't from awe anymore, it was calculation, fatigue, and fear. They didn't know where they were headed, only that they couldn't stay.

Sarah's left boot had split near the sole, soaking through. Dan had developed a slight limp after slipping on a loose piece of concrete. No one mentioned it. Marcus checked over his shoulder every few seconds, waiting to hear the buzz again.

At one point, Dan paused beside a pile of debris and crouched. Nestled beneath a charred metal panel was a small stash, an empty ration pouch with hand-stitched seams, not regulation. A melted battery casing, scavenged and modified, lay beside it. Someone had been here. Recently.

He didn't say anything. Just straightened and moved on.

They walked like that for hours, through the deepest part of night.

By the time the first blue tones of morning bled into the horizon, their bodies were aching, their clothes damp with cold. Hunger gnawed at them. Marcus's map was useless now, just a crumpled sheet with nothing to orient it. The street signs were long gone.

Sarah said nothing. She just walked.

Eventually, Dan held up a hand. "There. That building. Let's check it."

Sarah looked up at the stars—still brilliant, still infinite. But now they felt colder. Farther away. Fading into something unreachable.

Just before they stepped into the building, Dan paused again. In the distance, past the fractured skyline, a faint light blinked once. It was too far to read, too steady to be random. He squinted, but it was gone.

He didn't mention it.

"Alright," Sarah said quietly. "Let's disappear for a while."

Dan shot her a look he couldn't quite hide. "Careful what you wish for."

31

The screen glowed in the dark, casting a cold blue hue over Reverend Hightower's bedroom. He stood barefoot at the foot of his bed, wearing nothing but silk boxers and an open robe. The drone footage was paused on his tablet—Dan Clymer's face captured in crystalline clarity, a green facial recognition frame locked around his features.

"Fuck!"

He hurled the tablet across the room. It hit the far wall and clattered to the floor, screen still intact but flickering now, the footage still visible in spasms of light.

A voice called from the bathroom doorway. "Eli?"

A woman stood wrapped in one of his monogrammed towels, mascara slightly smudged from the steam. Her tone held half-concern, half-curiosity.

Hightower didn't look at her. He was staring at the fractured screen.

"Out," he said.

"What..."

"I said get out."

She hesitated only a second longer before vanishing into the bathroom. A minute later, the sound of the bedroom door clicking shut punctuated the silence.

Hightower knelt, picked up the tablet, and stared again at Dan's face.

The operator. The symbol. The saint.

And now? An infection in their myth.

He picked up the secure handset from the desk and keyed in a private channel.

"Patch me through to internal surveillance."

A soft beep.

"Tell me this is wrong," he said.

The voice on the other end was tight, practiced. "SST-2 drone. Surveillance grade. No doubt —confirmed ID of Dan Clymer inside the Sacrificial Zone. Accompanied by two others. We are running the scans for IDs on them now."

Hightower stood still for a long time. Then: "Who else has seen this feed?"

"Just your office, sir. Direct route, no cloud relay. Footage not yet indexed."

"Good. Keep it that way. Start sanitization protocol. And reroute the next patrol drone with immediate clearance. If they're still in that grid by sunrise, I want coordinates. And you have full clearance to deploy live fire."

"Yes, Reverend."

He ended the call and looked out the tall windows facing east. The sky was beginning to bleed with the first soft blush of morning.

The speakers in the corner of his bedroom hummed to life, on automatic schedule.

"May our hands be guided by the divine, our actions blessed with purpose, and our hearts unwavering in faith."

Hightower didn't move.

On the television across the room, a clean, pre-recorded image of himself faded in—polished, robed, eyes uplifted in serene devotion with the cross-emblazoned flag behind him.

Dan's face still hovered in the broken light of the tablet.

The contrast made the blessing feel like an indictment.

And Hightower, robe open and haloed in gold light, whispered to no one:

"We made you. And we'll unmake you."

He snatched up the handset again, rage spilling back to the surface.

"Get Knox on the line," he barked. "Tell him to get his ass over here. Now."

32

The restaurant was warm, quiet, and a little too upscale for how underdressed Greg felt. But his daughter was happy—sprawled across the booth with a placemat covered in crayon scribbles—and his wife looked relaxed for the first time in days. That was enough.

She reached for her glass of wine, then glanced across the table. "So? How's work?"

Greg hesitated, then shrugged. "Same as always. Boring unless something goes wrong."

She raised an eyebrow. "And does it? Go wrong?"

He chuckled softly. "Sometimes. Not today."

She watched him for a second longer, then nodded. "You've been quiet lately. Everything okay?"

Greg looked at his daughter, now fully absorbed in her coloring sheet and crayons. Her placemat was part of the restaurant's "Patriot Kids Menu," printed with a maze shaped like a missile and a coloring sheet titled "Color Your Hero!"

She'd scribbled a bright red uniform onto the cartoon soldier, who smiled beneath the words: "Real Strength Means Obedience!"

"Yeah, just tired. Been short-staffed this week. Dan hasn't been in."

"Dan?"

"Yeah. Clymer. You met him at the service dinner last year. The quiet one. Hall of Valor guy now."

"Oh, right," she said. "I remember. Didn't he used to be on your rotation?"

Greg nodded. "He was. We were on a lot of assignments together before all the promotions. Now I guess he's too important to answer texts."

"Maybe he's out of town?"

"Maybe. Him and Marcus both, actually. Neither of them have been in. I thought it was a joint op at first, but there's no log, no comms."

"Sounds like they're up to something."

Greg smiled faintly. "Maybe. Or maybe they're just being assholes."

He took a sip of wine. "I'll call him tomorrow."

He didn't think much more about it. Just leaned back as the server brought dessert—chocolate cake with two spoons.

His daughter squealed in delight. Greg passed her a bite with exaggerated flair.

A muted wall-screen near the bar played a highlight reel from the Valor Broadcast Network, sponsored by ProCore Solutions™. Footage of drone takeoffs and slow-motion explosions cycled under bold white text: **"Security Is Sacrifice. Obedience Is Peace."**

Nobody at the table looked up.

He tapped his tablet, which was propped beside the bread plate. A low-priority mission request blinked at the top of the screen—Class II, standard protocol. No details. There never were.

Greg authorized the strike without looking twice.

He pressed Confirm.

—STRIKE CONFIRMED.

He scooped a generous bite of cake—dense, glossy, and sweet—and fed it to his daughter who smiled up at him, mouth smeared in chocolate.

A soft chime. Confetti animation.

— +15 Patriot Points.

He muted the alert, turned back to his daughter, and took another sip of wine. The childlike confetti animation still flickered at the edge of his screen. He pushed it away.

Whatever Dan was doing, wherever Marcus had vanished to, it could wait.

Sarah hadn't answered any messages. Amelia had tried three different apps, two calls, and finally a blunt, direct knock on her door.

Nothing.

Now she stood inside Sarah's apartment, key still dangling from her hand. Everything was too quiet. Too still.

Cleo padded slowly around the corner, weaving against Amelia's legs and mewing. A quick glance showed that her food and water bowls were empty. Sarah would never leave Cleo like that... something was wrong.

Amelia quickly opened the cabinet and gave Cleo a triple portion of dinner and filled her water bowl. Then she scanned the living room. Blanket tossed across the couch. A half-finished cup of coffee. Nothing looked out of place, but nothing felt right either. Amelia checked the coat rack. One jacket missing. One of the hiking packs gone from the closet.

Her chest tightened.

"Shit," she murmured. "They've really done it."

On the counter, the scent of freshly ground coffee still lingered.

She stared at the empty bag.

If Sarah had restocked, that meant she had visited the vendor. And that meant a trail.

IT TOOK THREE CIRCUITS through the market before she found the right stall.

It didn't have a sign. Just a small table, a battered grinder, and a vendor who looked more like a faded relic than a shopkeeper.

Amelia stepped closer, lowering her voice.

"I heard you sell real beans."

The woman looked up slowly. Dark eyes, unreadable.

"I sell coffee."

Amelia nodded, tapping the edge of the table. "I'm looking for something a friend of mine used to buy. This blend. Earthy. Strong. Black market grade. She said she got it from here."

The woman blinked slowly. "A lot of people come and go."

"She has longish hair. Sharp eyes. Talks like she's always halfway to starting something dangerous. Ring a bell?"

A pause. Then the vendor poured a small scoop into a paper pouch without answering.

Amelia reached for it.

"You didn't ask how much," she said.

"Didn't need to."

As Amelia paid, the woman finally spoke. "Sarah. She's smart. Hope she stays that way."

Amelia opened her mouth to ask more, but the woman had already turned her back.

Then, quietly, as if to herself, Nama added, "Curiosity makes noise, even when you think you're being careful."

She stood there for a second, clutching the pouch, her mind racing.

Sarah was gone.

And this? This was confirmation.

Amelia left with the pouch clutched to her chest. The scent of coffee lingered in the air, too rich, too out of place. It didn't belong here. And maybe neither did she. It wasn't fear exactly. Just that familiar pressure, the kind that reminded you who was really allowed to ask questions...and who wasn't.

Now the only question left was: how far had Sarah gone?

THE SURVEILLANCE ROOM was colder than Knox remembered. The drone footage was already playing when he arrived, looped in silence across the central screen. Aerial angle. Three bodies in motion. Grainy, but recognizable. Dan. Sarah. Marcus.

Reverend Hightower stood with his arms behind his back, gaze locked on the image. He didn't turn.

"Tell me this isn't real," Knox said.

"It's real."

Knox stepped closer. The footage froze on Dan's face. The facial recognition frame blinked green.

"Why wasn't I told sooner?"

"You were told the moment it mattered," Hightower said.

A junior officer shifted uneasily at the terminal, eyes flicking between them. Knox didn't notice. Or pretended not to.

"And you're sure it was contained?" Knox asked. "No external uploads?"

"Only internal systems. The drone model is obsolete, broadcasts are localized. We scrubbed the feed before it hit network redundancy."

"Good," Knox said, but he didn't sound relieved.

He turned to Hightower. "And the drone? You authorized a follow-up?"

"Two, actually," Hightower said. "One recon. One prepared for strike."

Knox turned sharply. "You authorized a lethal drone without my sign-off?"

"It was a provisional order. Contingent on confirmation. They haven't reestablished visual."

Knox lowered his chin, eyes narrowing. "Don't forget who's the President here. You don't get to make that call without me."

Hightower finally turned to face him. "Then consider this a courtesy call. You've now been informed."

A long silence passed between them.

Knox's voice dropped. "So what do we do? Treat it as betrayal or revelation?"

Hightower's expression didn't change. "Neither."

He turned back to the screen, where Dan's face lingered in grainy green. "This never happened."

Knox blinked. "Excuse me?"

"We craft a cover story. Daniel Eustasius Clymer died in service to the Republic. A noble loss. An honorable sacrifice. And an irreplaceable martyr."

Knox muttered, half to himself, "People will riot. They love him."

"Then let them mourn him," Hightower said. "Grief unites. Questions divide."

THEY'D TAKEN SHELTER in the broken frame of what might've once been a maintenance hub; half a roof still intact, floor littered with debris and old cables. The wind had died down, but the cold still pressed in from the open edges of the walls.

Sarah sat cross-legged near the far wall, arms wrapped around her knees. Dan leaned against a collapsed support beam, coat pulled tight, face unreadable in the gray light.

Marcus was a few meters off, perched on a low ledge near the opening. He didn't say anything. Just watched them, idly rotating the worn bracelet around his wrist.

Sarah broke the silence. "This place isn't what I pictured."

Dan nodded. "Me either."

She didn't elaborate.

He shifted slightly, voice low. "I used to think war would feel... bigger."

She glanced at him, then away. "It's not big enough for you?"

He shook his head. "Not like that. I mean—older. Like the stories. Shield walls. Holding ground. Something clear."

She rubbed her hands together. "That ever seem real to you?"

He paused. "I wanted it to be."

"Was your strike, the one from the ceremony, real?"

They sat in the quiet for a moment, the wind making low, breathy sounds through the beams.

Dan looked down at the cracked floor. "I used to think, if I ended up in something like this, it'd feel like history. Like I could be... useful. In a way that meant something."

Sarah didn't respond. But her expression softened, just for a moment.

Marcus shifted. The bracelet clicked faintly against his knuckle.

Then he stood. Too fast.

"I'll take first watch," he said, voice tight, already heading toward the dark.

His footsteps were harder than they needed to be.

Neither of them said anything.

THE OTHERS SLEPT, Marcus hunched where he had staked out his watch. Sarah reached into her satchel, behind the lining. She carried it. Held it. But didn't read it. Not for many years. But tonight, illuminated only by starlight, she read. And beyond the childhood memories with her father, she truly felt in the words what it was to be the girl out beyond the known borders—losing, changing, remembering.

33

His wife had asked him to stop on the way home. Just a few things: milk, cereal, something for dinner. It should've been an easy task. Familiar. Automatic.

But Greg stood in the cereal aisle like he'd never seen food before.

He reached for a box of Faith Fruities, almost on autopilot. Something bright and familiar. The kind the kids usually liked. His hand was already closing around the edge of the box when he saw it...

Dan's face.

Smiling from a fresh display of Frosted Valor Flakes.

It was front and center. Full uniform. High-res image. The tagline beneath read: "Fuel Up Like a Hero. Faith First, Always." Below that, "Start Your Day With Honor."

Greg froze. His hand hovered midair, still touching the cartoon fruit rings. But his eyes were locked on Dan.

Behind him, a kid tugged on his mother's coat. "That's the one Dan eats! We saw it in the vid!"

Greg blinked. He pulled down the Faith Fruities. Bright box, sweet enough to keep the kids happy. His hand hovered over the shelf. Then, almost deliberately, he reached to the far end of the shelf for himself and his wife, grabbing something unbranded. No slogans, no smiling faces. Just Oats.

He continued down the aisles in a slow drift, turning toward frozen foods. His list was short. Cereal. Bread. Fruit. Milk. Something easy for dinner. He scanned the store cameras casually, then with a trace more focus. No one was paying attention. Just another loyal citizen out running errands.

He passed an endcap display of vacuum-sealed dinner kits—Rations With Righteousness! the sign proclaimed. Below it, a looping vid screen played muted footage of operators saluting in perfect sync. Greg looked away.

He wasn't sure why it unsettled him so much. Dan's face on a cereal box shouldn't have surprised him. It was the logical next step. First the ceremony, then the campaign, then the breakfast aisle.

But it was the speed of it. The way everything had slotted into place so smoothly. Like Dan had been packaged for public consumption from the beginning.

Greg hadn't said that out loud. Not to his wife. Not even to himself. But it gnawed at him now.

He turned the corner into produce, tried to remember if the kids still liked pears. He'd texted her earlier to ask, but the message still hadn't gone through.

He adjusted his grip on the cart. Finished the list. Paid in silence.

And as he stepped back into the sterile evening light, paper bags in hand, the grin on Dan's box had followed him out. Unshakable from his mind. He wasn't sure why it bothered him so much.

34

The room was dark except for the glow of the screen. Dan's frozen image still lingered, eyes locked on something just out of frame, grainy and haloed in static.

Hightower hadn't moved in minutes.

Knox paced.

"They'll start asking questions," he said, not for the first time. "The longer he's gone, the worse it looks. We need to release something."

"Not yet."

Hightower's voice was calm. Annoyingly calm. He stepped away from the console and folded his hands behind his back.

"We have time."

"No," Knox snapped. "We have a vacuum. And people fill vacuums with rumors."

Hightower turned slightly, just enough to glance at him. "So let them. Conspiracy is a symptom of faith. It means they're still watching."

Knox exhaled slowly through his nose. "And what do we do when someone spots him alive?"

"They won't."

"You don't know that."

"I do," Hightower said. "Because by the time it matters, he won't be."

Knox stared at him.

"You think I'm being cruel," Hightower said, finally turning. "I'm being kind. Dan will die a symbol. He'll be untouchable. A martyr who left this world to defend it."

He gestured toward the screen. "The Hall of Valor ceremony gave us the bones. But a memorial? A proper martyrdom? That gives us the blood. The soul. We don't lose Dan by letting him go. We make him bigger than ever."

Knox crossed to the table, where a printed draft lay waiting—an early version of the public memorial. He read the headline aloud: **"Daniel Eustasius Clymer: Light of the Republic, Called Home to Glory."**

He snorted. "This is theater."

Hightower didn't flinch. "It's scripture. And it will save lives."

Knox tossed the paper down. "We're not releasing it yet."

Hightower didn't argue. He simply walked to the wall terminal and tapped a new file into view. It was a playback loop. Dan's Hall of Valor ceremony, re-edited, slowed to half speed. Dan stood on the stage, his face a perfect portrait of reluctant grace. A subtle vignette faded in at the edges, softening the backdrop to something almost divine.

"Your media team is already recutting history," Knox said.

"No," Hightower replied. "I'm preserving it."

Knox ran a hand through his hair. "How long do you plan to wait?"

"As long as we can afford to."

Knox turned back to the screen. A new panel had opened. Facial recognition overlays blinking against a paused frame of the SST-2 drone footage.

"The other two?" he asked.

"Left is Marcus Vasquez," Hightower said. "Clean file. High potential. Off-grid since the night of the ceremony. No pings, no response. The match is solid."

"And the other?"

"No registry ID yet. But the algorithm's flagged potential contact nodes—transit cams, street-level logs. We're reviewing footage from the block where Vasquez lived."

"Anyone else pop?"

"Two confirmed identities: Clymer and Vasquez. Surveillance footage shows each of them leaving their respective residences early the previous morning. The interesting part is where the trails converge—an apartment complex near the market district. We have footage of the unidentified female entering Vasquez's car. Clymer doesn't stop, but follows in his vehicle. Shortly after, the vehicle exits the city limits. We lose visuals beyond that point."

He tapped a second screen. "Agents are en route to the apartment now. Once we determine which unit she exited from, we'll run the ID and get a name."

Knox crossed his arms. "And when we do?"

"If she matters, we control the narrative. If she doesn't, she disappears."

Knox said nothing.

"What about the drone?" he asked finally.

"It won't fire unless it sees a threat," Hightower said. "And if it does...well. Then we'll have a funeral worth televising."

"And what if it's not Dan it sees?"

Hightower didn't answer right away.

"Then it strikes. And the story holds."

Knox walked to the far wall, stared at nothing. "And Greg Halloway? He's tagged to operate the prototype next week. Does he know?"

"No one knows," Hightower said. "Not even the drone."

He returned to the terminal and tapped the screen once. Dan's image disappeared.

"We'll release the report when the world is ready to grieve," he said. "And not a minute before."

DAWN CAME GRAY and uneven, filtered through low clouds and the skeletal frames of collapsed buildings. The Sacrificial Zone didn't warm with the sun, it only sharpened. Every shadow looked deeper in daylight. Every ruined edge more jagged.

Dan stepped over a crumbling curb and paused, squinting into the pale horizon. No movement. No sound. Just the low hum in his ears. The kind that followed adrenaline and silence.

Behind him, Marcus slumped onto a half-sunken bench, his arms draped over his knees, chest rising and falling in shallow pulls.

"Anyone following?" he asked without looking up.

"No," Dan said. "Not yet."

Sarah didn't speak. She stood near a burned-out storefront, one boot nudging something half-buried in the dirt. A child's shoe. Melted at the heel. She didn't pick it up.

They'd walked for hours after the drone vanished. No one had slept. No one suggested it.

Marcus rubbed his face with both hands. "I thought we'd find something by now. A landmark. A road sign. A map. Anything."

"There's nothing left," Sarah said. Her voice was low, almost a whisper.

Dan looked around. She was right. The maps they'd studied didn't match what they were seeing. Buildings were missing. Whole blocks swallowed by decay or demolition. Even gravity seemed skewed. The streets canted and twisted, like the Zone had refused to rot in a straight line.

Marcus stood again, agitated. "This isn't what I trained for. I came out here to prove something, not..." He stopped himself.

Sarah turned to him. "Not what?"

Marcus didn't answer. He looked away.

Dan adjusted the strap on his shoulder. "We need cover. A place to rest. Regroup. We're exposed here."

They started walking again, heading east toward what remained of the outer neighborhoods.

The terrain shifted—less industrial, more suburban. Chain-link fences leaned inward. Driveways turned to cracked mosaics. Roofs had fallen like dominoes in a windstorm.

An hour passed before they reached the husk of a school. It sat half-sunken at the corner of what might have once been a cul-de-sac. No sign, no flag, just broken playground equipment tangled in rust and weeds.

Sarah slowed near the steps. A lunchbox lay open at the base, its cartoon print scorched but still visible. She crouched beside it. Inside, there was a fork. A scrap of paper. A name smudged out.

She didn't say anything, but her hand lingered on the metal edge.

Marcus hovered nearby, silent for once.

They moved inside.

The classrooms were worse. Desks scattered, chairs overturned. Someone had written on the chalkboard before the world ended: **"BE BRAVE. STAY STILL."**

Marcus stood in the doorway, his face unreadable. Then he turned and walked back into the hall.

Dan followed them through the school's side exit, and they walked until the rusted playground fences gave way to crooked sidewalks and collapsed single-story homes. The neighborhood had once been modest. Starter homes and trimmed hedges. Now the air smelled like wood rot and mold.

They picked one of the houses half-standing. Dan nudged the door open with his boot. It gave way easily.

Inside: a living room split by rot. Toys scattered across the floor. A family portrait facedown in dust.

Sarah stepped through the doorway into the kitchen. The cabinets hung off their hinges. One had collapsed entirely, spilling ancient cereal boxes with no regime branding...just a rabbit and fruit shapes, another with marshmallows and rainbows. Broken mugs were strewn across the counter and onto the floor.

Dan opened a low cupboard and paused. Nestled in the corner, blackened but intact, was a moka pot.

He pulled it out slowly. Brushed it off.

Sarah looked over. "You used to drink the branded stuff, right? That state-issued sludge?"

Dan smiled faintly. "Every morning. Before first light. It grounded me."

"I used to get contraband beans near the inner ring. Doesn't matter now, I guess. We are in this shit together from here on out. If we survive this, I'll make you a real cup."

"But coffee is coffee, ya' know," Dan teased.

"Oh, don't you dare...now we have to survive just so I can prove you wrong," she said with a wry grin.

She leaned against the counter. "Could use a cup right about now."

Then, suddenly. Quietly:

"I keep thinking about my cat."

Dan looked up.

"Cleo. I left out three days of food, and then I just... left."

A pause.

"She was probably waiting at the door."

From the hallway, Marcus lingered just out of sight. He could hear them talking—something about coffee, about survival. He didn't step in. Just watched. Listened. How had this gone so wrong? All he wanted was to show Sarah he could be enough. That he wasn't just another follower, tagging along behind heroes and golden boys. And she was in there with the most golden of all. And he had led them there. To this.

Dan turned the moka pot over in his hands. The bottom was dented, but the threads were clean. It would still work.

He stowed it gently in his pack.

"Maybe we'll get a chance to find out about that coffee," he said.

Sarah didn't respond. But she watched him longer than she needed to.

After a few minutes, Sarah stepped quietly out of the kitchen and into the hall. She paused at a crumbling wall where a child's drawing still clung to the plaster: families drawn in stick figures, holding hands beside suns and tanks and flags. Her jaw was tight.

"They told us no one survived," she murmured. "But this...this doesn't feel abandoned." She stepped back. "We should go."

Dan nodded. Marcus didn't speak.

They stepped out into the open again, silence trailing behind them. The wind picked up as they crossed the overgrown lawn, cold and indifferent. None of them looked back.

35

It looked like every other government sedan: boxy, matte gray, scrubbed of insignia. Parked just off-center from the curb, facing the wrong way. Engine off. No lights. No movement. Not nearly as inconspicuous as it was trying to be.

That meant they'd followed her. Or worse, they hadn't needed to. Which meant surveillance had picked her up near Sarah's apartment. Which meant... her place was already compromised.

Amelia couldn't go home.

Not ever again.

"Shit," she whispered.

Then she moved.

Not fast, but deliberate. She pivoted back toward the corner with the kind of casual ease that said she'd forgotten something, or remembered an errand. Her face neutral. Her pulse, already pounding.

At the end of the block, she ducked into a public convenience terminal and powered on her tablet. The screen flickered to life. She tapped through to her Citizen Portal, fingers moving with practiced calm.

—*Patriot Points: N/A.*

—*Status: Under Review.*

—*Please report to your local Loyalty Center to resolve a pending compliance flag.*

The message was sterile, friendly. Framed in soft blue edges. But her stomach turned.

She tried to access her banking app. Same result. Her medical records? Locked. Her housing contract? "No active residency file found."

They'd already started erasing her.

She powered the tablet off, glanced at the old man sitting on the bench nearby, then at the overhead drone making a lazy loop across the skyline. She tucked the device back into her bag and walked.

She needed to try one more thing.

Three blocks later, she stepped into a small corner hotel, one of those dated places people used for layovers or discreet affairs. The clerk didn't look up at first, just kept tapping away at a terminal. Amelia approached the desk with a calm, open smile.

"I'd like a room for the night," she said softly. "Just one. No extras."

The clerk finally looked up. Young. Slightly bored. His eyes flicked to her momentarily, then back to his screen.

"Of course. Can I scan your ID?"

Amelia slid her tablet across the counter without hesitation. He tapped it against the reader. The smile on his face faltered almost immediately. His eyes flicked back to her, quickly masked with a nervous sort of politeness.

"I'm sorry, there seems to be a system error." He swallowed. "Would you mind... checking in at a regional kiosk instead? We've had a few flag errors lately. Might be a Patriot Points sync issue."

She smiled back, full of warmth.

"Not a problem at all," she said. "Thanks for checking."

She picked up the tablet and walked out.

She didn't look back.

She kept walking.

Three more blocks. Then four. Past a café where she and Sarah used to meet after shifts. Past a florist with a cheerful poster that read "Faith In Bloom: Patriot Pots Now Half Off!"

She didn't stop until she found the edge of a construction site, sealed off with mesh fencing and caution tape. She ducked under a corner gap, found a pile of old ducting and rusted corrugated metal, and crouched behind it, shielded from view.

Amelia opened her bag with nervous care. Pulled out her phone, her tablet, her ID strip. Each one set neatly on the broken concrete.

Everything with a signal has to go.

She powered down the devices, but that wasn't enough. She pried open the back of the tablet with a piece of scrap metal, snapping off the access panel, exposing the circuits beneath. She found the SIM chip, dug it out with her fingernail, bit it in half, and flung it into the debris.

The phone came next. Same process—chip out, casing dismantled. She buried both devices under a heavy slab of insulation, then wedged the panel shut.

Her ID strip was thinner. Polycarbonate with a small transmitter embedded. She bent it in half, then half again, until it cracked with a brittle pop. SShe shoved one of the pieces into a narrow crevice between rusted pipes. The other, she dropped down a nearby storm drain.

Only then did she sit back, heart racing.

The implant requirement had almost caught her. She'd gotten the notice two weeks ago.

Mandatory internal chip for travel, healthcare, housing. Her appointment had been scheduled for next Thursday.

A chill passed through her.

If this had happened a week later, she wouldn't be hiding behind construction waste. She'd be traceable from the inside out. She would have been caught before she even turned the corner.

She pulled out the only thing she kept—a small bracelet, frayed at the edges, its woven band softened with time. Her sister had made it when they were kids. Back before either of them knew how far things could fall apart.

It wasn't worth anything to anyone else.

But she hadn't been able to leave it.

She slipped it into her bra and closed the bag.

She left the rest behind.

SHE STEPPED OUT from the construction site into the open night.

The street was brighter now. The ads louder. Billboards flashed digital blessings:

"Let us walk in unity, protected by truth."

"Operators Are Faith Made Visible."

She pulled her hood up and walked faster.

No plan yet. No contact. Just instincts and fear. She could try Nama. Maybe. Back at the market. But she wouldn't be there until at least the morning. Or there was that church near the lower district with rumors of sanctuary, even if it had been taken over by state clergy. Or maybe just a transit station. Ride the lines until the signal dropped.

But for now, she just needed to move.

She found herself drifting toward the central transit hub—wide, echoing, full of movement and anonymity. The perfect place to disappear without disappearing.

She sat on a bench near one of the older regional lines. No cameras in direct line of sight. No patrols. Just flickering announcements and the low drone of idling mag-trams.

She opened her bag again, almost empty now. Her fingers brushed a folded edge of paper. She paused, then pulled it free.

One of the flyers. The ones she and Sarah had distributed late at night, posting on notice boards and street lamps. A blend of scripture and plea. Resistance language buried inside sanctioned phrases.

She smoothed it flat on her lap.

Most of the verses were familiar. But her eyes caught on one she hadn't really noticed before:

ISAIAH 67:19 — "Deliverance will come not by way of the faithful, but by those who seek truth in all things. The road shall open before them."

The line struck her as off. The phrasing was too clean, too conveniently subversive. And something about the citation felt wrong.

She dug into memory. Isaiah didn't go that high. Or if it did, it wasn't a verse she'd ever heard quoted before. If she still had her tablet she could look it up, but she was almost certain. Beside it, a faint circle with two slashes below.

Now, it looked like a key....something waiting to be unlocked. She wracked her brain.

Deliverance comes by seeking truth... The road opens...

Then, suddenly, it hit her.

The road.

Isaiah 67:19 wasn't a verse. It was an address.

6719 Isaiah Rd.

She blinked. That stretch was one of the regime's Faithful Fulfillment Initiatives...pumping money in to support small businesses and rehabilitate homes, displacing those "less desirable." The ones Sarah worked with. Now it was populated with trendy brunch spots, boutique clothiers, and the residences of up-and-coming regime operatives.

But maybe someone waited.

She folded the flyer again, smaller this time, and slipped it into her coat.

She stood, slung the bag back over her shoulder, and scanned the route board.

One transfer. No ID needed if she stayed inside the zone.

She didn't know what she'd find at that address. But she knew she couldn't sit still.

36

The light was thinner now—silver and stretched, like it didn't want to commit to morning.

They moved in silence. Not out of strategy, but because there was nothing left to say.

Dan's leg dragged a little more with each step. Marcus's mood had worsened too, and he muttered under his breath every time the pavement shifted beneath him. Sarah's hands were scraped raw from crawling over broken concrete, dried blood forming thin seams across her fingers.

They'd found shelter in the ruins of what might have once been a municipal building, part city records office, part clinic. Half of it had collapsed into the street. The other half held just enough structure to shield them from wind.

Sarah sat against the interior wall, knees tucked to her chest, watching dust drift through a fractured window frame. Marcus paced what remained of the corridor, his movements jerky. He hadn't taken off his pack.

Dan leaned near the doorway, eyes scanning the horizon.

"We can't stay here long," he said. "Too exposed."

"We're exposed everywhere," Marcus snapped.

Dan didn't argue. He just kept watching.

When they moved again, it was through open ground, an overpass stripped of railings, sagging on one side. Beyond it, a field of fractured concrete stretched like a dry riverbed. They had to move fast. No cover.

Halfway across, Sarah paused. "Wait."

Dan stopped. "What?"

She turned her head slightly. "You didn't hear that?"

They froze. Wind scraped through the gaps in the rebar. Marcus turned slowly in a circle.

Nothing. Just the wind. And the sky.

Still, Dan moved faster after that. They all did.

On the far side, Sarah spotted something half-buried near a crumpled guard post. She knelt.

It was a cord-wrapped bundle—cloth torn from civilian wear, bundled and tied with a strip of copper wire. Inside: two protein bars. Not ration-grade. No barcode. No heat seal. Homemade

She held it up.

Marcus frowned. "That's not military issue."

Dan took it, turning the fabric in his hand. "Somebody packed this. Recently."

"Do you think they left it for us?" Sarah asked.

Dan didn't answer. He tucked it into his bag and stood.

They kept moving.

DAN AND SARAH were talking again. Discussing strategy.

The silence between Marcus and their conversation stretched as they moved forward again, broken only by footfalls and the faint creak of Dan's pack. No one had said it, but the direction they were heading, the confidence, had come from Sarah. Not Marcus.

He trailed behind, just slightly, watching the way she and Dan exchanged clipped thoughts about supplies and paths. They weren't ignoring him, exactly. But they weren't looking to him either. Not like before.

Marcus kicked at a rock with the edge of his boot. It skittered into the dust. He was hot. And hungry. And full of self-pity tinged with self-doubt.

Sarah crossed the pathway over to him, hoping to ease his nerves.

"Marcus,"

He glanced at her, but didn't stop walking. "You two seem to have it handled."

"It's not like that."

"You think I don't see it?" he said, not looking at her. "How you look at me. Like I'm pathetic. Like I don't belong here."

Sarah turned slowly.

"Stop. Just stop."

Her voice wasn't loud. But it cut clean.

"I can't do everything for you. I couldn't then. I can't now. And I shouldn't be expected to."

Marcus opened his mouth to speak, but nothing came out.

"None of us belong here. You brought us here to prove something," she said. "Prove it to us...to me. To prove it to yourself. But we didn't need that. And now we're here. You didn't ask. We just followed because we were afraid of what would happen if we didn't."

Dan shifted beside them but stayed quiet.

Sarah didn't raise her voice. She just stood there, breathing. Holding.

"You want to be seen? Then stop asking people to pretend you're someone else."

She turned away and knelt to retie her shoe.

Marcus didn't move.

He stared at the ground. And for the first time, he saw her clearly—not as the ideal he'd been chasing, but as a person who had already given more than she should have.

She hadn't followed him because she believed in him.

She'd followed because she was afraid he'd fall apart if she didn't.

It wasn't love.

It had never been love.

And was never going to have been.

It was a kindness he'd mistaken for something larger, because he needed it to be.

He turned slowly. Nothing in sight. But on the wall opposite their camp, scratched low into the brick, was a mark he didn't remember seeing before.

A circle. Two slashes beneath.

Deliberate. Recent.

Somehow familiar.

37

The sun climbed slow and dull, smothered by cloud cover and ash haze. No warmth came with it. Just more light to reveal how far they hadn't gotten.

Sarah's foot caught on a jagged lip of asphalt, and she stumbled. Dan caught her elbow without a word and steadied her. Marcus said nothing, just kept walking a few paces ahead, the scarf around his neck pulled high enough to hide most of his face.

They were all quieter now. Not from strategy, but resignation.

The streets had widened. Fewer buildings remained intact, and those that did looked wrong—it was hard to tell how much was a result of the attack and how much was the decade since. Twice they passed intersections Dan was sure they'd already crossed. Marcus insisted they hadn't. Sarah didn't argue. There was no point. They had no destination anyway. They were on a march to nowhere.

They paused under the shelter of a half-collapsed pedestrian bridge. Sarah leaned against the wall, her face pale beneath the grime.

Dan crouched to adjust his boot. That's when he felt it.

A low tremor. Not noise exactly, but a vibration. Subtle. Faint. Like a hum moving through stone.

He placed his hand on the ground. It pulsed through the concrete in irregular intervals. Not natural. Not seismic.

He looked up. Sarah was frowning.

"You feel that?" she asked quietly.

Dan nodded once.

Marcus hadn't noticed. He paced at the edge of the wall, agitated. "We need to move. Open ground's worse than ruins."

Dan didn't move. "Something's coming."

Sarah crouched beside him, hand brushing the pavement. She inhaled sharply. "This isn't normal."

"It's not a drone...it's coming through the ground," Dan said. "Could be machinery. Could be a signal. Or something big moving underground."

They waited. A minute. Then two.

The vibration faded.

No drone appeared.

No aircraft hum. No flash of metal in the sky.

But Dan's heartbeat didn't slow. Because that tremor, whatever it was, had known exactly where to find them.

They moved again.

Hours passed. The terrain shifted again—more industrial, full of exposed pipes and melted signage. Sarah spotted a toppled vending kiosk, its casing half-split. Inside, someone had scrawled a mark on the wall.

A circle. Two slashes.

Fresher than the one Dan had seen before.

He glanced at Sarah but said nothing. She saw it too. Her eyes lingered, then moved on.

By nightfall, they found the remnants of a dry drainage channel and took shelter in the curve beneath a collapsed overpass. The wind tunneled overhead, but it was quiet. Not safe, but quiet.

Dan took first watch this time. His eyes scanned the skyline, but he kept his palm pressed to the cracked stone beneath him.

Waiting.

And long after the others had gone still, the tremor returned, just for a second. Just enough to remind him: someone was out there.

And they were watching.

38

The air shifted just before dawn.

It wasn't the light. That came slowly, smeared by fog, the sky a flat gray with no direction. It wasn't the cold, either, though it cut deeper now, pressing in around the edges of their shelter beneath the overpass.

It was the ground.

A new tremor began, stronger this time. Not the faint pulse from the day before. This one rolled through the concrete in waves, like something massive was moving underfoot. Dan snapped awake first. His hand was already on the ground.

"Get up," he said.

Sarah stirred, groggy, but something in his voice pulled her upright. Marcus was slower, blinking hard.

Dan didn't wait. He grabbed his bag and slung it over his shoulder. "Move."

They didn't argue. The vibration was growing, a pattern, but not a rhythm. Not seismic. Measured. Mechanical. Sarah looked skyward as they broke from the shelter, squinting into the pale morning haze.

A low hum answered.

"Drone," Dan said.

Marcus stiffened. "It found us?"

"No. It's not circling. It's locking."

Then came the whine.

A rising tone, like pressure building in the air itself.

They ran.

Through the scattered bones of the outer neighborhood. Past overturned mailboxes, split driveways, collapsed garages. The sound followed them, always just behind.

They reached an intersection half-swallowed by a fallen traffic light. Dan shouted, "Left!" and shoved Marcus forward just as a flash seared the sky.

Impact.

The street behind them exploded. Concrete lifted like paper, metal screaming as it twisted. The sound hit a second later, a gut-punch of force that sent Sarah stumbling into a fence. Marcus was already down, arms over his head. Dan turned, caught a glimpse of the drone: matte black, angular, low-hovering.

Not surveillance.

He grabbed Sarah's arm. "Go!"

Another whine. Another flash.

The house ahead of them vanished in flame.

They veered off-course, slipping into the hollow of what had once been a mechanics garage. The roof had caved in, but some of the interior was intact. Smoke poured in after them. The heat stung Dan's face.

Then—movement.

Not from the sky. From the shadows.

Two figures. Silent. Covered in dirt, wrapped in dark, utilitarian layers. No armor. No insignia.

No words.

One reached for Marcus. The other pointed to Dan and Sarah, then toward a jagged hole in the wall.

Another impact nearby. The garage shuddered.

Sarah hesitated. Dan didn't. He grabbed her wrist and pulled.

The figures guided them down. Not into a tunnel exactly, but a crawlspace. Reinforced and narrow. They moved quickly, deliberately. Another blast. Dust rained from the ceiling.

It went black.

The ground tilted sideways, then stilled.

Dan didn't know how far they'd gone. Just that they were shielded now. His ears rang. His pulse wouldn't settle.

Someone moved near him. A hand gripped his shoulder. Not hard. Not comforting either.

Then a voice, close to his ear:

"Stay down."

And nothing more.

A WORLD AWAY, an operator saw their Patriot Points drop by 30 for a failed strike against the enemy.

39

The address on Isaiah Road took her next door to a brunch spot that served "Blessed Benedicts" beneath a neon cross glowing bright pink. The sign blinked 100% PATRIOT APPROVED, mounted above a patio of reclaimed church pews stamped with the FaithPoint™ seal. They were closed—one of those places that's only open until two. Nearby stood a Patriot Points™ verification kiosk. Between them sat a narrow, slumped building that looked like it had survived three rezoning initiatives just by being forgettable.

6719.

A chipped wooden placard hung beside the door, warped from sun and rain: *The Last Word*. A battered A-board stood just beside the door. The top half read:

Today's Selections: Devotionals, Reflections, and Seasonal Readings

Beneath that, handwritten in white chalk:

"Deliverance will come...by those who seek truth in all things..."

Below it, someone had drawn a circle with two faint diagonal lines beneath. The marks were half-erased, like they'd been wiped and redrawn a dozen times.

Amelia paused only a second, then stepped inside.

The bell overhead gave a dull clang. The shop was narrow and quiet—warmer than it looked from the outside, though still underheated. The air smelled of old glue and yellowed pages. Books leaned in uneven towers between shelves that had long since given up on standing straight. In the corners, the dust bunnies had staged a tent revival.

A man stood behind the front counter, mid-60s maybe, long-sleeved sweater under a faded vest. He was hunched over a ledger and didn't look up.

Amelia stepped further into the shop, lingering near the shelves. She moved slowly, letting her fingers brush the spines of old books, absorbing the quiet. Her eyes flicked between titles—mostly regime-approved at first, then stranger ones deeper in. Nothing obvious. Nothing certain. She wasn't ready to speak just yet.

A minute passed. Then another.

Only when the tightness in her chest began to ease, just a fraction, did she make her way to the counter.

Amelia approached slowly, flyer now in hand. She unfolded it, smoothing the paper along the counter.

"Excuse me," she said quietly, "I know this is a strange question, but... does this mean anything to you?"

The man glanced at the flyer. His eyes lingered on the verse.

"Where'd you get it?" he asked.

"A friend gave it to me," she replied. "Said it would give me encouragement...and answers."

He studied her for a moment longer. Then he nodded. Not a confirmation...but not a denial.

"You might find what you're looking for in the back," he said. "In the special selections. No returns."

He gestured toward a half-curtained doorway near the poetry alcove, then returned to his ledger without another word.

Behind the curtain, the space narrowed. A corridor with uneven floorboards and a faint ammonia smell led to a low-ceilinged room with no windows. The heater didn't reach back here. She rubbed her arms.

The shelves were stacked with older books—some banned, others obscure. The titles ranged from prohibited political memoirs to spiritual mysticism to once cherished children's classics now deemed subversive. Several bore no markings at all.

She moved slowly, scanning titles until one caught her eye.

Citizenship & You: Harmony Through Obedience.

It stood out mostly because it wouldn't stand out anywhere else. It was required reading in schools and loyalty centers everywhere. A book everyone had, everyone skimmed, everyone ignored.

But this copy was different.

It was filed among books on grief and poetry, where it didn't belong. And more than that, there was no barcode on the spine—a requirement for all approved texts since the regime implemented the Moral Literacy Standard shortly after the war began.

Instead, a faint symbol had been etched into the lower spine, barely visible unless you knew to look.

A circle. Two slashes.

She pulled it free and opened it. The pages were crisp, almost untouched. She flipped through the first few—standard language about duty, citizenship, social alignment.

But something slipped free from between the pages.

A folded receipt.

She caught it before it hit the floor. It had no note. Just a symbol drawn on the back in crayon—the circle and slashes—and on the front, the printed log:

Golden Circle Noodle House

Total: 0.00

Server: Liang

Time: 16:45

Table 7

She turned it over, looking again at the symbol on the back.

She refolded it, tucked it into her coat, and carefully replaced the book exactly where she'd found it.

When she stepped back into the front room, the shopkeeper was now sitting on a stool behind the counter with a takeout container balanced on one knee. He was using wooden chopsticks, slow and steady.

He looked up as she passed.

"Place down the street isn't bad," he said, gesturing toward the container. "Bit of a wait if you get there late."

Amelia gave a small nod. "Good to know."

"Take care of yourself," he added. Not warm, not cold, just deliberate.

"I will."

She stepped back into the street. The air had turned sharper.

40

The footage aired just after sunrise. It's not grainy or chaotic, it was pristine. Stabilized. Cropped. Color-corrected. The explosion is visible but distant, artfully framed between two crumbling towers. There was no audio. Just orchestral swells. Dan's face lingering on screen for twelve seconds. Long enough for reverence, but not grief.

The title card appeared in bold serif: **DANIEL EUSTATIUS CLYMER, PROTECTOR OF THE FAITH SACRIFICED IN THE OUTER WILDERNESS**

Then came the narration: a calm, almost liturgical voiceover about duty, valor, and sacrifice. It never says where. It never says how. Just that he gave everything "in defense of sanctity."

In a gilded control room within the capital's ministry complex, Knox stood before a massive screen, still wearing last night's suit. Someone powdered the oil from his forehead, but nothing could hide the dark crescents under his eyes.

Hightower watched from a few paces back, arms folded. His eyes unreadable.

"This'll work," Knox said quietly, almost to himself. "They needed a death to believe in."

"A death with purpose," Hightower replied.

Onscreen, a second broadcast began: a montage of candlelight vigils, both real and staged, already playing out in major cities.

Knox gestured to the footage. "See? They're buying it. The death, the ascension, the myth. Clean. We're not just controlling the story anymore—we're controlling the faith."

Hightower smiled, but it was thin. "The line between the two has always been artificial."

The strike should be complete any minute now. Hightower no longer cared if it was. Belief outran the truth a long time ago.

Across the city, a new mural began going up. Dan's face, rendered ten feet high in grayscale, gazing toward the sky. Below it, in gold:

IN MEMORY OF DANIEL E. CLYMER: PATRIOT, PROTECTOR, HERO

Then, below it:

MAY EVERY CITIZEN BE WORTHY OF HIS GIFT.

41

"Stay down."

Sarah didn't question it, just obeyed.

"Don't move yet," the voice said again. "They scan for motion. We're shielded here—no thermal signature. Stay still, and they'll read you as debris."

That didn't sound like myth. That sounded like experience.

Sarah nodded once, just enough.

Someone else shifted near Marcus. She heard a low grunt—alive, but fading. Then hands, careful ones, checking his breathing. No words. No introductions.

The air was thick and stale. Dust stirred with every breath. Dan's ears still rang, and the pulse in his neck beat faster than he could track.

Sarah lay beside him, blinking against grit. Her ribs ached. Her mouth was dry, and full of dirt.

She turned toward the voice. A silhouette crouched beside her, wrapped in fabric the color of dried mud. No badge. No armor. Just rough clothes layered for silence and survival.

A subtle tremor ran through the ground. Not a strike. Not anymore. This one had rhythm. Precise. Calibrated. Beneath her, through the floor.

A signal.

The one beside her tapped two fingers to their collarbone.

"Clear," someone else whispered from the dark. "We have to move."

Hands helped her sit up. Another arm under Dan's shoulder. Marcus stirred, dazed and slow, but moving.

No one spoke to them. No one asked who they were. Just motion. Forward.

They passed through a crawlspace barely wider than their shoulders. Down. Deep. Deeper. The walls pressed in from every side—scrap metal, broken brick, old timber. Then a turn. Then another. Then a door.

Wooden. Scarred. Reinforced from within. The symbol was carved faintly into its center:

A circle, with two diagonal slashes beneath it.

Sarah paused. She'd seen it before, scratched into rock, etched in corners, but only now did she place it. The flyers. The verse. The quiet signal buried in plain sight.

One of the strangers knocked once. Then again. Rhythmic.

The door opened.

A type of warmth spilled out—not light, not heat. Just the sense of people. Of breath and closeness and motion. Of survival.

They were pulled through. The door shut behind them.

No one spoke.

Sarah didn't know if they'd been rescued or rerouted into something worse. But they had entered the unknown, and it had not yet decided what to make of them.

42

They didn't speak for a long time.

The three of them sat in a narrow concrete room with a low ceiling and no visible door. The walls were smooth, sealed, as if carved out rather than built. A single light strip buzzed above them, dim and flickering, casting more shadow than clarity.

No one told them to sit. No one told them anything.

Dan leaned forward on his knees, elbows pressed to his thighs, head down. His breathing had slowed, but his hands still shook occasionally. Just enough to betray him.

Marcus had stopped asking questions after the third time. He paced in uneven loops near the back wall, muttering under his breath. He was fiddling with the bracelet again, this time more openly, the frayed band pulled tight against his wrist, his fingers working at the knots as if trying to remember the motion.

Dan noticed. He glanced at Sarah. "What's the story with that?"

Sarah's eyes flicked to the bracelet. She lowered her voice. "His grandmother taught him a song when he was little, said to hum it whenever he was scared. The bracelet goes with it. He said the beads helped him to remember."

Dan didn't press further.

The bandage on Marcus's forehead—new, clean —had been applied while he was unconscious. Sarah sat cross-legged, spine straight, watching the makeshift door.

Hours passed. A tray of food appeared at some point without sound or warning, bowls of something warm, spiced, unfamiliar. Stew, maybe. None of them spoke when it arrived. They ate in silence.

At what might have been night, or just another power cycle, the door slid open.

A woman stood there.

Same layers. Same dark clothes. Older than Sarah had first guessed. Her skin was weatherworn, her face composed. She held no weapon, but she didn't need one. Authority radiated from her like heat.

"Follow me," she said.

They didn't argue.

She led them down a sloped corridor lined with repurposed lights and coiled cables. The space grew wider, the air cooler. They passed doors without markings, paths that split off and vanished. This was no shelter. It was a system. A network.

They emerged into a larger room—low-ceilinged, layered with bunks and crates. A fireless heat source hummed from one corner. People turned to look but didn't speak.

A small girl sat cross-legged near a storage bin, sorting dried herbs into paper sachets. Another person, young, maybe sixteen, was scraping labels off old food tins. The atmosphere wasn't hostile, just wary.

"You're not guests," the woman said, turning to face them fully. "You're a liability. Until we know what you are, you stay here."

Dan opened his mouth, but she raised a hand.

"You stay," she repeated. "You work, you eat, you shut up. You don't wander. We watch everything."

Her eyes lingered on Marcus. "If that's going to be a problem, you can leave the way you came."

Marcus looked away.

The woman turned to go.

Just before she disappeared into the corridor again, she paused.

"Someone will be back. Eventually."

Then she was gone.

Marcus sank onto a crate near the far wall, rubbing his temples. The bandage on his head was streaked with dust, and his eyes were sunken, dull.

"What the hell was that?" he muttered finally, not to anyone in particular.

Dan didn't answer. He stood with his back to one of the support beams, arms folded, scanning the faces in the room—the quiet workers, the narrow bunks, the makeshift lights. He looked like he wanted to take it all apart and put it back together in a way that made sense.

Sarah sat down beside Marcus, slowly, carefully.

"I think we're alive," she said. "That's something."

Marcus gave a dry laugh. "Doesn't feel like it."

Dan stepped forward. "They saved us. That's what matters."

"She didn't even ask our names," he said quietly. "Like we don't matter. Like we're livestock." His fingers continued working the beads. "I guess I already knew that about myself, but you two..."

Sarah looked at him, then at the bracelet.

"You matter," she said.

Marcus's hand clenched around the beads. His jaw tightened. "You don't get it."

Sarah started to speak, but he kept going, voice low, rushed, unraveling.

"This is my fault. All of it. I pushed for the Zone. I thought..." He shook his head. "I wanted to see it, prove something. I don't even know what. And now we're here. We almost died because I couldn't shut up."

Sarah opened her mouth, then stopped. She wanted to argue. But she didn't.

Dan sat down across from them, his posture still but alert. He didn't offer comfort. Just a long, quiet look at Marcus.

"We're not dead," he said finally. "Let's keep it that way."

For once, Marcus didn't have a comeback. He just nodded, eyes fixed on the floor.

For a while, none of them said anything more.

43

The national anthem played softly in the background, re-scored in a minor key for solemnity. Screens across the city flickered with curated tribute footage of Daniel Clymer, lit in gold, standing before the Hall of Valor. Daniel Clymer, headset in place, guiding holy fire from the heavens. Daniel Clymer, now a martyr, now a saint.

The broadcast had begun at dawn. President Knox appeared first, his voice grave and full of false humility. "Daniel Clymer was the best of us," he declared. "A servant of faith and justice. A warrior of clarity in a world clouded by sin."

Then came Reverend Hightower, robed and radiant, hands raised before the pulpit in the Hall of Valor. "He did not die. He ascended," he proclaimed. "He has gone ahead to prepare the way."

Across the city, candles were handed out in the streets. Choirs sang. Children practiced their pledges. Every broadcast looped the same montage: Dan smiling with his fellow operators. Dan walking in slow motion past a glowing console. Dan's final strike footage—cut to black before impact.

It was a production. And for many, it worked.

But not for all.

VICTOR SLOANE ADJUSTED his lapel as the cameras rolled. His studio lighting was dimmer than usual, an aesthetic choice. Somber tone. Regal, subdued.

"Good evening, citizens," he said, smooth as ever. "Tonight, I want to talk about belief."

A pause. Then a slow zoom as he leaned forward, elbows on the desk.

"We were told Daniel Clymer died in service to the Sanctified State. We watched the tribute. We bowed our heads. We taught our children his name. And yet... something feels off, doesn't it?"

He folded his hands.

"I'm not here to accuse. I'm here to ask. Because faith thrives on truth, not manipulation. And if Daniel Clymer is truly gone, why the need for such overwhelming performance? Why so many reminders? Why so much insistence?"

He leaned forward again.

"Unless, of course, the story isn't finished."

The camera cut to a four-person panel. Sloane sat at the center, flanked by two regime-affiliated analysts and one new face: a mid-level political commentator known for treading the line between acceptable doubt and subversive curiosity.

"We're not saying there's a cover-up," the new guest said, eyes flicking toward the camera, "but if there were, hypothetically, wouldn't this be how you'd do it? Roll out the tribute, close the loop fast, and bury the questions in candles and choirs."

One of the regime loyalists scoffed. "That's dangerous speculation."

"Of course," Sloane interjected smoothly. "We're just exploring the 'what-ifs.' That's our job. To ask questions. Because questions are patriotic."

He turned back to the camera, smile practiced. "We're not saying Daniel Clymer is alive. But if he were, would we even know?"

44

The war room was silent except for the faint hum of the overhead display. On the massive screen, the failed strike played on loop, the drone's targeting system locking onto the structure, the payload dropping, and then the figures below scattering just before impact. Dust and debris obscured the view, and by the time the smoke cleared, it was obvious: the target had escaped.

A glass shattered against the far wall.

"Unacceptable," President Alexander Knox seethed, his breath coming in sharp bursts as he ran a hand through his thinning hair. His usual smirk, the expression he had perfected for the cameras and the masses, was absent. His jaw twitched with restrained fury. "How the fuck does footage of a failed strike get to the press?!"

"This was supposed to be a moment of control," he continued, voice rising. "Clymer was supposed to be eliminated—quietly, cleanly. No footage. No feed. Just...gone."

He jabbed a finger at the screen. "Do you know what's playing right now on the goddamn morning news? Clips of this."

"And speculation. Questions." His voice dropped to a venomous whisper. "I do not tolerate questions."

Across the table, Reverend Eli Hightower sat perfectly still, hands steepled together in front of him. His lined face betrayed no emotion, no irritation, only the same calculated calm that had always allowed him to maneuver Knox like a puppet.

"We do not panic," Hightower said smoothly. "We correct."

Knox's nostrils flared, but the words settled him. He exhaled sharply, rolling his shoulders before turning to the cluster of military brass and advisors surrounding the table. "What went wrong?"

A nervous shuffle. Then, one of the senior commanders spoke up. "The new operator lost lock at the last second. There was unexpected movement. It..."

Knox slammed a fist on the table. "I don't give a shit about unexpected movement! I care about results!"

On a side screen, the broadcast continued to loop. Victor Sloane's face filled the frame, wrapping up a segment speculating on Dan Clymer's survival—and the regime's possible cover-up.

Knox stared at the screen, jaw tight.

"I want Sloane gone," he said flatly.

He turned to Hightower. "And what happens if Clymer *does* show up again? We already aired the memorial, Eli. His face is ten stories tall downtown. If he resurfaces..."

Hightower met his glare without flinching. "He won't."

Knox didn't look convinced.

"We didn't kill half the country to give up that easily."

The words cut through the silence like a blade. Knox's expression shifted, just slightly. Hightower didn't flinch.

"We made a decision a decade ago. We burned the Zone because we had to," Hightower said, voice low and cold. "Because fear is control. And you needed a goddamn stage."

Knox sneered. "And you needed a pulpit."

They stared at each other, a decade's worth of resentment threading the air between them.

"And if he does reappear, it changes nothing," Hightower continued. "The people already mourned. They believe the story we gave them. Truth is whatever we amplify. Clymer is no longer a problem."

Knox said nothing.

IN THE OUTSKIRTS of the city, in flickering cafes and quiet terminals, people were still watching. Still replaying. The montage had gone out to millions.

Some said the tribute felt too staged. Some questioned the scale, the timing, the speed with which the sainthood campaign had been rolled out.

A few conspiracy forums began to churn: What if Dan Clymer had never died? What if the ceremony was cover? What if the regime needed a martyr more than they needed the man himself?

Most dismissed it. Most wanted to believe.

But not everyone did.

45

I n the dimly lit operations center, the young operator sat frozen, staring at the flashing red deduction on his screen. His Patriot Points—the measure of his worth, his status—were plummeting.

His colleagues stood behind him, some exchanging silent glances of relief that it hadn't been them, others smirking at his misfortune. Failure was a rarity in their profession, but when it happened, it was brutal. The ranking system didn't just encourage competition; it ensured that one man's downfall was another's advancement.

Greg stood at the back of the room, arms crossed, watching the scene unfold. He had been Dan's colleague, and now, with Dan missing, he was the top operator. He had tried to mentor this one, but clearly, the kid wasn't cut out for it. Greg's expression didn't shift as the failed operator pushed away from his console, hands shaking.

"Maybe... maybe the system glitched," the operator muttered, looking up at Greg desperately.

Greg exhaled through his nose. "You missed. That's all that matters."

A message flashed across the operator's screen. Official Demotion: Security Risk Status Pending. His breathing hitched. This wasn't just a performance penalty. It was a step toward erasure.

Security would be waiting outside.

BACK IN THE WAR ROOM, the tension was beginning to shift, from the heat of Knox's anger to the cold calculation of Hightower's next move.

"This is an opportunity," Hightower said. "A failed strike will not demoralize the faithful. It will embolden them to demand justice." He let the word hang, savoring the weight of it before continuing. "We increase the strikes. We use this moment to fuel righteous outrage. The enemy is mocking us, striking at the very heart of our nation's resolve. We will not allow it."

Knox listened, his breathing evening out. Hightower was already controlling the narrative, shifting failure into divine necessity.

"Double the strikes," Knox ordered, now regaining his composure. "Make sure it's a spectacle."

Hightower inclined his head slightly. "And let us not forget the spiritual angle. A Cleansing Ceremony, a declaration that we are purging the enemy of its corruption."

Knox hesitated, narrowing his eyes. "We still need to keep the public's focus on the canonization. We can't have distractions."

Hightower smiled. "It will not be a distraction. It will be reinforcement. Dan Clymer's ascension is a symbol of our divine military might. A living testament to our cause. And to mark it, we ensure the biggest strike yet."

Knox let out a low chuckle. "Poetic."

THE DISGRACED OPERATOR stood before a tribunal of stern-faced military and faith leaders. His failure had not just cost him his career, it had cost him his identity.

The ranking clergyman sat in the center of the room, a picture of measured disappointment. He sighed, shaking his head. "You were given a sacred task."

The operator swallowed hard. "I—I miscalculated."

The gaze sharpened. "Miscalculations lead to doubt. Doubt leads to chaos."

The tribunal's decision was swift. He was no longer an operator. No longer a warrior of the faith. His security access was revoked, his clearance wiped. He was now indistinguishable from the average citizen.

And in this society, the average citizen was nothing.

Greg watched from the sidelines, expression unreadable. Another one gone. Another position open. He turned to leave, knowing exactly what came next.

46

ilith shut the door behind her and exhaled into the dim. Her boots echoed down the corridor as she moved away from the holding area, not quickly, not quietly, but with the weight of someone who owned responsibility far beyond what they are able to control.

She turned down a narrower passage, stepped through a reinforced arch, and entered a cramped room no bigger than a point redemption kiosk. There were five others already waiting, seated on scavenged chairs and upturned crates. The air smelled faintly of petroleum and root vegetables.

No one spoke right away.

An older man with deep-set eyes and a grease-streaked apron was the first to break the silence. "You brought them in."

Lilith didn't sit. "They were already well past the perimeter when the drone hit. We didn't invite them. We didn't mark their path."

"They were seen." This came from a younger woman near the back, arms crossed, eyes sharp. "The footage was cleaned, but I recognized him. The tall one. That's Dan Clymer."

A few heads turned. One man muttered something under his breath.

"You're sure?" another asked.

"Positive." The woman didn't blink. "The state's been pumping out martyr reels since dawn. They're calling him a 'fallen defender of sanctity.'"

Someone snorted. "He's not very dead for a dead man."

"He won't stay not-very-dead for long," the apron man replied. "Not if they know he's down here."

"I've got a mind to help them out with that, after what he's done."

A murmur passed through the room, unease, not fear. This group had lived too long underground for panic. But concern had weight here, and Lilith could feel it settling.

"They're not who we expected," said the younger woman. "And you put them in the workers' hall. With the children."

"They're not soldiers," Lilith said. "Not anymore."

"Spoken like someone who hasn't lost anyone to the upper air."

Lilith turned toward her slowly. "You think I haven't?"

The woman looked away.

The silence held. Then the old man leaned forward, elbows on his knees. "We've been watching them since they crossed the perimeter. They didn't turn back, even when they had the chance."

"They were loud," the woman muttered.

"But they stayed," another said. "Even after the warning tremors. Most wouldn't have.".

Lilith let that hang. Then: "You all want to protect this place. So do I. But if we start acting like them—judging on suspicion, turning fear into law—this place won't last another season."

No one spoke.

She turned toward the door.

"They stay," she said. "We observe. We don't offer trust. Yet. But we offer space."

As she reached the threshold, the apron man cleared his throat. "They brought the strike with them," someone muttered. "We should drop them back outside."

Another voice, tense: "If the regime sends another..."

"Then we prepare for the worst," Lilith said, without turning. "But they stay. For now."

A third voice, sharper now: "Why risk it?"

Lilith finally turned, voice low but firm. "Because we've already been watching them. "And because if we abandon everyone the moment things get hard, then we've already lost."

She turned and left without another word, her footfalls fading into the corridor.

Only once she was alone did she pause beside a scratched mark on the tunnel wall—faint, worn, almost invisible unless you knew where to look.

The circle with two slashes.

Her fingers hovered near it. Not touching. Just remembering.

They'd all seen too much to trust easily.

But trust was the point.

From the beginning, the symbol had pointed the way—to shelter, to others, to something like hope.

It had always meant: we don't survive alone.

She just hoped it still meant that now.

47

They didn't wake to alarms or shouting. There was no siren, no formal reveille. Just the hum of generators and the distant scrape of metal. Life moved down here without spectacle. People rose because there was work to do, not because anyone told them to.

Dan, Sarah, and Marcus stirred slowly from their bunks. The lights had brightened by degrees, simulating morning in a place that had none. Nearby, others moved quietly, folding blankets, sorting tools, preparing supplies. No one greeted them. But no one stopped them, either.

Marcus stood first, still wearing the fatigue of injury and guilt, but steadier than the night before. He glanced around the room as though searching for his place in it. Sarah watched him tug the bracelet tighter on his wrist, fingers brushing each bead in sequence. She thought he might be praying.

Dan sat up and swung his feet to the floor. He didn't stretch or sigh or shake off sleep. He simply stood, already alert, eyes sweeping the space as if taking stock of exits, vulnerabilities, and routines.

Sarah was slower. She blinked against the artificial light and felt the stiffness in her limbs. But what lingered more than discomfort was curiosity. The people here moved like they had lived in the shadows forever, and yet there was order, rhythm, purpose.

A small woman passed with a stack of folded garments. She paused just long enough to nod at a crate of supplies nearby. "Clothes. Soap. You'll need both."

No introduction. No welcome. Just what was necessary.

THE WATER WAS COLD. Not freezing, but enough to make Marcus hiss when it hit his skin. The bathing area was a series of stalls made from hanging tarps and old shipping pallets—partitioned, but barely. Privacy was implied, not enforced.

Dan rinsed efficiently, methodically, as if this were just another part of the regimen. Sarah scrubbed the grime from her arms and stared at the rust stains on the floor. She couldn't remember the last time she'd showered—days, maybe longer. The water ran dark at her feet before fading to clear.

When finished, they dressed in the offered clothes—neutral fabrics, slightly too large, but clean. Sarah found herself grateful just for socks that weren't stiff with dust.

When they returned to the main space, breakfast was being distributed: a dense loaf of protein bread, two slices per person, and a hot liquid that smelled vaguely familiar. Sarah took a sip and paused.

It wasn't good. Bitter. Gritty. No sweetness. No cardamom. But something about it scratched at memory. A comfort she couldn't fully grasp.

She took another sip and looked over at Dan, who held the cup near his face, studying the steam.

He looked like he was weighing something.

Then, without a word, he reached into his bag and pulled out the moka pot.

A few people nearby noticed. One of the cooks, a wiry older woman with a patched apron, tilted her head. Dan stepped forward, extended the pot.

"Might be useful," he said.

She didn't smile, but she took it, gave a single nod, and turned away.

Sarah stared at him. "You just gave that up?"

"It was never mine," Dan replied.

Marcus gave a short laugh. "You're gonna be the most popular guy down here."

Dan didn't respond. But something in the room had shifted. The act had been noticed. And maybe, just maybe, it mattered.

THEY WERE ASSIGNED tasks by mid-morning. Sarah was sent to assist in the storerooms, organizing salvage from the upper levels. Marcus went to maintenance, where someone apparently decided that giving him a wrench would help channel his nervous energy. Dan was assigned to security watch, escorted to a low-level tunnel junction where a young girl showed him how to monitor vibration sensors.

She couldn't have been more than ten.

He watched her small fingers dance over a touchpad, then glance up at him.

"You ever done sensor work before?" she asked.

Dan hesitated. "Not like this."

She nodded seriously, then gestured for him to sit. "Just feel for patterns. Most of it's noise, but if it repeats... that's when you tell someone."

He sat beside her. The touchpad hummed faintly under his fingertips.

Not a drone. Not yet.

There was silence.

Then she added, quieter: "The surface sensors pick up rotor vibrations. Drones make a signature pulse in the air, even before they're in sight."

"We used to try sirens on the surface," she went on. "But the drones found them. Blew them up fast. So now we use old machines—manual weights on pressure plates, some rigged from freight elevators and interstate weigh station scales."

Dan looked at her. She couldn't weigh more than seventy pounds, and yet she was talking about counterweights and improvised machinery like a field veteran.

She shrugged. "Sometimes they get through anyway."

The touchpad fluttered briefly beneath their hands. Two faint taps. Then nothing.

She stared for a second, then shook her head. "Just windshift."

Dan glanced down at her. "You know, I used to lead missions that ran strikes off less than this. One pulse, one signal—poof. Dust and silence."

She didn't laugh. Didn't even look at him.

"Yeah," she said flatly. "We noticed."

Dan blinked. Whatever small satisfaction he'd been about to savor disintegrated. Her voice had drawn a line, and he knew better than to cross it.

The girl tapped the pad again. "Patterns, not pulses. It's not about reaction. It's about reading the signal right."

He nodded, humbled. "Understood."

She passed him a piece of salvaged slate. "You can sketch to pass the time if you like. just make sure to keep a feel on the touchpad."

Dan took it. The pulsing continued beneath his fingers.

This wasn't glory. This was something more real. Vigilance.

IN THE STOREROOM, Sarah stacked old wiring spools into color-coded bins. It was mindless, but strangely calming. At one point, she passed a crate of dried goods and stopped.

A torn burlap sack sat half-spilled on the floor. Coffee beans. The label on the side was mostly gone, but she could still make out the shape of the printed logo.

She'd seen it before. In the market. The woman who sold it, Nama, had claimed it came from outside the border. No one ever believed her.

But she had told the truth.

Marcus fumbled with a pipe fitting under a sink that hadn't drained properly since the last strike. The man beside him grunted something unintelligible and yanked the tool from his hands.

"Left thread, not right. You're stripping it."

"Sorry," Marcus muttered.

The man didn't respond. Just kept working.

Marcus leaned back and wiped his forehead. Everything here was recycled. The walls, the clothes, even the air. He felt useless.

"Do you ever get used to it?" he asked finally.

The man didn't look up. "You don't."

He didn't say anything after that.

By late afternoon, the three were back in the common space. Their assigned jobs done, their clothes dustier than before.

Dan sat alone at a table, sketching faint arcs and lines on a piece of salvaged packaging. Sarah joined him, quietly. Marcus followed, slumping onto a crate.

"I'm bad at pipes," he said. "Like, impressively bad."

Dan didn't look up. "I don't think they care."

"They do," Marcus muttered. "They just won't say it."

Sarah rested her elbows on the table. "They've survived a long time without us."

Dan set down his pencil. "Which means they're watching us. Deciding if we belong."

They sat in silence for a while. The lights dimmed fractionally.

Sarah looked toward the corridor where Lilith had vanished earlier.

"She said we weren't guests," Sarah murmured. "But I think... maybe we're becoming something else."

Marcus looked at her. "What's that?"

She didn't answer.

Dan's eyes tracked the shadow of a child running past.

"Still alive," he said.

Sarah didn't reply, but she brushed a few crumbs from the table. For the first time in days, she let herself settle. Not relaxed—just a little less braced.

Across the room, someone muttered, "Coffee's better today."

Another voice answered, just loud enough to carry: "Probably that pot the new guy brought."

Marcus glanced over at Dan.

Sarah followed his gaze—and gave Dan a slight sideways smile.

Dan didn't look up. He just kept sketching, the faint trace of a grin barely detectable on his face.

"And there shall be upon every high mountain, and upon every high hill, rivers and streams of waters in the day of the great slaughter, when the towers fall."

-Isaiah 30:25

PART 3

48

It had been a week, maybe two. Time passed differently underground. There were no sunrises, no weather patterns, only the soft pulse of light cycles and the drone of recycled air. But some rhythms had returned; tasks, routines, meals. Patterns of movement that hinted at belonging.

Dan, Sarah, and Marcus had found a kind of footing, enough to move without being watched at every turn. People still didn't talk to them much, but the silence had changed. It was less suspicious, more indifferent. Or maybe it was a kind of earned tolerance.

Their names were known now, if not spoken. Sarah had been moved from storage to sorting, then to repair tagging, where she helped inventory what could be salvaged from surface runs. Dan had been shifted twice—first to sensors, then to perimeter relay check-ins. Marcus, still bruised from the strike, remained with maintenance. He was getting better with a wrench.

They had been to the surface. Not far. Not anywhere near the perimeter. But enough to feel the change in air pressure, the shift in light. Enough to see the sky, grey, streaked with ash, and feel how exposed it made you. The trips weren't explained, only assigned. Retrieve this. Mark that. Leave this bundle. Memorize the path back.

Sarah asked no questions. But she committed every step to memory.

SHE FIRST NOTICED the scent before she saw the flame. It caught her just outside the kitchen corridor. A bitter, earthy note layered with something warmer. Memory, almost.

She followed it around the bend and paused.

A small copper pot rested over a makeshift burner—narrow-waisted, long-handled, blackened at the base. The flame beneath it was low and steady. The woman tending it stood quietly, arms folded, watching the pot with the reverence of someone protecting an old song.

Sarah lingered near the edge of the room, caught by the smell—sharp, rich, familiar in a way that made her stomach ache.

"I had an ibrik like that back home," she said quietly. "Belonged to my dad. Nobody could make coffee like him."

The woman glanced over, one brow lifted—not quite a smile, but something near it.

"We called it a cezve in my family," she said with what might have been a smile. "My mother made it perfectly. Once. Every other time was a disaster."

The woman considered her. Then gestured slightly to the side. "I'm Ish."

"Sarah."

"I know."

The ibrik bubbled softly as the foam began to rise. Ish removed it from the flame, swirled it gently, then poured into two small cups. One she handed off to an older man who passed without a word. The other she set down without drinking.

"You make it differently?" she asked.

Sarah nodded. "Same steps. Just... more spice."

"Cardamom."

Sarah smiled. "If I can ever find it again."

Ish gave a small nod. "If you do, we'll brew it your way."

She picked up the cup she had set down and handed it to Sarah.

Sarah accepted it quietly. "Thank you."

She lingered a moment longer, letting the scent anchor her to the memory it stirred.

Dan was tightening a bolt on one of the lower tunnel locks when someone passed behind him and muttered, "You're not bad at this."

He looked up, surprised.

The speaker didn't stop, didn't look back. Just kept walking, a toolbelt slung low across one shoulder.

It wasn't praise. But it wasn't nothing.

Three days later, Sarah crossed paths with one of the market runners—a girl maybe sixteen, with wind-chafed skin and a bag strapped tight across her back. She was checking the straps on a small satchel of coffee beans near the main exit tunnel.

Sarah recognized the logo on the sack, faded but familiar. "You trade that up top?"

The girl nodded. "Drop it with a contact across the west barrier. She pays in grain or medicine."

Sarah hesitated. Then: "If I asked for something—something small—would that be possible?"

The runner eyed her. "Depends."

"Cardamom," Sarah said. "Dried pods. Just a few."

The girl blinked. "You cooking or conjuring?"

Sarah smiled. "Just trying to remember."

The girl studied her for a second longer. "You've been steady. People notice."

Sarah didn't know what that meant, but it sounded something close to acceptance.

" I'll ask. No promises."

"Thank you."

"Oh—" Sarah added as the girl started to turn, "and tell Nama that Sarah said hello."

The girl gave a half-nod and a smile, secured the bag, and disappeared down the tunnel.

IT WAS ALMOST A WEEK before the girl returned. Sarah didn't see her come in, but found the bundle tucked into her sorting crate, wrapped in waxed cloth, marked with a single slash of ink.

Five pods.

THAT EVENING, Sarah found Ish cleaning out the ibrik again. Same posture. Same quiet.

Sarah approached and held out the bundle.

Ish opened it slowly. Her eyes lingered on the pods. "Where?"

Sarah didn't answer.

Ish gave a small nod. "You grind."

They moved without further words. Sarah measured the grounds, crushed the pods with the flat of a blade, and stirred both together before adding water.

The coffee bubbled and bloomed.

Across the room, Marcus was demonstrating how not to juggle bolts to a patient teenager. He spoke louder than necessary, sighing with each dropped bolt, like he was trying to turn failure into charm.

Dan sat near a vent shaft, sketching quietly. He glanced toward the coffee corner now and then, expression unreadable. Not jealous, not quite—just watching, one hand idly smudging the charcoal on his sketch. Calculating where he stood in a system he didn't yet understand.

Neither of them looked over.

Marcus dropped one of the bolts and cursed under his breath. The teen laughed gently, but Marcus didn't. His eyes flicked across the room, to Sarah, seated with Ish, and lingered a moment too long. He adjusted his posture, more upright, more performative. Then he picked up the bolt again, this time slower. Less show. More silence.

Sarah glanced toward Marcus and Dan but didn't cross the room. Not out of avoidance, just... not out of need. The distance felt natural now, a quiet reshuffling she hadn't meant to begin.

Ish sipped first this time. Paused. Then nodded.

"That's...different," she said.

Sarah met her eyes. "Better?"

Ish looked into her cup for a moment. "My mother used to talk about cardamom. Said she drank her coffee that way before the strike... before everything changed."

She took another sip. "It lingers. I like it."

Sarah poured herself a cup. The steam carried her father's voice, not words, just the rhythm of mornings. In a world that erased the past, holding onto flavor felt like rebellion. She let it settle inside her.

She would remember this.

She would remember all of it.

HIGHTOWER AND KNOX stood alone now, the others dismissed.

"We'll need more precision," Knox mused, swirling the amber liquid in his glass. "More than these... fallible operators."

Hightower nodded. "Then we move up the timeline. The DAN drone prototype debuts at Clymer's canonization ceremony, complete with its first live strike. Full production ramps a month later —assuming prototype testing holds. We could push full rollout the week after, if needed."

Knox raised an eyebrow. "That quickly?"

Hightower smirked. "Faith demands sacrifice."

Knox let out a slow exhale, then nodded. "Do it."

Hightower reached for the phone beside him and pressed a single button.

"Accelerate production."

49

Amelia stepped into the Golden Circle Noodle House just before the dinner rush. The walls were a mix of faded red paint and greasy beige tile. A laminated poster near the counter read: "Loyalty begins at the table." A framed photo of President Knox and Reverend Hightower hung slightly crooked near the register, its glass smudged. Below it, an electronic Patriot Points sticker blinked dutifully from the window, untouched. The air smelled of soy and ginger and something deeper, like scorched sesame oil. The glow from the window signage cast a dull gold hue across the tabletops.

Her eyes scanned the room casually. The logo on the glass, an elegant gold circle with two chopsticks beneath, might've meant nothing to anyone else. But to her, those chopsticks angled just so were unmistakable.

She scanned the room and noticed small brass table numbers mounted discreetly on the wall above each booth. Table 7 sat near the back, tucked beside a dusty window. She made her way toward it and slid into the seat without hesitation.

She sat, picked up a laminated menu, printed with patriotic borders and dish names like 'Freedom Pho' and 'Devotion Dumplings', then looked around as if still deciding. Toward the front of the shop, a quote board offered a daily 'thought for reflection': "He who seeks shall not find, but the blind shall be shown the way." The handwriting was casual. Unremarkable, unless you knew what to look for. A man cleaned nearby tables in silence. His apron bore the faintest outline of a logo where something had once been printed, faded now, like a memory worn thin. She noticed the shape almost unconsciously: a circle, maybe, and two lines, just barely there. It could've been nothing. But it wasn't.

A server approached, quiet, middle-aged, with soft steps and a dish towel tucked at his waist. "What can I get you?" he asked, voice casual.

Amelia glanced at the menu but didn't really see it. "I was just over at The Last Word," she said lightly. "Ever been? They've got some interesting titles."

The server's expression didn't change. He simply nodded once, then moved away without another word. A few minutes passed.

Then Liang approached, wiping down a nearby table. His posture was casual, but his eyes didn't miss a thing.

"We don't carry everything on the menu," he murmured, barely audible. "Just what people are hungry enough to ask for."

Amelia didn't respond. He set a small dish down in front of her, nothing on it but a single fortune cookie, unwrapped.

She cracked it open.

"Midnight devotional. Jeremiah 18:2."

Stamped at the bottom, faint but unmistakable, was the circle and slashes.

By the time she looked up again, Liang was already back at the sink.

A new customer had taken the table beside her. The noise returned. The moment was gone. She pocketed the slip. And stayed a few minutes longer, pretending to read the menu.

50

The alley behind the Ministry annex still smelled like fryer oil. Amelia kept her head down, hood drawn low, a paper bag of leftover noodles tucked under one arm. The food was lukewarm, but it had been free, an extra portion from a kind cook who didn't ask questions. That kind of kindness was becoming rarer.

She moved quickly but without urgency. Just another woman walking home in the after-dusk lull. Just another quiet shadow.

Voices echoed from the end of the block.

Two regime officers stood outside a storefront, their posture stiff and performative. A third figure, young, maybe late teens, was pressed against the wall, hands up, backpack at his feet. He wasn't resisting. Wasn't even speaking.

Amelia slowed.

"You ran your ID too many times today," one officer was saying. His voice was bored. "What are you hiding?"

"I just got turned around. My sister lives on this street..."

"Uh-huh. That's what the last one said."

The other officer nudged the bag with his boot. Something inside clinked. "Well, well. Contraband or charity?"

Amelia's pulse climbed. She didn't know the boy. Didn't know if he was resistance or just unlucky. But she knew this routine. If they took him in, he wouldn't come back.

She stepped forward. Bracing herself. Hoping the officers wouldn't ask too many questions.

"Excuse me," she called. Her voice was calm. Measured.

Three heads turned. The boy's eyes were wide.

One officer narrowed his gaze. "Keep walking, ma'am."

"I'm sorry," she said, shifting the bag in her arms. "That's my cousin. I told him to wait for me. He's not supposed to be out alone after curfew."

The officers exchanged a glance. "Identification?"

Amelia reached slowly into her coat. Pulled out her badge. It was real, expired but real. Left over from a short-lived placement in Ministry logistics. Her thumb covered the deactivation mark. The only identification she hadn't destroyed.

"Field errands," she said. "District food repurposing. Look, I get it, you're just doing your job. But if he misses another check-in, it's my audit."

The officer with the bag frowned. "He your responsibility?"

She nodded. "He's not smart, but he's not dangerous."

A long pause.

Then: "Fine." The officer kicked the backpack toward the boy. "Keep him out of trouble. Next time, we won't ask."

They turned and walked off, boots loud on the pavement.

The boy stared at her, frozen.

"Pick it up," she murmured. "Walk like you know me."

He did.

They moved two blocks in silence before he finally spoke. "You didn't have to do that."

Amelia kept her eyes ahead. "I know."

"Why did you?"

She didn't answer.

The silence stretched.

But as they reached the intersection and parted ways—no names, no promises—she felt the adrenaline finally begin to ebb.

51

Marcus sat on the hard-packed dirt, running his fingers through the fraying strands of rope in his hands. He had tried again and again to get the knot right, but it just wasn't clicking. It wasn't just the knots. Everything here felt like an uphill battle. Hunting, rationing supplies, evading drone detection —every skill he was expected to master, he failed at.

It had been over a month since their arrival in the Sacrificial Zone, and yet he still felt like an outsider. Worse, he felt like dead weight. Sarah had adapted quickly, earning trust and respect. Dan, despite his struggles, was at least making progress. But Marcus? He was drowning, and no one was coming to save him.

He glanced up at Sarah as she worked with one of the older resistance women, the two of them focused and in sync. He had never seen her like this;

confident, self-assured, needed. And she was slipping away from him, aligning herself with these people, this life. The very same life he had dragged her into in an effort to impress her.

The realization left a bitter taste in his mouth.

A voice startled him. "You're making this harder on yourself."

Marcus turned to see Lilith squatting beside him. Steady. Practical. Observant. She took the rope from his hands and looped it effortlessly into a tight, secure knot.

"You're trying to force things," she said. "This isn't like back home. No promotions, no Patriot Points, no shortcuts. You earn what you take."

Marcus exhaled sharply, rubbing his face. "And what if I don't? What if I never catch up?"

She studied him. "Then you die."

The bluntness sent a chill through Marcus. She wasn't being cruel, just honest. There was no safety net here, no infrastructure designed to keep people comfortable. You either contributed, or you were a liability. And Marcus had been a liability since day one.

He hated it. Hated the way Sarah looked at him now. Not with admiration or intrigue, but with the kind of patience you had for someone who couldn't keep up. Hated that Dan, of all people, was adjusting better than he was.

Dan. The celebrated operator. The golden boy of the regime. The one who had spent his entire life behind screens, who had never set foot on a battlefield, now being treated like a peer while Marcus—Marcus was still the weakest link.

And, most of all—he hated that he believed it, too.

His fingers found the edge of the woven bracelet beneath his sleeve. He twisted it once around his wrist, tighter. A quiet reflex.

That night, Marcus lay awake on his cot, staring at the ceiling of the underground shelter. The flickering lanterns cast shadows along the earthen walls, giving the space an eerie, restless quality.

He turned his head slightly. Sarah was across the room, speaking quietly with Lilith and one of the surface runners. She didn't look back.

He watched her, hoping she might glance his way. She didn't. Maybe she was just focused. Maybe she was tired. But in the silence, his mind translated it into something colder.

She belonged here now. He could see it. She had found something in this place that resonated with her in a way he hadn't. And maybe never would.

He closed his eyes, exhaling slowly. He had brought them into the Zone to impress her.

Instead, he had lost her to it.

THE NEXT MORNING, Marcus forced himself into the routine. He dragged his exhausted body up with the others, swallowing his pride as someone handed him a dull blade for sharpening signal arrows—low-tech decoys meant to draw drones off course. Simple. Basic. A task even he couldn't mess up.

His fingers trembled slightly as he worked, frustration bubbling up with each uneven stroke against the whetstone. Around him, the others moved fluidly, resistance members loading supplies, Sarah discussing scouting rotations, Dan listening carefully to quiet instruction.

Dan. Always watching. Always absorbing. The silent competence made Marcus want to scream.

A sudden snap rang out through the air. Marcus looked down to see the arrow in his hands had splintered—his grip too forceful in his frustration.

Someone nearby sighed. "Marcus..."

But he was already on his feet, heart pounding. "No. I'm done."

He threw the broken arrow to the ground. "I've been trying. I've done everything you've told me, and it's never enough. You all look at me like I'm some kind of joke."

Sarah stepped forward, concern in her eyes. "Marcus, no one thinks that..."

"Don't," he snapped. "I know what this is. I see how you look at me. Like I'm pathetic."

The others paused, tension hanging in the air. Dan stood nearby, silent.

Someone crossed their arms. "Then prove us wrong."

Marcus clenched his fists, his nails digging into his palms. He looked briefly toward Sarah.

She didn't move.

He turned and stormed off, heading toward the training grounds with a fierce determination burning in his chest. If survival was all that mattered here, then he would make damn sure he survived.

52

It was raining by the time Amelia reached her destination, still gripping the fortune slip—the verse printed on the paper.

She had unfolded it twice to be sure. Blocky black text, hand-pressed. No smiley face. No lucky numbers. Just:

Midnight devotional. Jeremiah 18:2.

And the circle with two slashes.

She hadn't known the verse offhand and had to look it up:

"Arise, and go down to the potter's house, and there I will cause thee to hear my words."

She read it again.

Go down.

The potter's house.

It wasn't an address. It was a riddle.

She spent the afternoon circling blocks, staring at plaques and reviewing zoning overlays, searching for anything—anything—that fit.

Eventually, a name surfaced: Potters' Row.

A narrow stretch near the river, where artisans once worked clay—before the war, before the regime deemed such work impractical. Most of the kilns had been bulldozed, but the name lingered: in local mouths, in half-erased maps, in buried city records.

She couldn't be sure this was what the verse meant. But it was the best guess she had.

It was still there. A few windows were lit—fringe artists, sanctioned creatives clinging to just enough patriotism to survive. Bohemians hung on at the edges, painting regime-approved murals, selling "heritage ceramics" stamped with loyalty oaths.

A couple of late-night joints blinked between shuttered warehouses.

She walked the block, uncertain, each step louder than she wanted.

Then she saw it.

Two blocks ahead, sprayed in looping red paint on the side of a boarded-up corner store:

The circle with two slashes.

By the time she reached the corner, the rain had set in for real. It was 11:06. A steady, whispering drizzle softened the edges of everything—headlights, footsteps, doubt.

No one was there.

She stood across from the symbol, the flyer heavy in her pocket. It wasn't the first time she'd seen the mark. The flyer. The bookstore window. That old sign at the noodle shop. Even the fortune cookie itself, it had been stamped onto the slip's edge, almost invisible in the folds.

It might have meant nothing. A gang tag, a remnant. But it matched the mark on the slip, and that was enough.

The minutes dragged on, Amelia's nerves none the better for wear.

Exactly on the hour, someone turned the corner.

They wore a poncho the color of wet asphalt, hood low. No umbrella. Just a steady presence in the rain.

"You made it," they said, voice low and genderless under the static of weather.

Amelia tensed. "I was told there'd be a devotional. I'd assumed indoors."

The figure nodded once. "There will be. But not here. Come on."

They turned without waiting for a reply, moving down the street with the quiet efficiency of someone who knew exactly how many cameras they were passing.

The rain soaked into her shoes, the cold creeping up her legs. Her coat grew heavier with each step. But something about the figure—maybe the stillness, maybe the way they didn't ask questions—made her trust just enough to keep moving.

They cut down an alley behind a closed laundromat, then crossed under a rusting scaffold where wind chimes tinkled softly in the rain. Eventually, they stopped in front of a warehouse that looked no different from the dozens she'd passed, except the door was cracked open, and warmth spilled through.

The figure turned to her. "Inside. Second floor. Don't touch anything unless you're asked."

Then they slipped away, lost to the rain like they'd never been there.

Amelia hesitated at the threshold, then stepped in.

INSIDE, THE AIR changed.

It wasn't warm, exactly, but it was dry. Dust hung in the light from a bare bulb overhead. The floorboards creaked under her boots, loud in the silence. Somewhere far off, a pipe ticked with expanding heat.

She closed the door behind her and stood for a moment, letting her eyes adjust. The warehouse stretched wide, half storage, half forgotten. Stacks of crates formed narrow corridors, some labeled in fading ink. Others were blank.

She found the stairs tucked along the far wall. Iron and wood, bolted together, not meant to be decorative. She climbed slowly, heart steady now but alert, each step louder than it should've been.

At the top was a landing, and a single door.

She knocked once. Nothing.

Then, on instinct, she tried the handle.

It opened with a reluctant groan.

Inside: a makeshift room. Not exactly homey, but lived-in. A stove patched with old parts and patience. A couch with one armrest broken clean off. Piles of blankets. Books. Cans. A desk scattered with paper and ink pens.

A woman sat by the stove, hands wrapped around a chipped mug.

"You made it," she said, still watching the steam.

The voice pulled at something in Amelia's memory. She stepped inside slowly, closing the door behind her.

The woman looked up.

Recognition clicked.

"You're—"

"Nama," the woman said. "From the market."

Amelia nodded. "You sent me."

Nama stood, crossed the room, and held out the mug.

"Ginger and lemongrass. Not much, but it's hot."

Amelia took it, fingers brushing ceramic.

"Towel's by the couch," Nama added. "You can dry off. We'll talk after."

Amelia didn't move right away. She looked around the room, then back at Nama.

"Why not just bring me here in the first place?"

Nama's expression didn't shift. "Because getting here was part of the answer."

A pause. Then, quietly:

"We don't bring people in. We see who finds their way."

"You can sleep here. There's a blanket over in the corner," and Nama disappeared into another room.

Amelia sat. Let the steam rise to her face. For the first time in days, the quiet didn't feel dangerous.

53

The sky was clear.

Across the city's skyline, the banners hung motionless in the early morning stillness, their sharp reds and golds glowing in the crisp light of dawn. Towers blinked with silent surveillance nodes. Air patrols made slow, ceremonial loops. And from every public screen, the voice of Reverend Hightower rang with solemn clarity.

"This is a day of sanctification."

In the drone operations center, Greg adjusted his headset.

The room was unusually quiet. Not reverent, exactly, but attentive. They had all been ordered to wear dress blacks today. Even the consoles had been re-skinned with gold interface overlays, cosmetic and unnecessary, but in keeping with the optics of a holy broadcast.

Greg's station glowed with live telemetry. The DAN drone—prototype, fully armed, and newly christened as the cornerstone of a divine new doctrine—was already in position. Operation Requiem.

And Greg had been chosen to launch it.

He hadn't told his wife, not in exact terms, but he had seen the pride in her eyes when the assignment came through. The inaugural strike. The weapon bearing Dan Clymer's name. It was the highest possible honor for an operator: to shepherd the faith, to carry the legacy forward.

He glanced at the mission packet again. A confirmed enemy redoubt deep within abandoned territory. Uplink feed was live. Target coordinates were locked. Weather optimal. Collateral estimates minimal.

He slowed the prestrike footage, frame by frame.

The camera panned over fractured rooftops, wind-blasted alleys, and charred remnants of what might once have been a school. Symbols caught the light, something scratched into concrete. A circle. Two slashes.

Greg blinked. Probably old graffiti. Didn't matter. The packet had been vetted. He wasn't here to question, only to execute.

Behind him, a junior tech murmured a prayer under their breath.

The speaker system echoed Hightower's voice: "By fire we shall be made clean."

Greg leaned back slightly in his chair and exhaled.

The feed had already gone live. It played across every public channel, every school terminal, every devotional sanctuary. Citizens were watching this strike as a holy event.

A tribute to the life and legacy of the fallen hero, Daniel Eustatius Clymer.

A celebration of his canonization.

A righteous blow against those who had attacked the homeland—who turned cities to ash and carved the Sacrificial Zone into the earth.

Not just war.

The Lord's vengeance.

Redemption. By fire.

Greg checked the final diagnostics. The DAN drone's systems were perfect. No anomalies. No flags. Just righteous precision.

He rested his fingertips on the console.

Five minutes to launch.

He didn't move.

Not yet.

54

They moved without speaking.

Sarah, Dan, and Marcus had been above ground for nearly an hour. The surface runners had left a salvage marker two nights ago, an old rail junction repurposed as a drop site, and Lilith had sent them out at first light. Supplies were thin. Wiring, tubing, salvaged pipe fittings. Whatever could be pulled from the bones of the city.

It was supposed to be routine.

Sarah crouched beside an overturned console terminal, brushing away soot and rat droppings with her sleeve. A few wires spilled out from the rusted back panel. She clipped them with a borrowed tool and coiled the cleanest lengths into her satchel.

Dan stood several meters away, half-shadowed beneath the bent canopy of a collapsed awning. His eyes weren't on the ground. They hadn't been since they arrived.

Marcus paced. Not obviously, but enough for Sarah to notice. He was checking every corner, every glint of motion between buildings. The wind dragged a brittle strip of plastic across the street and he flinched. Barely, but it was there.

"You good?" she asked, not unkindly.

He nodded too quickly. "Just being careful."

Sarah didn't press. She turned back toward Dan, and saw him frozen.

He was staring at a ruin just ahead, halfway caved in but unmistakable in its outline: gutted, its roof collapsed inward, beams sagging like broken ribs. Part of the street was cratered. A shell of a corner store stood at the far end, its windows long blown out.

Something about the layout made him stop.

He turned slowly, eyes scanning the angles—the bend in the road, the spacing between buildings, the skeletal remains of what might have once been a balcony.

A flicker at the back of his mind.

The way it had looked through the feed.

Grainy. Obscured. Just shapes and shadows from above.

But the spacing was right. The arch in the rubble. The void where a roof should have been.

His stomach sank.

This wasn't just familiar.

It was one of his.

He'd seen it on screen—seconds before the strike.

A shadow had moved.

A pause. A question.

Then fire.

He stepped back, heart hammering now. Not from exertion—something else.

This had been an enemy site.

Overseas.

But it wasn't.

It was here.

At home.

Inside the border.

Inside the Zone.

Inside the Community.

SARAH APPROACHED slowly. "Dan?"

His lips parted, but no sound came. His body was motionless, eyes locked on the ruin.

Dan turned toward her, eyes wide. "This is the site. The one from the footage. From my... my strike."

"What do you mean? What strike?" Marcus wasn't following.

"The Hall of Valor," Sarah said quietly. "The strike that got you inducted."

Marcus gave a half-laugh, half-scoff. "Dan, that strike was across the ocean. That was the whole point, right? Retribution. Foreign target. Big win."

Dan's voice dropped. "They said it was enemy infrastructure. Weapons cache. Minimal presence. Authorized. Clean."

He turned slowly, gesturing to the ruin around them. "But it was this. This exact block. Same roofline. Same collapse pattern. Same angles from the feed. They didn't even edit it. They just slapped a different label on it and fed it to everyone as proof of vengeance."

Sarah's brow furrowed. "Are you sure?"

"I centered the crosshairs myself." His voice cracked. "I remember the hesitation. I saw something move. Right over there. And I pressed anyway."

Marcus fell silent, the earlier flippancy bleeding away. He looked around, like the world might rearrange itself to make this untrue.

Dan moved forward, steps unsteady. They followed. At the base of a crumbling wall, he reached out and brushed away a layer of dust.

A faint symbol revealed itself beneath—etched into the concrete.

A circle. Two diagonal slashes.

He inhaled sharply.

"It's the same building," he said. "Same structure, same angle. Nothing has changed."

Sarah turned slowly in place. "So there was no enemy?"

Marcus's smile faded. "That can't be. That would mean..."

"It was never foreign," Dan said. "It was never war."

He looked between them, eyes wide, voice cracking. "I didn't kill soldiers. I killed civilians. Survivors. The ones who lived through the first blast and kept going."

He gestured back toward the buildings behind them. "The ones who built this. Who took us in. This was the Community."

Marcus stepped back, stunned. "But...why?"

Dan shook his head. "I don't know. They said it would stop another attack. That it was justice. That it was necessary."

"Suppression," Sarah said quietly.

"They also said the Zone was uninhabitable."

"They said a lot of things," Dan said. "And I never questioned any of them."

Silence gathered.

"They built a war out of our loss," he said quietly. "Out of our need for retribution. And sold it to us as divine. Sanctified."

"And I made myself a hero in the middle of it."

His voice dropped to a whisper. "I helped erase them."

THEN, A RUMBLING—

Followed by a low hum overhead.

Marcus looked up first. "Drone."

Dan followed his gaze. A flicker in the sky. Distant. Moving with purpose.

"Back inside?" Marcus asked, voice tight.

Dan didn't move.

Sarah grabbed his arm. "We have to go."

Dan looked at the ruin one last time, jaw clenched.

Then they ran.

55

They didn't stop running until the old street grid reappeared beneath their feet—cracked asphalt and fire-scarred concrete leading back to the surface camp.

They must have felt to signal tremor, too. By the time they reached the outer barricades, a crowd had already started to gather—runners, lookouts, resistance teams pulling themselves into defensive positions.

Dan didn't speak. He couldn't. The truth still roared in his skull.

And so did the hum; low, steady, mechanical. A predator's growl vibrating through the air. The sky, murky with dust and distant fires, parted slightly to reveal a sleek, predatory machine descending. The prototype DAN drone, state-of-the-art, a monstrous extension of the very system that had once hailed Dan as its greatest operator.

As he finally turned to look over his shoulder, Dan froze at the sight of it. The drone that bore his name.

And emblazoned on its metallic shell, beneath the insignia of the state, was the bright red and blue PowerUp Patriot logo.

It was the same drink he had bought casually at a convenience store all those weeks ago. The same drink that had fueled them in the early days of their suffering in the Zone. Now, it was stamped on a machine built to kill them.

Dan felt physically ill.

Shouts rang through the encampment as people scrambled for cover, weapons hastily drawn.

"EMP?" Ish barked, eyes locked onto the incoming drone.

"Still not at full charge!" a resistance fighter shouted back.

"Shit."

They weren't ready. The generator had been struggling for weeks, and the drone had come too soon.

Dan's mind worked on instinct, recalling every tactic, every maneuver, every weakness in these machines.

He turned to Marcus, who stood stiffly beside him.

"We have to take out its sensors," Dan said. "Blind it."

But Marcus barely heard him. He was staring at the drone, his expression unreadable.

"That's it," he murmured, eyes locked on the machine. "That's the future, isn't it?"

Dan had no time to process the words. The drone released a blast of suppressing fire, sending bodies diving in every direction. It moved with inhuman precision, scanning the terrain, calculating targets.

"We could split and distract..." Sarah began.

"We don't have time for this!" Dan said. "If we don't blind it now..."

But Marcus was already moving.

He sprinted toward the wreckage of an old transport vehicle, debris and shrapnel littering the sand. His fingers closed around something heavy, something cold and metallic.

It was a steel rod, jagged, about four feet long, the broken end twisted into a wickedly sharp point.

A weapon.

A crude, ancient weapon against a god of war.

Marcus turned back, gripping the makeshift spear with white-knuckled determination.

"Marcus, what the hell are you doing?!" Sarah's voice rang out, frantic.

Dan saw it too late.

Marcus had no gun. No modern armor. No training for this kind of fight.

Yet he ran straight toward the drone.

The resistance fighters shouted for him to stop, but Marcus was past the point of stopping.

The drone recalibrated. Target acquired.

A missile locked on.

Dan's breath caught in his throat.

He's dead. He's already dead.

But Marcus dodged.

He moved not like a soldier, but like something older, something primal. He used the terrain, weaving between debris, rolling low, keeping the drone's line of sight broken.

And then, with a terrifying leap, he launched himself at it.

The drone adjusted, but not fast enough. Marcus grabbed onto the landing strut, hanging on for dear life as it veered erratically, trying to shake him off.

Dan couldn't breathe.

Marcus climbed.

Hand over hand.

The drone swerved violently, trying to regain control, but Marcus held on.

Then...

he reached the core.

One chance.

With a guttural yell, Marcus drove the steel spear deep into the machine's underbelly.

Sparks erupted.

The drone shuddered, its stabilizers failing, its targeting scrambling.

Marcus ripped the weapon free and stabbed again.

A final, fatal blow.

The machine lurched, spiraling, its automated systems failing—

—and then it crashed.

A cloud of dust and flame erupted from the wreckage.

The DAN drone, the pinnacle of warfare, was dead.

DAN RAN. Sarah ran.

They reached Marcus just as he slumped onto his side, blood pooling beneath him.

Sarah fell to her knees, pressing her hands against his wounds, her breath ragged. "Marcus! Marcus, stay with me...!"

His eyes flickered.

Dan knelt beside him. He was struggling to process what he had just seen.

Marcus—the one they had underestimated, the one who had always been in the background, always struggling to prove himself—had done what no one else could.

Marcus had been the real warrior.

Not for glory. Not for points. Just to prove, maybe even to himself, that he could still matter.

Dan's throat tightened. "You stupid bastard."

Marcus smiled faintly, a weak, breathless chuckle escaping his lips. "You're welcome."

Sarah pressed harder against his wounds. "Just hold on, okay? You're gonna be fine."

Marcus's gaze drifted upward, past them, to the sky. The drone's carcass burned, its wreckage flickering against the distant skyline. The first real victory.

Marcus exhaled softly. "I was right," he murmured, voice barely above a whisper.

Sarah leaned in. "Right about what?"

A pause. A faint, fading smirk. "I did impress you."

His body went still.

Sarah squeezed her eyes shut. She didn't sob. She didn't scream. She just knelt there, one hand on his chest, trying to memorize the weight of him before it left.

Dan stared down at him, unable to speak. A part of him, some part he barely let himself name, had always longed for this kind of courage. The kind of heroism he'd read about as a boy, that they had seen in the stars. The kind that bled.

The moment stretched, heavy and unbreakable.

Then, finally, Sarah whispered: "You did."

The resistance fighters gathered. They had lost Marcus, but they had won something else.

The drone, a weapon of absolute authority, was beaten by nothing but human will.

Before they lifted him, Sarah reached down and unfastened the beaded bracelet from Marcus's wrist. She held it in her palm for a long time before slipping it into her pocket.

The final seconds had aired without censorship. The camera, mounted on the drone's hull, had captured it all. Not just the crash. But the man who brought it down.

For the first time, the regime had failed.

And somewhere, on the other side of the country, millions had just watched it happen.

56

The wreckage of the DAN drone still burned, its metal shell warped and half-buried in the dirt. The PowerUp Patriot logo was barely visible beneath the soot, a jagged reminder of the machine's origins. Dan stood over it, unmoving, his breath shallow.

It had his name.

His name.

He had spent years sitting in a temperature-controlled room, guiding these drones across screens, watching targets evaporate from a safe distance. He had earned promotions for precision, for efficiency, for striking targets exactly as expected. He had won awards, been praised, been cheered. All for a lie.

And now he was staring at his own weapon, the weapon they named after him, as it hunted him down like an animal.

It wasn't just the drone that lay in ruins.

Marcus was dead.

Sarah was kneeling beside the body, clutching the bracelet, her fingers wrapped so tightly around it that her knuckles had gone white. Dan's gaze flicked to her, then to Marcus's motionless form—his body still, his chest unmoving, his fingers slack against the dirt. The expression on his face was almost one of peace, as if, for the first time in his life, he had found certainty in something.

Dan had never respected Marcus. He had seen him as a foolish, desperate follower, a man trying to prove something that didn't need proving. Someone needing to be protected.

And yet.

Marcus had charged a machine designed for mass destruction with nothing but his own hands and a piece of scrap metal. And he had won.

Dan felt something collapse inside him.

He had spent his entire life believing himself to be a warrior. A protector. A hero.

But the heroes of old faced their enemies. They bled, they endured, they fought. They didn't sit in comfortable chairs, sipping lukewarm office coffee, pressing buttons that erased entire cities.

Dan hadn't been a hero.

But Marcus?

Marcus had died facing his enemy.

Dan swallowed against the tightness in his throat.

Marcus had been the strongest of them all.

SARAH PRESSED HER FOREHEAD against Marcus's cold hand. Her breath hitched.

She had not loved him, not in the way he had wanted.

But he had been hers, in a way. Her responsibility. Her companion. He had followed her, believing that if he proved himself, she would see him. And she had followed him. Here.

And now he was gone.

She uncurled her fingers, staring at the bracelet in her palm. She traced the beads, whispering the tune he had taught her beneath her breath. The same one he had used to calm himself when he was nervous.

It was the only thing of his left in the world.

A shadow fell over her.

Sarah lifted her gaze. Ish was looking at her. Not at Marcus, not at Dan, but at her.

"We have to move," she said quietly.

Sarah nodded.

Dan was still standing by the wreckage, staring at the machine that had almost killed them. Dan lingered behind as the others moved, the ruined drone still smoking behind him.

He looked down at what was left of Marcus.

The man who had always tried too hard. Who cracked jokes to cover the silence. Who wanted to matter so badly it ached.

Dan had once pitied him for that.

Now he understood.

Marcus had charged a machine named for a man who had never bled.

Had fought the gods of war with nothing but grit and a broken spear.

And he'd won.

Dan felt something in his chest fracture. Quietly. Finally.

This was what heroism looked like. Not banners. Not medals. Not points or broadcasts or precision strikes.

It was mud. Fire. The sound of your own breath in the moment before it stopped.

Dan swallowed hard, the taste of ash still on his tongue.

He had spent his life aspiring to be a hero.

But Marcus had become one.

SARAH TURNED to him.

"We need to go."

He didn't move.

Sarah's patience snapped. She shoved him. Hard.

"Dan." Her voice was sharp, cutting through the haze that surrounded him. He blinked.

"It's over," she said. "But if we don't move, we'll all end up just like Marcus."

The words hit him like a slap.

Dan inhaled sharply, closing his eyes for just a moment. Then he nodded. "Okay."

Sarah turned to Ish. "We need to tend to the wounded first. I'm not leaving anyone behind."

Ish hesitated.

And then she nodded. "Alright."

THE CEILING WAS already cracked before the first impact. The second one shook it loose. Dust drifted down in lazy spirals as Lilith reached out to hush the little girl clinging to her side. Her granddaughter had just turned 4 a few weeks ago.

Outside, the sound was faint: a mechanical hum, steady and circular. The kind that arrived before you knew to run.

They didn't run. There was nowhere to go.

The walls trembled. The moka pot on the stove tipped, sending a thin line of coffee across the burner. It hissed sharply, then continued in a stream along the cracked floor. The girl flinched at the sound.

The room was cobbled together, rough concrete walls, salvaged furniture, a stove patched with old parts and patience. A decade of living under threat left no room for beauty.

In the background, a radio crackled, half-buried in static. A flickering screen mounted above it displayed a regime broadcast she hadn't asked for. The language was familiar. The accent, familiar. The name, unmistakable.

A tribute. A voice spoke of sacrifice. Of cleansing. Of peace.

Lilith turned her head. She knew that face well.

Dan Clymer. Not just the boy from the broadcasts, but the man she had helped pull from the rubble not long ago. The one who still winced when rising too fast, who brewed strong coffee every morning as if ritual could banish guilt. They had shared silence more often than words, but the truth had passed between them all the same.

She'd seen him with Sarah. With the boy, Marcus. She knew his grief, his guilt, and the stubborn resolve that had kept him breathing.

They were on salvage duty today. Quiet and low-risk, at least in theory.

The roof creaked again. She pulled the child closer. Held her steady.

She didn't speak. There was nothing to say.

The drone passed. Just for today.

"...in honor of Daniel Eustatius Clymer..."

The child looked up. "Is that Dan from..."

"Shh," Lilith said. "Be still. You are so brave."

She moved to the stove, reaching for a towel. The coffee had already begun to cool.

Then another blast hit. Closer this time.

The screen above the radio flickered again. The tribute dissolved into a live feed. Lilith's breath caught.

Footage from the drone. The strike. The flash of a figure climbing the machine. Marcus, unmistakably, even in silhouette. And for a fraction of a second—Dan's face.

Another blast followed. Louder, sharper, closer. The screen cut to static as the signal died. The ceiling groaned above them. Dust poured down in sheets as something massive hit the surface overhead.

She turned sharply. No more time.

"Go to Mira," she said quickly, gripping the child's shoulders. "She'll keep you safe."

Then Lilith ran.

57

Sarah sat with her back to the stone wall, the cold seeping through her jacket. The hum of the underground shelter had quieted since the blast. Conversations had dulled to murmurs, and the space between people had grown wider.

She turned Marcus's bracelet in her fingers.

The beads were matte from wear, soft with ash. They didn't shine anymore. She didn't want them to.

She wasn't crying. Not now. There was no sobbing now. Just that thin edge of feeling, somewhere behind the teeth. What lingered now was quieter. Heavy.

He had died in front of her. Not a sacrifice. Not a symbol. A person. Her person.

She remembered the night he told her about it. They were walking home after the bar, the streets dim and mostly empty. He'd been quiet for a stretch, then started fiddling with the bracelet, rolling it between his fingers like he always did when he was thinking. "Just something my abuela gave me. From when I was a kid," he'd said. "She used to say the world would try to make me forget who I was. So she gave me this. Said if I ever felt lost, I should hold onto it."

She rolled one now. "Uno por coraje," she whispered. One for courage. Her fingers moved. "Dos por esperanza." Two for hope. And the last—her hand trembled. "Y tres..." Her voice caught. "Por no perderte." And yet, she had.

The bracelet clicked softly in her palm.

Someone passed by without speaking. She didn't look up.

They were still underground, still recovering. Ish had taken over logistics. Dan was resting, barely speaking since the strike. People looked to her sometimes, but she wasn't sure what they saw. She didn't feel strong. She felt threadbare.

She tucked the bracelet into her pocket.

There was work to be done. Communications to rebuild. Supplies to salvage. Memories to hold.

She stood slowly, her knees stiff. In the corner, the ibrik pot waited.

She'd make the coffee today.

Not because it fixed anything.

But because life still mattered.

DAN WAS UNDERGROUND again.

The dirt was still under his nails. His arms streaked with blood and dust, ash and grease.

Dan sat on the ground against the wall, knees bent, hands loose in his lap. His shoulders ached. His jaw. He hadn't spoken since—

No.

He kept wiping his hands. Jeans, sleeve, the floor.

Still there.

He wouldn't look.

Dirt. Blood. His. Marcus's.

He ground his palms against the rough concrete.

Not just Marcus.

The community.

The strikes.

The past.

The truth.

The blood on his hands wouldn't come clean.

And he knew it never would.

He screamed. He thought. Or maybe he hadn't.

The sound of it was still in his throat.

He hadn't moved in a long time. After this, he didn't know how he ever could again.

58

Lilith had been with her grandchild when the strike hit.

One moment she was crouched in the corner of the shelter, arms wrapped tight around the girl's tiny frame. Then came the thunder, the tremble, the dust. The child screamed. Lilith held her until the worst passed. Then she sent her running to the others, heart cracking as she let go. The child needed to be with the rest. Lilith needed to stay.

Now she stood alone outside the scorched edge of the compound, smoke still curling from shattered beams. Her ribs ached. Her throat was raw. But she was alive.

Ish emerged from the side of the rubble, jacket dusted with ash. Her face was smudged and tight, jaw clenched in quiet fury.

Lilith gave a grunt. "We keep waiting for the end. It keeps not coming."

Ish approached slowly, glancing once at Lilith's side. "You okay?"

Lilith nodded. "Battered, not broken." She lowered herself onto a crate, knees creaking. "It's the rest of you I'm worried about."

Ish sat beside her, silent.

Lilith studied her face. "You're steady. That's good. People need steady."

"You've always been the steady one."

"Not anymore."

Ish blinked. Lilith continued. "I've been doing this for ten years. Guiding, coaxing, carrying truth through shadows. But I'm not the future, Ishtar. You are."

"You're not dying."

"No," Lilith said with a rough laugh. "But I am tired. And you, your generation, is the last one that remembers what was lost. That makes you dangerous. That makes you essential."

Ish stared ahead. "I don't know if I'm ready."

"No one ever is." Lilith put a hand on her arm. "But when you speak, people listen. When you act, they follow. I've seen it."

They sat in silence a moment longer. Somewhere behind them, a child cried, and a voice soothed them. Life, pushing forward.

"You're not just surviving anymore," Lilith whispered. "You're leading. Don't forget where you come from. But don't be afraid to walk toward where we're going."

59

The Hall of Valor was packed. The same place where Dan Clymer had once stood before the nation's adoration now echoed with chants and prayers. Banners lined the towering walls, emblazoned with the nation's insignia, each one framed by a golden cross intertwined with military laurels. Patriots stood shoulder to shoulder, their voices unified in fervent devotion.

At the center of it all stood Reverend Eli Hightower, radiating triumph. Behind him, Knox watched stone-faced, arms folded tightly as the ceremony continued.

This was meant to be the moment of victory. The war was ending. Or at least, that was what they had engineered the people to believe. And the final proof would be delivered in real-time.

A nationwide broadcast. A canonization. A live execution. The Cleansing Ceremony.

Hightower's voice boomed across the hall, projected to every citizen watching.

"Brothers and sisters, today is the day of righteous reckoning! The enemy who destroyed our cities, who murdered our loved ones in the Sacrificial Zone, shall be no more. Over a decade of war has brought us to this final moment of justice. And you, the faithful, shall bear witness to the righteous hand of deliverance!"

The crowd erupted.

Above the Hall, a hologram of the DAN drone rotated slowly in the air, sleek and lethal. A PowerUp Patriot logo gleamed across the simulation. The real drone was already en route to its target, but this projection kept the spectacle alive.

Knox's jaw tightened. He was beginning to hate this.

THE NATION WATCHED through the DAN drone's eyes as its camera feed took over every screen.

Dan, Sarah, Marcus, and the resistance forces ran through the ruins below. They didn't know the world was watching. And the world didn't know who they were.

To the audience at home, they were just distant, blurry figures, targets marked for elimination. The anchors filled the silence with cold analysis.

"As you can see, the DAN prototype is tracking its targets with absolute precision. These foreign enemies have evaded us for too long, but tonight, we wipe them from existence."

Then, unexpectedly, one of the figures could be seen separating from the other two, vanishing off the bottom edge of the screen.

"We see that one of the enemies has left the strike zone. Have no fear, those of you watching at home. The DAN drone is perfectly suited for multiple strikes," the anchor intoned.

The crosshairs locked. A missile was armed. And then...

Something changed.

THE CAMERA SWAYED. A glitch? A malfunction? No. A shadow blurred past the lens. The drone jerked violently, as Marcus climbed it, gripping for his life.

And then—a face. Magnified fifty feet high across the nation, Marcus's eyes burned with fury. A collective gasp swept through the Hall of Valor.

Viewers at home could see every bead of sweat, the strain in his arms, the sheer feral determination on his face.

He plunged his blade into the drone's metal hull as it spiraled from the sky.

A breath. A flicker of an image. For one second, before the feed collapsed, the nation saw two figures running toward the drone. A woman. And a man. The camera tumbled. And, for a fraction of a second, Dan Clymer's face came into view.

The nation saw him. Their hero. Their idol. Their Dan.

He belonged to them. Fighting against them.

The screen cut to static. Then color bars.

THE HALL OF VALOR erupted. The faithful roared in confusion, in anger, in disbelief.

Hightower—sweating, but grinning—raised his hands in an attempt to reclaim the moment.

"This is proof! Proof of their desperation! Proof of their fear! The enemy is crumbling! Do not be deceived by the tricks of the faithless..."

But the crowd wasn't listening. Some still cheered blindly. But others...they whispered. Doubted.

They had seen something they weren't meant to see. For the first time... the illusion wavered.

Knox, expression unreadable, slowly turned toward Hightower. And then, without a word, he turned on his heel and walked into the building, leaving Hightower to face the crowd alone.

60

Greg flexed his fingers, cracked his knuckles, and settled into the seat.

It was Dan's seat. The one Dan had once occupied, the one he'd left behind. Greg hadn't expected it to feel this heavy, this empty. It should've been Dan in the control room today, executing the mission, but instead, it was Greg. A quiet weight pressed on his chest. Pride, certainly. He'd earned this position And yet, it felt like a betrayal. Dan had been his friend. Greg hadn't wanted this, hadn't wanted to take Dan's place, but here he was. The mission, the moment, was his now, and it was still hard to believe.

The console before him lit up. A small pulse of power. His name was at the top of the mission log: Operator: Greg Halloway.

Finally, Greg thought. This was it.

The room was almost too quiet. In the distance, a door opened and shut, but Greg's attention remained fixed. There were no words exchanged. His fingers hovered over the controls.

The room felt cold, isolating. The DAN drone's interface flickered before him. Its target was locked. Greg had expected to feel something more—pride, accomplishment—but all he felt was a gnawing emptiness.

The AI engaged itself, cutting through the tension. His role was reduced to a passive observer, as the system executed its mission with unsettling precision.

The real-time feed began flashing across the screens.

GREG'S JOB was now nothing more than a spectator until it came time for targeting.

The DAN drone soared across the wasteland, sleek, cold, deadly, tracking insurgent heat signatures. Greg had no control over it. Not anymore.

He knew what was coming. This was routine. The drone was programmed for precise action, after all. As it arrived at its destination, Greg's hands moved back into position above the screen.

Then, a sudden flash.

AUTONOMOUS TARGETING ENGAGED –
MANUAL OVERRIDE DISABLED.

Greg's fingers hovered midair.

What?

He had trained for nuance. For precision under pressure. Now the system didn't even want him to confirm.

His gut twisted. It wasn't supposed to be this way.

A voice echoed from a distance, quiet but clear enough to hear:

"That's the beauty of it. No hesitation. Just pure execution."

Greg clenched his jaw. No hesitation. But wasn't that the point of an operator?

THE FEED REMAINED STEADY. The AI executed the mission with the usual, cold efficiency. And Greg sat there, frozen. His entire purpose had just been usurped.

And then, unexpected movement.

The camera shifted. It jerked violently, tilting as if in panic.

Greg sat forward. What the hell?

A face.

Marcus.

His wild, unflinching eyes were inches from the camera. His mouth twisted into a scream.

Marcus had scaled the drone.

Greg's breath caught in his throat.

What the hell was happening?

Marcus held something...a spear of some sort... muscles coiled, and then, with a sudden, visceral movement, he struck.

The drone rocked violently in the air, camera whirling as sparks exploded from its seams.

Greg's heart pounded as he watched the screen shudder. The audio picked up Marcus's screams, the echoes of desperation.

Dan's face. Just for an instant.

And the screen cut to static.

The feed was gone.

THE ROOM ERUPTED in chaos. Supervisors moved like panicked soldiers, trying to salvage whatever they could from the failed operation.

"What the hell was that?!" someone shouted.

Greg's hands stayed frozen, hovering over the console. He could feel his heart hammering in his chest.

But then, the voices carried through the room, giving orders.

"Run the damage reports! I want a full analysis —NOW."

Greg's heartbeat thundered in his skull as the feed on the screen looped back to a controlled, sterile broadcast of Knox addressing the nation. The regime was already spinning it. They were already working on their narrative.

Greg's mind raced. He could say something. But his mouth stayed shut. Eyes turned to him, narrowing.

"Did you see anything unusual before the feed cut?"

Greg hesitated.

He thought of Dan's face. Clear. Unmistakable. Burned into every screen.

He swallowed hard.

"Glitch in the telemetry," he said. "Could've been artifacting from the impact. Hard to confirm. The impact might have caused it to pull in an old feed."

Silence. A few exchanged looks. But no one pressed.

The regime didn't need truth. It needed options.

61

The streets were charged with a strange energy. Something in the air felt different.

Every screen around him replayed the regime's heavily edited footage. The DAN drone's failure had been rebranded as a "minor setback in a glorious campaign."

But the crowd wasn't buying it.

Protests had started. The whispers were growing. People were beginning to doubt.

Greg walked through the crowd, head lowered. His eyes darted nervously, avoiding the faces around him. Then, as he passed a massive screen, the raw, unedited footage flashed for a brief moment.

A blurred figure.

Dan.

Greg's stomach twisted. He looked away, panic rising in his chest.

He didn't know what he was going to do, but one thing was certain:

The illusion was breaking.

62

Amelia woke to the smell of coffee.

Not the acrid instant powder she'd grown used to, but something deeper, earthier. It filled the air like a memory, one she hadn't realized she'd lost until it returned. For a moment, she lay still, blinking up at the ceiling of the safehouse, the thin blanket tangled around her legs.

She had slept.

Truly slept, for the first time in days.

The silence of the place was its own kind of insulation. No patrols. No alerts. No apartment walls thin enough to hear your neighbors breathe. Just the low hum of an old heating unit and the sound of someone, Nama, moving in the next room.

Amelia sat up slowly, the ache in her body protesting as if waking meant returning to danger. But there was no danger here. Not yet.

She padded softly into the kitchen. Nama stood at the stove, one hand steadying a small ibrik over the flame, the other holding the long spoon she stirred with deliberate care. She didn't look up.

"Coffee's ready," Nama said.

Amelia hovered in the doorway, unsure of whether she was being invited in or warned away. She stepped forward anyway.

"I haven't slept like that in... I don't know. Before all of it."

Nama poured the coffee with the same quiet efficiency she seemed to apply to everything. Two cups. No ceremony. Just presence. She slid one across the table.

Amelia sat.

For a moment, they drank in silence.

The coffee was strong and rich, familiar. It reminded her of the kind Sarah used to make during their early morning chats, back when everything still felt salvageable. Same depth. Same bitterness. Same grounding warmth. It was the same coffee.

Then Amelia's eyes flicked to the wall behind Nama. A scrap of paper was pinned there. Worn and rain-warped, but unmistakable. One of the flyers. The same design Sarah had pressed into her hands, asking her to help post them in the alleys, the stations, anywhere eyes might land without permission. The same one still folded in the bottom of her purse.

She stared at it. At the edges curling away from the thumbtack. At the smudge of ink where a raindrop had bled the message into itself.

"Sarah got those from you in the market, didn't she?" Amelia said quietly.

Nama didn't answer right away. She sipped her coffee, gaze unreadable.

"She believed people would see what they needed to," Nama said. "You helped her. That was enough."

Amelia looked down at her cup, the steam rising in soft spirals.

From the other room, a voice, flat and polished, filtered through the air. A broadcast.

They both turned toward the small screen tucked between stacked books and a faded radio.

The Cleansing Ceremony was underway.

At first, it was the same as always. Anchors in pressed suits, tones of certainty. A drone's-eye view of a city reduced to ash. Preapproved phrases. Glorious precision.

Then the feed stuttered.

A jolt. A sudden tilt in the horizon.

The camera lurched. The smooth hum became static and rotors and panic. And then...

Marcus.

His face filled the screen, sweat-slicked and wild, eyes locked on some impossible target. The blade flashed. Sparks erupted.

The feed buckled.

And then, amid the chaos...

Dan.

Not a phantom. Not a name in a eulogy. Dan Clymer, alive.

And then the drone fell. The screen cut. A crimson emblem. An emergency override. The hymn.

Amelia didn't realize she'd stood.

She stared at the screen, the echoes of the final frame still burning in her mind.

"That was Marcus," she said. "And Dan Clymer. That was them. They're alive."

Nama rose, began to clear the cups without speaking.

Amelia's voice sharpened. "If they're alive, then Sarah might be too!"

Nama's silence stretched. A nearly invisible clench in her jaw.

"It's possible," Amelia said. "Hell, it's more than possible. Sarah would've followed them."

"She did," Nama said at last, not looking at her.

Amelia blinked. "What?"

Nama set the cups gently in the sink.

"They were seen," she said. "We have channels. Eyes in places the state doesn't think to look. We knew long before the drone feed glitched. Word reached us days ago. We just couldn't confirm it until now."

"Then we have to do something," she said. "We can't just sit here while Sarah, while any of them..."

Amelia lowered herself slowly back into the chair.

Something brushed against her ankle.

She flinched, startled, then looked down.

A familiar gray shape circled her leg, purring softly.

"Cleo?"

The cat blinked up at her, then rubbed her head against Amelia's shin with casual insistence, as if no time had passed at all.

Amelia reached down, scooping her up. "I thought...I didn't know what happened to you."

Nama's voice came gently from across the room.

"She found her way here."

Amelia looked up, still holding the cat.

"But how?"

Nama didn't answer right away. She just watched as Cleo nestled into Amelia's arms.

"We've had people keeping watch. Quietly. Sarah had more protection than she ever knew. Some things we couldn't stop. But others..."

She reached over and scratched behind Cleo's ears.

"Not everything is lost when someone disappears. Some things find their way."

Nama's voice shifted, calm but firm. "We are doing something. But not like this."

Amelia looked at her, frustration flickering behind her eyes.

"They're exposed now," Nama continued. "The state will move fast. But so will we. We have people closer than you think. People who know how to disappear."

Amelia swallowed hard. "But what if..."

"No heroics," Nama said. "Not now. That's not how we win."

Amelia closed her mouth, the words catching behind her teeth.

"You're in danger too," Nama added quietly. "The best thing you can do now is stay alive."

They sat with it a moment. The silence this time was heavier, weighted with the shape of possibility.

"What happens now?" Amelia asked.

"Now," Nama said, "we wait. We watch. And when the moment comes, we move.""

Outside the window, voices rose, not in conversation, but in cadence. A chant. A call.

The unrest had begun.

Amelia turned to the sound and didn't flinch.

ISH CROUCHED BESIDE one of the support columns, absentmindedly scratching a grid into the dust with the end of a broken spoon. Mapping. Or maybe just thinking in lines.

Sarah sat nearby, the quiet weight of Marcus's bracelet still coiled in her palm. She hadn't spoken since the end of the ritual. The silence didn't press between them, it settled, familiar.

"Surviving's just the first half of the work," Ish said finally.

Sarah looked up, her voice low. "And the second?"

"Building something better than the shit that tried to kill us."

The torchlight flickered faintly along the walls, shadows stretching.

Ish continued, still drawing lines. "People think resistance ends when the bullets stop flying. It doesn't. That's when it gets harder. When everything's broken, and nobody wants to admit they don't know how to fix it."

Sarah traced one of the bracelet's faded beads with her thumb. Her voice was almost a whisper. "So what, you want to lead something?"

Ish glanced at her, not smiling. "I want it to mean something. What Marcus did. What any of us did. Someone's got to keep track of the shape of things. Make sure we don't trade one cage for another."

She rose slowly, brushing the dust from her palms. "I'm not into building a new regime, if that's what you're asking."

Sarah gave a faint nod. "Good. One's enough."

Ish looked toward the dark beyond the tunnel. "Still, someone has to start drawing the map."

63

"And we're back. Welcome to Eyes Forward, I'm Victor Sloane, and tonight...well, let's just say some of us owe the benefit of the doubt an apology."

He leaned forward into the camera. His expression wasn't smug, exactly. It was something colder. Tired, but sharpened. Vindicated.

"Three nights ago, during what was meant to be a national moment of unity, millions of citizens witnessed something they weren't supposed to see. Not a symbol. Not a statue. A face."

The screen split. One half held Sloane in the studio. The other, paused footage from the drone strike, grainy but unmistakable. Marcus climbing. A figure below. A brief turn toward the camera.

Dan Clymer.

"Now, some would have you believe this is fake. That this is AI-generated propaganda crafted by subversive actors to destabilize the Union. Others claim it's deepfake material seeded through compromised channels. But let me ask you, if that's true, why is the regime working so hard to erase it?"

He gestured offscreen. The image changed again: newsreel clips of street monitors blinking out, regime feeds cutting to emergency screens, patrol drones tearing down paper printouts and murals. In one video, a teenager gets tackled for chalking a symbol on a curb: a circle, with two slashes beneath it.

"If it's fake, why the panic?"

A familiar jingle played, followed by a cut to the panel: four figures, each in their own remote frame.

"Let's bring in the table. We've got Dr. Amina Keller, civil historian. Retired General Stavos. Tech correspondent Remy Lang. And—yes, she's back—former faith liaison Marla Jette."

They greeted one another, some more stiffly than others. Sloane didn't wait.

"Remy, you first. We've got footage. We've got a regime that can't keep its story straight. What do you make of the scramble to rewrite the last seventy-two hours?"

Remy shook her head. "The footage is real. It's not just one source. It came from the drone's own feed and was intercepted mid-broadcast. Yes, some bootlegs have distortions, but the core material has been authenticated by independent labs. If this were a fabrication, it'd be the most sophisticated one in history. *And* the regime's damage control wouldn't make sense."

"Stavos?"

The general grimaced. "Frankly, the regime screwed up. Whatever they were trying to orchestrate with that ceremony—martyrdom, rebirth, whatever spin they were after—it backfired. You can't unring that bell."

"Marla, you're awfully quiet."

The former liaison pressed her lips together. "People see what they want to see. I've spoken with members of the Temple Core, some of them think this is a test of faith. Others claim it's a holy deception. The footage has... shaken people."

"Dr. Keller?"

"There are protests across the city. Murals appearing overnight. Children asking questions their parents can't answer. Whatever happens next, we've entered the age of fracture. The regime's version of reality is no longer the only one available."

Sloane looked back to the camera.

"There you have it. For some, the footage is gospel. For others, it's heresy. But for all of us, it's a reckoning."

The screen faded to black. But the footage played on, bootlegged, mirrored, encoded, and reshared faster than it could be erased.

Dan Clymer was alive.

And the world was watching.

IN A SECOND-FLOOR apartment on the east side, a mother passed her son a tablet with both hands. It shook slightly as she did.

"Just watch," she said.

The footage flickered. Grainy Distorted Real. Marcus climbed. Dan turned.

"Is he dead?" the boy asked.

"No," she said. "That's what they want you to think."

Outside, a patrol drone buzzed low over the rooftops. She didn't flinch.

"We remember the truth," she said. "And we don't let them take it from us."

Outside, distant shouting rose and fell like waves. The protests hadn't reached their building yet, but the tension had. Every knock at the door felt louder. Every flicker of the lights meant something.

Two blocks away, a mural had gone up in a matter of hours: Marcus, standing atop the drone, hand outstretched. A local artist had painted him in profile, one eye turned skyward, the other shadowed.

Below him: the symbol.

It had started appearing across the city— scratched into brick, chalked on pavement, etched into foggy windows: a circle, with two slashes beneath it.

Someone had tried to scrub it at dawn. By midday, it was repainted. Larger.

Across the street, a bus stop shelter still held one of the regime's printed ads. Weathered at the edges but intact, the image showed Dan Clymer mid-salute, his face solemn, heroic. Bold text below read: HE GAVE EVERYTHING.

A young woman stepped up to the glass. Hood up. Marker in hand.

Without hesitation, she wrote one word across the image:

ALIVE.

Near the edge of the square, a vendor's cart had been overturned, its contents spilling across the pavement. T-shirts from the Hall of Valor tribute flapped in the wind, Dan's face printed over bold text that once read: THERE IS NO GREATER GIFT.

Someone had stitched a red X through the slogan. Beneath it, a rough line of black thread spelled out: TELL US THE TRUTH.

A patrol drone buzzed into view. The crowd scattered.

The woman dropped the marker and ran.

But the word remained.

And even after the drone passed, a child paused beside the glass, looked up at Dan's image, and whispered the word back.

THE TRANSIT STATION was too quiet.

Not silent, there were still shuffling footsteps, the hiss of steam from vending grates, the whir of ceiling fans, but something beneath it had stilled. Like the station itself was holding its breath.

No one waiting at the station spoke. A courier shifted her weight from foot to foot. A child clutched a plastic toy in the shape of a DAN drone. An older man squinted at the screen and said nothing. The man at the ticket kiosk didn't speak. He took his receipt with a gloved hand and shuffled to the bench along the wall.

The screen above the ticket window blinked on. Soundless but bright.

Dan Clymer appeared mid-salute, a golden glow behind him.

"CLEANSING CEREMONY," read the caption. *"COMPLETE FOOTAGE: MEMORIAL CEREMONY FOR DANIEL E. CLYMER."*

But it wasn't the footage. Not really.

No fire. No falling drone. No Marcus.

Just a slow montage of honor and obedience. Looped smiles, still frames, and a voiceover promising stability.

The man scoffed quietly. "Sanitized bullshit."

He didn't say it loud. Just loud enough.

Someone behind him heard. Didn't reply, but didn't correct him, either.

Across the terminal, a girl with a utility badge reached for her tablet, then paused. Her eyes flicked to the screen. She frowned, then closed the device.

The platform lights flickered once.

A flier peeled loose from the shelter wall and fluttered to the ground. On its front: a photo of Marcus overlaid with the words, "What do you believe in now?"

No one spoke

The child let go of the drone toy. It hit the pavement with a dull, plastic clack.

No one picked it up.

The train arrived on time.
Everyone boarded.

64

The crates didn't hold weapons.

That was the first thing Amelia realized when Nama led her into the storage area beneath the safehouse, the same ones she had passed when she first arrived. Rows of stacked boxes stretched to the far wall, each carefully marked and weather-worn.

From the first time she cautiously stepped through the warehouse door and climbed the stairs, the crates had always looked like clutter. Dusty, mismatched, shoved against the walls of the safehouse like forgotten donations from another era. But Nama had led Amelia to them with a reverence that felt almost sacred.

"It's not a safehouse," Nama said quietly. "Not just. It's a library."

Amelia raised an eyebrow. "Doesn't look like one."

Nama crouched beside a stack, prying open a weathered wooden lid. Inside: newspapers, yellowed pamphlets, plastic-bound journals, data cards labeled in faded ink. "We collect anything that can still tell the truth," she said. "The Zone sends what it can. From old basements, abandoned newsrooms, ruined schools. If something might not survive out there, or if it's something the regime wants quiet, we keep it here."

The air smelled of mildew and ink. Amelia stepped closer, brushing her fingers across the brittle edge of a newspaper. The headline was a decade old. "Cities Destroyed: President Knox Vows Retribution, Christens 'Sacrificial Zone'."

She pulled it free. The ink bled slightly on her fingers, and the paper crackled lightly in her hand. Too loud in the silence of the warehouse. She looked up, suddenly self-conscious.

The article was short, sterile. Just a few lines about "necessary containment" and "unavoidable loss." A photograph sat beneath: an aerial shot of smoke, rubble, and the outline of a city once called home.

She kept digging. A sealed plastic bag held a schoolbook, spine burned. Pages filled with children's handwriting. A notebook of sermons, some with Hightower's signature, others with frantic scribbles crossing his words out.

Then she found it.

An internal memo. Unmarked. But the language was sharp. "Operational integrity requires decisive framing. Civilian casualties must be categorized under Phase II Displacement Policy. Reframe loss as sanctified sacrifice. Maintain message discipline. Standby for instructions on eliminating collateral."

Amelia's breath hitched.

She sat down, knees buckling onto the cold stone floor, documents spreading across her lap like confession. More memos followed. Early drafts of press releases, evidently written in the days and weeks leading up to the strike. Notes from "Faith & Patriotism Media Council." Word-for-word scripts delivered as spontaneous sermons. Names of journalists who went missing. Families relocated. Suppression orders.

Her fingers trembled as she turned each page. She had always suspected. But suspicion was safe. This was real. Brutal. Intentional.

She heard footsteps behind her. Nama stood in the doorway, arms crossed gently.

"They didn't just kill the Zone," Amelia whispered. "They buried it."

Nama nodded. "That's why we gather what we can. Before they bury the rest."

The light caught the edge of a photograph. Nama, twenty years younger, standing with another woman her age beside a barricade marked with spray-painted scripture. Her eyes were fierce, her arms crossed. Behind her, children held signs: "We Remember."

Amelia stared at the photo. At the articles. At the weight of everything she'd never been meant to know.

Amelia pulled out another paper. This photograph- a protest. The faces were blurred. The caption read: "Traitors Gather in Defiance."

But scrawled across the bottom in red ink were six words:

They were teachers. They were mothers.

Amelia felt her breath catch.

"Take your time," Nama said. "There's more. Always more."

Amelia hesitated, then looked back at her. "But what about the enemy? Why did they attack?"

Nama met her gaze. Said nothing.

And Amelia understood.

Nama left Amelia alone with the past. The room buzzed with silence. The kind that feels like it's waiting.

And Amelia began to read.

65

The doors to Knox's private office slammed open, sending a sharp crack echoing through the high-ceilinged chamber. Reverend Eli Hightower stormed inside, his heavy steps reverberating against the polished marble floors. His face, flushed with rage, twisted into something ugly as he bellowed.

"This is your fault, Knox!" His voice filled the space, raw with unchecked fury. "Your weakness—your lack of vision! We were supposed to be celebrating today, and instead..." He jabbed a finger toward the massive floor-to-ceiling windows that framed the city skyline. "Instead, there are protests! Protests, Knox! Do you hear me? Our great Cleansing Ceremony—the one I designed to unite the people—has turned into a disaster!"

Knox didn't turn. He stood with his back to the room, hands clasped behind him, half hidden by the spill of window light, gazing out over the city below. The skyline stretched endlessly, the towering structures of the capital looming over the lesser districts. A spectacle of power. But not his power. Not yet.

Hightower seethed. "You should have crushed that damned operator the moment he went missing. You should have put his face on every screen as a traitor instead of letting it fester into a spectacle!"

Still, Knox said nothing.

Hightower took a step closer, his chest heaving. "They saw him, Knox. They saw Dan Clymer alive. After he was declared a martyr. After you let me stand before millions and bless his memory! Do you have any idea what that does to our credibility?" He scoffed, eyes narrowing. "Then again, what would you know of credibility? You wouldn't even be in that seat if it weren't for me."

Knox's fingers curled slightly behind his back, but his expression remained neutral as he finally spoke. "You're very loud today, Reverend."

Hightower's lips pressed into a thin line, his frustration bubbling over. "Loud? You're damn right I'm loud! You have no idea what's coming, do you? They're already whispering in the halls of the

Ministry. The people are questioning us. The military is losing confidence in you. And if you don't fix this *immediately* you won't have a government left to lead!"

Knox stood in the silence. Then, slowly, deliberately, he turned, hands shifting.

The light from the window cut a sharp line across his face, casting half of it in shadow. One arm hung at his side now, no longer behind his back.

And in his hand, plain and quiet, was a gun.

A simple, unadorned pistol, held loosely in Knox's grip. Casual. Almost lazy.

Hightower's mouth opened slightly, but no sound came out.

Knox exhaled, shaking his head as if disappointed in a disobedient child. "You always did like to talk, Eli."

Hightower took a step back, swallowing hard. "Knox," he began, his voice faltering for the first time. "Let's—let's not be rash. We've worked together for years. I put you in power. I made you what you are."

He took a shaky breath, words coming faster now, like a dam cracking under pressure.

"You were going to lose reelection.

It wasn't about him. It was about what his voters represented.

Those people still believed in choice. In process. In doubt. Opening our borders. Standing in the way of the righteous: family values, obedience to scripture, keeping heresy out of schools—A world where everyone knew their place: Men, women, children. God above all.

A leader like that—living openly, unapologetically—it would've shattered the illusion.

That's what had to go.

So we went big.

Together."

His voice cracked slightly on the last word. Not defiant.

Afraid.

Desperate.

Knox lifted the gun slightly, rolling his wrist, as if testing the weight of it. "We did," he admitted. "And you made a mistake. So now, well, *I* have to go big."

Hightower's throat bobbed. He glanced toward the door. "The council..."

"The council already knows." Knox's lips twitched into something that wasn't quite a smile. "You've lost them, Eli. They're loyal to me now."

Hightower's fingers clenched at his sides. "You're not a killer," he said, though the tremor in his voice betrayed the thinness of his conviction. "You're a politician. You don't have the stomach for this."

Knox lifted his brow. "Are you sure?"

Hightower hesitated, his hands rising slightly in a placating gesture. He licked his lips. "Knox. Think carefully. You may not need me, but you need the Church. Without me..."

The shot cracked through the air, sharp and final.

Hightower staggered backward, his breath catching as a dark bloom spread across his chest. He looked down, stunned, as if struggling to comprehend that it had actually happened.

Knox exhaled, lowering the pistol slightly. "I don't need the Church," he said coolly. "I only need the people to believe I already have it."

Hightower's knees buckled. He reached for something, anything, to steady himself, but his hands grasped at empty air. He crumpled to the floor, his weight landing heavily against the marble, his mouth opening and closing in silent protest.

Knox stepped forward, staring down at him with something almost like curiosity.

Knox watched him stutter for breath. Then fired again, without a word.

This time, Hightower didn't move.

Knox adjusted his tie.

A knock sounded at the door.

He turned his head slightly. "Enter."

The door opened, and a military official stepped inside, eyes flicking briefly to the crumpled form of Reverend Hightower before snapping back to attention. He showed no reaction.

Knox holstered the gun, smoothing down his suit jacket. "Have the body taken care of. Quietly."

"Yes, sir."

The officer made a quick gesture, and two guards entered, swiftly collecting the corpse and hauling it away. Knox watched them go, then turned back to the window, staring down at the city once more.

The world was already moving forward.

Knox adjusted his cuffs. He had plans of his own.

66

After the DAN drone, he had asked to know more. He needed to know what he'd been a part of.

The file was slim. Just a folded sheet, half-creased, passed to him by one of the Resistance medics. No names. Just grid coordinates. Timestamps. Confirmed hits. A few with notes: civilian shelter, aid convoy, neutral zone relay tower.

He scanned the list, not quickly.

He recognized several timestamped targets. Had seen them through a monitor.

Someone behind him said, "We didn't think they'd ever figure out who was on the other end. Guess we were wrong."

Dan didn't answer right away.

Then, quietly: "I told myself it was all enemy territory. I didn't even know there were still people alive out here."

The other person didn't respond right away.

Then, softly: "But you knew they were human."

Dan folded the sheet and tucked it away.

"I don't need to be forgiven," he said. "I won't pretend I didn't do it All I can do now is do better. Be better."

He stood. There were batteries to sort. Wiring to reroute. Trenches to dig.

67

Greg hadn't returned to Central Command since the strike.

No one had said he couldn't. But no one had asked him to, either.

They called it a transfer, but everyone knew what it really was. His Patriot Points had taken a hit. He wasn't fired, just folded, filed, and reassigned. Out of the chair. Out of sight.

Now he sat in a room that hummed.

Banks of monitors stretched across one wall, each tuned to a different channel of regime infrastructure: maintenance lines, border cameras, low-priority chatter from outer districts. Officially, he was now part of Tactical Communications Routing —Tier C. Unofficially, he was warehoused.

Fine.

They thought they'd buried him in static. But sometimes static said more than silence.

He leaned back in his chair and scanned the logs, fingers resting lightly on the console. His screen flickered with coded packets, most of them gibberish, others too encrypted for Tier C clearance.

Then, at 19:43, a blip.

Just a flicker.

He paused. Rewound. Slowed it down.

The transmission wasn't long, just a burst of compressed data. But it carried a signature. Not a name, not a voice. A shape. A waveform tucked between pulses, repeating every four seconds.

A circle. Two slashes beneath it.

Greg's pulse quickened. He isolated the burst and ran it through diagnostics. Twice. The metadata was scrubbed. No origin tag. No destination field. Whoever sent it knew what they were doing.

He could have flagged it.

He could have called it in.

He didn't.

Instead, he logged it to a private notebook and stared at the terminal.

Not a glitch.

Not an echo.

A signal.

He leaned back again and stared at the ceiling.

He had always believed in service. Believed in order. Believed in the machine.

But now?

He believed in what remained of truth.

He reached beneath the console and removed a slim chip wrapped in soft cloth. There was a faint etching on it, a circle with two slashes underneath. The chip slid into the port with a soft click. A new line of code blinked to life—brief and deliberate.

He entered the words as he had been instructed: *Java. Valkyrie. Ramen. Receipt.*

The signal pulsed outward. Not traceable. Not official.

He took a sip of coffee from the tin mug beside him. The aroma was deeper than anything from the rations.

He smiled faintly. "Fresh beans really do make a better cup."

He waited patiently to see if the signal would be received, if the courier had been successful.

The screen flickered once, then held steady.

Somewhere, far beyond the noise, through the darkness, someone whispered back.

"Here."

68

The bunker still smelled like old metal and disinfectant, like someone had once tried to scrub the war out of it and failed. Maps bled into each other on the walls, layers of notes and corrections from a dozen hands. The overhead lights buzzed softly, powered by an aging generator that hiccuped every few minutes like a cough.

No one sat at the head of the table. No one ever did.

Ishtar Imanna leaned forward, elbows on the scarred metal, fingers steepled. Around her were the familiar ones Runners, medics, coordinators, the archivist from the library compound still smelling faintly of ink. Half-empty mugs cluttered the corners. The air tasted like copper.

Dan stood near the door. The jacket he wore didn't quite fit...like it had belonged to someone else, or someone he no longer was. He looked like someone who had wandered into the wrong room and decided not to leave. He hadn't asked why he'd been called. He figured if it was important, someone would tell him.

Ish glanced his way.

"The cities are cracking," someone said, voice low but certain. "Three riots this week. That's just the ones we heard about."

"Knox's name gets shouted less," added the medic. "Yours gets shouted more."

A small shuffle of papers. The archivist laid something down. Printouts, old-channel messages.

"People are saying this could really be the end. The opposition wants a face," they said. "Someone who can stand in front of a crowd and convince them to believe again. To trust again. They need a champion."

"There are a few names being tossed around," another added. "But in the streets, there's only one. They're asking for Dan."

"He does have the experience in front of a crowd... and the integrity to lead."

A quiet filled the room. Not expectant, not demanding. Just... waiting.

Dan didn't flinch. Just breathed out slowly, his gaze resting somewhere near the far wall.

"I'm happy to help where I can," he said. "If that's sharing intel, fine. If it's fixing wiring or digging latrines, also fine."

A pause. Ish didn't interrupt. Someone across the room gave a nervous shuffle.

"I was worshipped once," he added. "I don't need it again."

There was no bitterness in it. No speech. Just a fact.

"We need a new system," he said. "Not another symbol."

No one argued. No one needed to.

The conversation moved on: routes, ration concerns, scattered intel. Dan offered what he could. When someone handed him a folder, he took it. He found a seat.

Not central. Not separate. Just present. Helpful.

Dan was done with heroes.

"Is this... where you keep the records?"

Sarah's voice barely rose above the low hum of the oil lamps.

Lilith gave a slight shake of her head, slow and solemn.

"No," she said. "This is where we keep the people."

Sarah looked around in awe at the expanse of the archive. Rows of carved stone, clothbound journals, plastic crates, and etched tin were stacked like sediment, layered and uneven, but clearly placed with intention.

"We don't catalog by date," Lilith added. "Only by memory. It's messier, but truer."

Sarah stepped forward. She could feel the weight of it. It wasn't just the objects that got to her— it was the reverence, the tenderness. It was the unapologetic remembering. She saw a rusted lunch pail with a name written in chalk. A strip of film nailed to a piece of driftwood. A child's coat, mended again and again.

"Things that indict Knox and Hightower we send back inside to be preserved...can't risk them getting hit by a strike out here. But these are the other memories. From before."

Sarah reached into her satchel and felt into the lining. The book felt smaller now, but heavier somehow. The cloth-bound cover, sun-faded. The spine slightly warped from years of being read, hidden, carried.

She turned it in her hands once before offering it to Lilith.

"It's not political," she said. "It's just... a story." But her hands didn't believe that. "A girl follows a river, leaves home, loses and remembers. My father read it to me when I was little. Gave it to me before I left for college."

Lilith took it carefully, as though it might burn.

"They banned it?"

"Years ago. Not for what it says. For what it remembers."

Lilith opened the cover and read the inscription. Her eyes paused, not blinking.

For Sarah, May you always walk the harder path, even when it disappears beneath your feet.

Sarah looked down, blinked once, and exhaled too fast. A thread of breath caught at the back of her throat. She rubbed the corner of her eye like dust had settled there, but the sting stayed.

"This belongs here," Lilith said.

Sarah gave the smallest nod. Her fingers hovered for a moment before she let go of the linen wrap. She didn't speak again. But when she turned away, there was something quieter in her shoulders. Not peace, but a kind of stillness. Like something she'd carried too long had finally been set down.

69

Amelia didn't ask where the package was going. She had been training with Nama for weeks—routes, signals, emergency protocols—but this was the first time she'd take a delivery all the way into the Zone. The work was starting to feel almost routine, though the stakes kept increasing.

She didn't need to know. If Nama was handing it to her, it mattered. That was enough.

The satchel was old, canvas faded to ash-gray and stitched at the seams with care and repetition. Inside, wrapped in soft cloth, were three sealed parcels, two light, one dense. One carried the familiar aroma of dried cardamom pods. Another was tightly folded paper. The third was heavier, metallic.

"What's in them?" she asked quietly.

Nama's hands paused. "What matters."

Amelia nodded once, adjusting the strap over her shoulder.

She had come to accept these half-answers. They weren't evasions, they were a form of trust.

"This is the last run for a while," Nama added. "After today, we go quiet. Eyes are opening. Too many. Too fast."

Amelia nodded again, slower this time. The air between them was thick with meaning. No goodbyes. Just shared understanding.

"It's not far," Nama said. "But it's not easy. The route's changed again. You'll take the passage under the river and emerge north of the old checkpoint. From there, the signals will guide you. They'll be watching."

Amelia adjusted the satchel again. "How will they know it's me?"

Nama stepped forward and tucked a strip of cloth into Amelia's pocket: a scrap of fabric with a circle and two slashes, the mark she'd once thought was graffiti. A signal. A promise.

"They already do," Nama said.

The city was shifting beneath her feet.

She moved through its bones like she belonged to them—hood low, gait even, alert but not hurried. The outer perimeter of the Sacrificial Zone had softened in recent weeks, not from any formal policy change, but because the regime's grip was slipping. They were trying to reassert control, new patrols, stricter scans, but their resources were stretched thin. Too many fires to put out. Too many eyes turning inward. The unrest outside the Zone was bleeding into its borders.

She passed the old checkpoint at dusk, ducked into a service tunnel choked with moss and broken wire, and emerged near what had once been a municipal rail yard. The quiet was vast.

Somewhere above, a tremor sounded. Not thunder, not machinery, but the kind of low vibration that had become familiar. She stopped briefly, scanning her surroundings.

Ahead, barely visible in the fading light, a resistance symbol had been painted on a broken wall: two slashes beneath a circle. She followed it, then the next, then the next, tracing a hidden path laid out in code.

By the time she saw them, the sun had dipped below the broken skyline.

She passed through the outer limits of the Zone, deeper than she'd ever gone. The city fell quiet in strange ways here. No sirens. No engines. Just wind and wire and the echo.

She walked on, deeper into the Zone.

Toward the lights that weren't supposed to exist.

Toward the myth.

Toward something she hadn't expected.

SARAH MOVED through the ruins with practiced ease, her boots crunching over loose gravel and glass. The deliveries came irregularly, but when they came, they mattered.

She stepped into the clearing.

She was cautious at first, eyes scanning for the courier she'd been told to expect. Then she froze.

Amelia stopped, her breath catching in her throat.

They stared at each other, two versions of a life neither had imagined. The seconds stretched.

Then, without a word, they closed the distance and embraced.

It wasn't long or showy. It didn't need to be.

Just contact. Flesh and certainty.

Amelia pulled the small parcel from inside her coat and pressed it into Sarah's hand.

"From Nama," she said.

Sarah nodded, still stunned. Her fingers closed around it.

"Cleo says hello."

Sarah began to speak, but was cut short by a low hum rippling through the air, faint but unmistakable. Both women turned instinctively.

Amelia stepped back. "Go."

Sarah reached into her satchel without thinking, pulled out a small cloth bag, and pressed it into Amelia's hand. "For Nama," she said.

The scent hit her instantly. Smoky, rich, unmistakable.

Amelia nodded, eyes already scanning the horizon. She tucked it away and turned to run.

Sarah hesitated. She wanted more. Answers. Words. Time.

But Amelia was already retreating into the shadows, vanishing into rubble and quiet.

Sarah turned the other way, the package clutched to her chest.

Behind her, the hum grew louder. But neither of them looked back.

ONLY WHEN THE RUINS had stilled again, when the sound of the surveillance drone had fully faded, did Sarah let herself exhale.

She had ducked behind the partial wall of a collapsed storefront and crouched, letting the weight of it catch up to her as the danger passed. She rose to her feet just in time to see the horizon swallow the last of Amelia's silhouette.

Amelia. After all this time.

She hadn't known who the courier would be. She hadn't asked. In the resistance, questions like that invited risk, not clarity. But the second she saw her, really saw her, something cracked open.

She touched the edge of Nama's scarf wrapping the package, fingers brushing the stitched seal. It could have been anyone. It was Amelia.

Here she was. In the Zone. Running supplies. With Nama's mark in her pocket. But...how?

Sarah stood slowly, clutching the parcel tighter. The tremor in her hand wasn't fear. Not exactly. It was awe. Gratitude. Something that sat between grief and relief.

Dan was waiting.

She turned back toward the community, her pace quick but measured. The path was dangerous, but familiar. Her boots struck the ground with renewed purpose.

"It was Amelia."

Dan looked up.

"The courier," she added. "She didn't say anything. Just... handed it off. Like it was nothing."

"She used to show up at my place with knockoff wine and gossip about who was secretly in the resistance," she said, her voice somewhere between a smile and a sigh. "Half of it was guesswork. But she always made it feel like the world wasn't already broken."

Dan waited. The moment wasn't for him, but he stayed in it.

"She's the one who first told me about the Service Center backlogs. How people were slipping through. We'd talk about what we'd do if we ever really did something. I didn't think she'd..."

She stopped.

Sarah touched the edge of Nama's scarf, running her fingers across the stitched seal again.

Dan looked down at the package, then back to her. "You proud of her?"

She nodded, slowly. "Yeah. I am."

She lingered in the silence a moment longer.

"She's the one who told me to go to the other bar that night. Said I should humor Marcus. That maybe I should meet the famous Dan Clymer while I had the chance."

A soft smile tugged at the corner of her mouth. "I wasn't going to go. We were halfway through a bottle of something terrible, but she said, 'just go, make him nervous.'"

Dan huffed something close to a laugh.

"She liked stories," Sarah said. "And making them happen for other people. She made that one happen. Even if we didn't know it yet."

She looked down at the parcel again, the weight of it pressing into her hands. "It's strange. All the things we talked about back then. Resistance as theory. Jokes. Rage over wine. And now..."

Dan didn't interrupt.

"She didn't say a word," Sarah added. "But she didn't have to. She knew what she was doing. And who she was handing it to."

Dan looked at the parcel. "What do you think she's risking?"

Sarah didn't answer right away.

Then: "Everything."

"Whoever survives a test, whatever it may be, must tell the story. That is his duty."

-Elie Wiesel

Epilogue

The embers had long since cooled, but the crater still scarred the earth.

The DAN drone was just wreckage now—twisted metal and scorched carbon, its sleek edges blackened, its purpose broken. Near its flank, barely visible through soot, the PowerUp Patriot logo had melted into slag. A machine of purity, undone by its own violence.

Dan stood at the edge of the crater. He hadn't moved in a while. Sarah watched him from a short distance, then knelt beside the ruin and brushed a thin layer of dust away from the ground. Marcus's bracelet was still looped around her wrist. She ran her thumb along its edge.

They had made it out. Somehow. But not all of them.

Behind her, Dan stirred. "They're still out there," he said.

She looked up. "The protests?"

He nodded toward the haze where the skyline flickered in the distance. "The feed was live. People saw what happened. They saw us."

Sarah wasn't sure what "us" meant anymore. But she nodded. "Do you think it matters?"

Dan was quiet for a long time. "It might."

They didn't speak after that. There wasn't much left to say out here. Just dust, and memory, and something beneath them shifting that none of them could name yet.

Weeks passed.

Knox struggled to maintain his grip. The regime was cracking, but it wasn't broken. Not yet.

In the tunnels, the air grew colder. People whispered when they passed. Someone nodded to Sarah. Another placed a hand over their heart. A quiet ritual had begun to form in Marcus's absence, built not from doctrine but from need.

Dan drifted toward the mechanicals, where a busted water purifier had gone still. He'd taken to fixing things. Small, quiet tasks that kept his hands moving and his mind tethered. She let him go.

In her corner, Sarah sat cross-legged and unwrapped the cloth bundle Amelia had brought.

The fabric was familiar, one of Nama's scarves, dark blue and softened by time. Inside: a small transmission device. Rugged. Black. With an antenna folded tight, small screen, and a pulse light flickering.

She stared at it. Her throat tightened.

Two-way. Encrypted. Nama's note had been simple: You are not alone. Others are listening. Some are inside.

And a date.

Today's.

Her fingers hovered over the casing. She felt the moment's weight, not just for herself, but for everyone who had survived in silence, believing the world had turned its back.

Dan reappeared, crouching nearby. He didn't ask questions. He only looked, then nodded.

"They got it to us," she said.

He exhaled slowly. "Then it's starting."

She didn't know if he meant the revolution, or the reckoning, or just the next chapter. But either way, she believed him.

Far from them, in a city where every surface was watched and every voice could be tracked, Nama stood by her stove.

She was alone in her apartment. Curtains drawn. Lights low.

She added the dark beans, freshly ground into the ibrik, A pinch of dried cardamom, as a faraway friend had once suggested. Poured the water.

A quiet defiance.

As it heated, the scent filled the air. Strong. Bitter. Alive.

And beneath the rising steam, Nama allowed herself a moment to smile.

THE DEVICE BLINKED once, then again. Steady and deliberate. The scarf in Sarah's lap still held the faint scent of beans—rich, bitter, real.

She looked toward the horizon.

The ridgeline in the distance—blurred and uneven—caught her eye.

She knew those shapes.

Not from a map. From memory. Somehow both distant and close.

From the sketch her grandmother had made for her.

The one that had once hung above her bed.

The device blinked again, the screen flickering to life. Then, an image. A circle. Two slashes.

Sarah answered with two taps, whispering back across the dark:

"Here."

She had been brave.

And now, just this once, Sarah was still.

Author's Note

Valor Flakes: Part of a Complete Breakdown was born out of quiet dread and a deep sense of responsibility. My background is in teaching fourth and fifth graders—brilliant, resilient kids who ask better questions than most adults. I now work as an elementary school administrator, and I still carry that same conviction into every day: that we've left the next generation with a mess. I often told my students, honestly, that it isn't fair—but they're going to be the ones who have to fix it. This novel grew from that reckoning. It's not written for children, but it's shaped by the world we're leaving them. It's a story about complicity and awakening. About the machinery of belief, and what happens when war becomes clean and truth becomes a product. But underneath all of that, it's a message meant for anyone paying close attention—a quiet reminder that seeing clearly is the first act of resistance, and the beginning of something better.

-drb

Acknowledgements

TO MY WIFE, ROXANNE, for putting up with the late nights of me typing on my computer, not even knowing what I was working on until it was nearly complete (due to my insecurities about trying to write a whole-ass novel). Thank you for your patience, support, and belief when I had none of my own.

To my kids, Auggie and CeCe, for being amazing and inspiring and so much better than I could ever be. Thank you for being understanding when an idea would pop into my head in the middle of gymnastics, baseball, softball, soccer, or taekwondo and I would rush to capture it before it disappeared. And to Aug, for being the only person I was brave enough to speak of this project aloud to for many months... and for being an amazing ten-year-old who can keep a secret (even if it was only because you caught me reading over my shoulder as I typed).

To the amazing staff at Telva at The Ridge and Perennial on Lockwood for graciously tolerating me as I sat and worked in your spaces, and for providing such welcoming places for our community to gather and grow.

To The Novel Neighbor bookstore, for showing me that local authors can be seen and for bringing the joy of reading to children and adults across our community.

To Ryan and Nicole, for Chili's date nights with triple dippers and dip trios. To Joe and Hannah, for keeping me grounded and sane through the day-to-day minutiae that comes so close to overwhelming me. To Michael, for being Michael. To Brad, for sharing so much of life's journey, in and out, yet always somehow parallel. To Bob. To Melanie, for being my first reader and offering such encouraging feedback (again, by catching me mid-edit).

To every teacher, librarian, and mentor who ever encouraged my love of books and writing, and who showed me that stories were worth telling.

To each of my students, for teaching me more than I could ever teach you, and for striving to right the wrongs we have left you with. You deserve so much better than what we are leaving behind, but you are up to the challenge.

To the early readers, ARC supporters, and brave explorers who uncovered pieces of this project before it was even fully formed—you were the first to believe in the characters and lives lived in this world.

And finally, to you—the reader. Thank you for opening this book. I hope you find something in these pages worth carrying forward.

All errors, as always, are my own.

About the Author

DEREK BRIDGES is an award-winning public school educator and administrator. His experiences include being awarded the Federal Bar Association's Excellence in Civics Education Award, receiving the Missouri Association of Elementary School Principal's Exemplary New Principal Award, presenting at the National Association of Educational Renewal's national conference, serving as a mentor to master teachers from the Saudi Arabia Cultural Ministry's Educational Improvement Initiative, serving on the Teacher Advisory Council for the Judicial Learning Center at the Thomas Eagleton Federal Courthouse, and curriculum development for the National Park Service, among others. His work across a wide range of school and educational environments has shaped a deep understanding of the systems young people inherit—and the stories we use to explain, justify, or resist them. His fiction blends emotional realism with speculative structure, exploring themes like state control, spiritual performance, and the cost of complicity. Valor Flakes: Part of a Complete Breakdown is his first novel. He currently resides in Saint Louis with his wife and two children.

an imprint of Viaduct Publishing
www.viaductpublishing.com

Salt Circle Press is devoted to publishing fiction forged at
the fragile edges of survival, memory, and myth.

www.ingramcontent.com/pod-product-compliance
Lightning Source LLC
Chambersburg PA
CBHW020004120726
47903CB00004B/1126